B.J. McCall
Paige Tyler

Pirate's Prize

ELLORA'S CAVE
ROMANTICA®
www.ELLORASCAVE.COM

PIRATE'S WOMAN
Paige Tyler

To honor the debt her family owes Slayter Cardona, beautiful Teyla Dunai agrees to let him sell her as a sex slave in the markets of Arkhon. Determined to bring as much value as she can on the auction block, but inexperienced where men are concerned, she asks the handsome pirate if he'll teach her how to pleasure a man. Intrigued, and more than a little attracted to the lavender-eyed beauty, Slayter agrees. As he initiates her into the world of bondage, spanking and out-of-this-galaxy sex, though, both Teyla and Slayter find themselves falling for each other.

But Slayter has a responsibility to his crew, and Teyla knows it is her duty to pay off her family's debt. With the deal already agreed upon, there doesn't seem to be any way for their story to have a happy ending. Until Teyla is kidnapped...and they reach the slave auction house...and Slayter has to find a way to reclaim his own "sex slave".

SCARLET TEAR
B.J. McCall

Captain Wytt Sann is given the mission of a lifetime. Impersonating the notorious pirate Kirxx, Wytt must participate in a *zap* tournament sponsored by the pirate king. Wytt's objective is to play the bloody game, beat the competition and win the prizes—a beautiful Glacidian woman and the coveted scarlet tear gem.

Ceyla is offered as a prize in a tournament and embroiled in the pirate king's vengeful scheme to steal back the gem. Refusing to spend the rest of her life as a prize, Ceyla plots her escape.

Ceyla is drawn to the handsome pirate who fights like a warrior and fires her Glacidian blood. Seducing Kirxx is the key to winning her freedom, but will she lose it all in the process? His true identity could tear this lusty couple apart.

An Ellora's Cave Publication

www.ellorascave.com

Pirate's Prize

ISBN 9781419964893
ALL RIGHTS RESERVED.
Pirate's Woman Copyright © 2011 Paige Tyler
Scarlet Tear Copyright © 2011 B.J. McCall
Edited by Raelene Gorlinsky and Briana St. James.
Designer and Photographer: Syneca.
Model: Kory.

Trade paperback publication 2011

PIRATE'S PRIZE

ഔ

PIRATE'S WOMAN
Paige Tyler
~9~

SCARLET TEAR
B.J. McCall
~131~

PIRATE'S WOMAN
Paige Tyler

ജ

Dedication

ဆာ

With special thanks to my extremely patient and understanding husband, without whose help and support I couldn't have pursued my dream job of becoming a writer. You're my sounding board, my idea man, my critique partner and the absolute best research assistant any girl could ask for! Thank you for talking me into finally taking the plunge and submitting to Ellora's Cave.

Chapter One

လ

Slayter Cardona propped a booted foot on the edge of the desk and eyed the portly man sitting across from him. Agus Dunai frowned, but didn't say anything. Slayter knew he wouldn't. The expensive Tekorian wood was the least of the man's worries. If Dunai didn't pay the money he owed — with interest — then the ornate desk, and everything else he owned, was going to belong to Slayter by day's end.

"Two years is a long time to wait for my money, Agus," Slayter said. "I think I've been more than patient, don't you?"

Sweat beaded on Dunai's brow and he licked his lips nervously. "Yes, you have. You've been very patient."

"Then where is my money?"

The other man wet his lips again. "I—I don't have it."

Slayter lifted a brow. "I find that difficult to believe. That ore processor I procured for you on Zenoral 5—at the cost of one of my crewmen's lives, I might add—put your competitors out of business and made you the only manufacturer of polysilicate within light-years of this backwater planet you live on. I know you have money. Lots of it."

"But I don't." Dunai lifted his chin, puffing up his enormous chest. "Running a business takes money. Lots of it. I've had to invest in shiploads full of specialized equipment and pour credits into upgrading facilities. On top of that, I have hundreds of workers to pay. You're not the only creditor I owe money. I'm stretched very thin."

Slayter doubted that. "Not my problem."

Dunai sighed. "Slayter, please. I have a wife and five daughters to feed."

11

He should have known the bastard would drag his family into this sooner or later. Dunai probably thought mentioning them would appeal to Slayter's softer, gentler side. Any other time it might have, but not today. While he could have a heart on occasion, this wasn't one of them. Dunai had been trying to weasel his way out of the debt for far too long as it was. If Slayter went easy on the man, then everyone would expect him to go easy on them. Not only would he be out of business, but he'd be the laughingstock of the pirating world, too. He had a reputation to maintain.

"Like I said before, Agus, that's not my problem. You should have thought of that before you decided to do business with a pirate. If you don't pay me the money you owe today, along with the interest you've accrued, then this company and everything else you own is mine."

Dunai went pale. "You can't do that! H-how will my family and I live?"

Slayter shrugged. "I'll allow you to keep working here. Your wife and daughters, too." His mouth curved into a mocking smile. "I'm not as heartless as it seems, you know."

The other man opened his mouth, then closed it again. Maybe because he finally figured out it wouldn't do any good to argue with a pirate. From the calculating look in his gray eyes, though, Slayter didn't think so.

"What if I could offer you something of equal value?" Dunai finally asked. "Would you release me from my debt and consider us even?"

Slayter's eyes narrowed. He didn't want to be saddled with Dunai's damn company. What the hell was a pirate supposed to do with a silicate-processing plant? But at the same time, he wanted the money the man owed him. He had to be careful, though. Dunai was a shrewd negotiator and could screw him over if he wasn't careful.

"It depends," he said to the man. "What are you offering?"

"Something that will bring you a great deal of money if you sell it to the right buyer in the right locale. Something I guarantee will be worth more than what I currently owe you, even with all the interest."

That didn't answer his question, but it did pique his interest. What the hell did Dunai have that would be worth all that money, and why would he give it up? What choice did Slayter have, though? If he didn't take the deal, he'd be stuck with a company that might as well be an anchor tied around his neck. He was a pirate, for a God's sake, not a dirt dweller.

"All right. Meet me in one hour at my ship. If this thing is as valuable as you say, then we have a deal and you can consider your debt paid in full." Slayter leveled his gaze at the other man as he got to his feet. "One hour. Don't be late."

* * * * *

Slayter was in the ship's cargo hold with his crew when Agus arrived. He wasn't surprised Dunai was on time. The man knew better than to get on his bad side, particularly after the pain in the ass he'd been. Slayter was a little amazed to see two women hurrying up the gangway after the heavyset businessman, however. Slayter had met the older woman on an earlier visit, so he knew she was Dunai's wife. From the striking resemblance the younger woman bore to her, Slayter assumed she was one of the couple's many daughters. Dunai must have brought them along hoping they could appeal to Slayter if he refused to accept whatever it was the man had brought for payment.

Shit.

He hoped to hell they didn't start crying. He'd always been a sucker for a woman's tears. Especially if the woman was attractive. And while Dunai's wife was very lovely, the man's slender daughter was absolutely gorgeous. A fact every member of his crew seemed to have noticed as well.

13

Slayter dragged his gaze away from dark-haired beauty to turn his attention to Dunai. He'd been so intent on the women he hadn't noticed Agus wasn't holding anything in his hands. From the way Dunai talked, he'd expected the man to show up with a locked box and security guards.

He folded his arms over his chest. "Where is this thing you claim is so valuable, Agus? Or didn't you bring it with you?"

"I brought it."

Slayter waited for the man to produce whatever it was, but instead Dunai glanced at his wife. The look he gave her was almost apologetic. Tears welled in her eyes and she lowered her gaze to stare down at the floor.

Slayter frowned. What the hell was that about? He hadn't even seen the merchandise yet and she was already crying. "My patience is wearing thin, Agus. Hand it over. Now."

Dunai took a deep breath, then looked at his daughter and gave her a nod. She walked across the cargo hold to stand before Slayter, her head held high. Her exotic lavender eyes met his resolutely, but she didn't say anything. She didn't take anything out of the small satchel she held, either, which annoyed Slayter even more.

He looked past her to where Dunai stood. "Okay, Agus, enough with the games. Where is my payment?"

"Standing right in front of you," the man said.

Behind Slayter, his men murmured among themselves, but he barely heard them. He was too busy trying to wrap his head around what Dunai had said. Surely the man couldn't be offering his daughter as payment. "Run that by me again."

The portly man drew himself up. "My daughter Teyla is very beautiful. She'll bring you a fortune from any man looking to possess her."

Slayter narrowed his eyes. "You're suggesting I sell your daughter as a slave? That won't bring the money you owe me."

Dunai lifted his chin. "It will if you sell her in the markets of Arkhon."

Slayter looked at him incredulously. The slave markets of Arkhon were only known for two things—the buying and selling of sex slaves. "Are you serious?"

Beside Dunai, his wife choked back a sob, but the man ignored her. "You said if I brought you something valuable enough to cover my debt, then it would be paid in full. You set the terms of the deal."

Slayter ground his jaw. That was before he knew it was Dunai's daughter they were talking about. Damn the man to the lowest depths of hell. He knew Slayter wasn't a slaver. Then again, maybe that was why the crafty businessman was offering Teyla up as payment. Maybe he was counting on Slayter refusing. If he backed out on the deal because he was squeamish about selling her on the blocks, it was as good as forfeiting the money Dunai owed him. The man was right about Teyla bringing a good price in the sex slave markets. Slayter couldn't make as much from selling off Dunai's company, that was for sure, which is what he would end up doing if he demanded the man's business as payment instead. Selling the girl would be a hell of a lot smarter, not to mention easier, even if it did leave a bad taste in his mouth.

He looked at Teyla. "Did you agree to this?"

She seemed taken aback by the question for a moment, but then she nodded. "Yes. It's my duty."

Slayter hoped she would have said no. At least then he could have had something to argue about. As it was, the man had neatly backed him into a corner.

He turned his attention to the older man with a sigh. "All right, Agus. You have a deal. I'll take your daughter as payment."

If Dunai was surprised, or even upset, he didn't look it. In fact, he seemed relieved. He nodded stoically. "Then our business is done."

The man's wife wasn't as adept at hiding her emotions. The tears Slayter had seen in her eyes earlier flowed freely down her face now. Ignoring him and every other man on the ship, she ran forward to pull her daughter into her arms.

"You don't have to do this, Teyla," she sobbed. "Your father and I will find another way to repay the debt."

Teyla wrapped her arms around the older woman, holding her close. "Yes, I do. As the oldest, it's my responsibility." She took a step back to give her mother a small smile. "I'll think of you and my sisters every day."

Fresh tears filled the older woman's eyes at Teyla's words. Slayter swore under his breath. It felt like he was ripping a newborn babe from a mother's arms. He was on the verge of saying to hell with Dunai and forgiving his debt altogether regardless of what it cost his reputation when the man stepped forward and gently pulled his wife away from their daughter.

"Bronwyn, please," he said quietly. "Teyla is a strong woman. She'll be fine. Let's go before Slayter changes his mind."

Slayter clenched his jaw. The ease with which the man handed over his daughter turned his stomach. He supposed he shouldn't be surprised. The Kallorians were well known for using female children as a commodity for barter. It was practically a way of life on the planet, which for some reason seemed to produce more female children than male. If Slayter hadn't agreed to accept Teyla as payment, then Dunai would have sold her to some other pirate along with the rest of his daughters, if that was what it took to honor his debt.

Although the woman allowed her husband to lead her down the gangway, she couldn't resist stopping at the bottom to give her daughter one more tearful glance over her shoulder. Teyla watched them go, waiting until her parents had disappeared in the crowd of people milling around the spaceport before turning back to face him. Her lavender eyes were bright with unshed tears, and as one rolled down her cheek, Slayter had to fight the urge to gently wipe it away.

He swore silently, cursing the weakness. The woman was headed for the slave market. She was nothing more than a piece of merchandise, albeit a beautiful one.

"Have you lost your damn mind?"

Slayter stiffened at the words. He turned to see Genoone, his communications officer, glaring at him. As men went, the red-haired Belkin was one of the toughest on his crew, which sometimes made the man forget his place.

He fixed the man with a hard look. "What did you say to me?"

"I asked if you'd lost your damn mind." Genoone jerked his head in Teyla's direction. "It's bad luck to bring a woman on a ship. Everyone knows that."

Behind Genoone, the rest of the crew eyed Teyla, too. Either the other men didn't know about the old pirates' tale, or they didn't care, because they weren't looking at her with the same aversion. Instead, most of them were regarding her with open lust on their faces. That wasn't shocking. They weren't used to having women on board, especially one as attractive as Teyla. Those looks told him there was trouble brewing.

"Whatever you're thinking, you can forget it right now," Slayter said to them. "The woman is off-limits to every man on this ship. She's meant for the markets of Arkhon, and anyone who damages the goods will answer to me personally. Touch her and I'll cut off your hand with a metal blowtorch."

From the corner of his eye, Slayter saw Teyla blanch at the mention of the infamous slave market. He swore silently, wishing he hadn't said it so harshly.

Slayter looked from one man to the other, letting his gaze linger long enough on each to put the fear of God in them. "Is that understood?"

A few of the men muttered something under their breaths, but after a moment each member of his crew nodded.

"Then get back to work," he ordered tersely. "We leave in less than an hour."

The men moved off to finish stowing the cargo they'd picked up on Kallor, leaving Slayter standing there with Teyla and his first officer, Hewson. The older man stepped close.

"Since when did we become slavers?" he asked in a voice too low for Teyla or the crew to overhear.

Slayter didn't answer right away. More than thirty years his senior, Hewson was more of a father to Slayter than his real parent had been, which was why the man was the only one on the ship who could question him and get away with it.

"Since now," Slayter replied.

Hewson's mouth tightened behind his bushy mustache. "Well, I don't like it."

Slayter clenched his jaw. "I don't like it either, but we need the money."

It was true. A ship the size of his didn't run on good looks and a charming smile. It needed cold, hard Imperial credits.

Hewson grunted, though whether in agreement or distaste, Slayter wasn't sure. "Where are you going to put the woman until we get to Arkhon? If you put her in one of the general quarters, you'd better get your blowtorch ready now."

Slayter gave Teyla a sidelong glance as he considered the question. She was still standing in the same spot, a resigned, faraway look in her pretty eyes. Hewson was right. Regardless of the warning he'd given his crew to keep their hands off her, there was no telling what stupid ideas might make it into their brain buckets after a few days with her on board. If he put her in one of the empty cabins, he'd have to stand guard outside it 24/7. He might intend to sell Teyla into a life of slavery, but he still felt an obligation to keep her safe. How stupid was that?

"She'll stay in my personal quarters," he said to Hewson.

The older man said nothing for a moment, then nodded. "I'll take her there now and get her settled."

As he watched his first officer escort Teyla up the steps and along the catwalk, Slayter felt another twinge of guilt. He'd never stooped to the selling of another human being before, but it seemed as if that last moral barrier was about to go by the wayside like all the previous ones. Hard times made for hard men, though, and life in the outer reaches of the Imperial realm definitely qualified as hard times.

That didn't mean he had to like it, though. He sighed. Just one more stamp on his passport to hell.

* * * * *

Teyla followed the first officer along the passageway with her head held high. She refused to allow herself to feel even one single second of self-pity. She'd known this day was coming since she was old enough to start understanding the ways of her planet, had always known she would be used as a chip in one of her father's business schemes. She had naturally thought he would put her on the marriage block in return for capital, not sell her into slavery. That had been unexpected.

Her father wasn't being cruel when he'd handed her over to the pirate Slayter, though. He was simply doing what was best for his family. Offering her as payment had relieved the family business of a massive amount of debt, and now her sisters probably wouldn't have to suffer the same fate.

Still, hearing the pirate announce he intended to take her to Arkhon had made her resolve tremble a little. Even on her backwater planet, Arkhon had a reputation as a dreadful place no woman wanted to end up.

She swallowed hard. She would survive this, no matter what she had to do. In fact, she would find some way to thrive. It was how her people lived. The Kallorians were known throughout the galaxy as the kind of people who could handle any burden and come out on top. Perseverance was bred into them from the day they were born. Small children were frequently left unattended in the boundless forests of her planet as a way of teaching them to survive on their own.

19

Other families would set impossible tasks for their children, like pushing a boulder to the top of a hill by themselves in an effort to teach them to never give up. While her parents hadn't asked her to do either of those things, she had turned out just as stubborn and determined as the rest of her people. If she was going to be a slave, she would be the best slave ever. And if she was going to be a sex slave, then she would be the best damn sex slave ever. She would make her family proud.

There was only one problem. While she'd fooled around with guys some, she didn't have a lot of experience when it came to sex. She wasn't sure how a man interested in making her a sex slave could tell if she would be good in bed or not, but she worried if she didn't bring enough money on the block, Slayter might go back and demand additional payment from her father.

Teyla frowned as she thought of the pirate. Slayter wasn't anything like she imagined. Her father had made him out to be a cold, ruthless man, but he didn't seem like either of those. Not only had he asked her if she'd agreed to the deal before telling her father he would accept it, but he'd threatened the men on his crew with dismemberment if they laid a hand on her. Although she was sure he'd only said it to make sure she retained her value for the auction block, she appreciated his protection anyway.

Slayter didn't look like she'd pictured, either. She'd heard pirates were nasty, sweaty-smelling men with bad teeth and full beards to hide their pockmarked skin, but that couldn't be more wrong. At least not where Slayter was concerned. Tall and dark-haired, he was well-muscled with powerful shoulders, a broad chest and a strong, chiseled jaw. While his good looks and incredible body were enough to turn any woman's head, it was his eyes that had captured her attention from the moment she'd stepped on board the ship. Brown and soulful, they had a touch of gold that made them mesmerizing. If a man like him purchased her to be his sex slave, perhaps this new life of servitude wouldn't be so bad after all.

Ahead of her, the first officer stopped in front of a door in the passageway. He pushed a button beside it and the door slid open. Turning to her, he gestured with his hand.

"After you."

Teyla hesitated, then took a deep breath and stepped inside the cabin. It was bigger than she'd expected. Nicer, too. She'd pictured a small room with a narrow bed, a tiny dresser and a cramped writing desk. Instead, it was a suite of rooms. One was large enough to accommodate a huge bed and night tables, while the other contained a big desk with a computer and a holographic map. Like the man, the rooms were somewhat of a contradiction. While much of the ship was sleek steel and polished surfaces, the inside of these rooms hearkened back to another era. Almost all of the furniture, from the bed to the ornate desk, was oversized and made of antique wood. On one wall hung what she could only guess was a porthole from a seafaring ship. On another was a wood and wrought iron coat rack. Though most of the pegs were empty, one of them held a long, leather duster.

"I'll have one of the crew set up a cot for you in the captain's study," the first officer said. "You're welcome to go about the ship, but the men can be a little rough around the edges sometimes, so it'd probably be best if you keep to the cabin."

She nodded, but didn't say anything. She'd naturally assumed she would be confined to the captain's quarters for the duration of the journey. She supposed there wasn't much harm in giving her freedom to roam around, though. It wasn't like she could escape. Even if she could, she wouldn't.

"If you hear the alarm sound, though," the man added, "get back to the captain's cabin and stay here."

"What does the alarm mean?"

"Nothing for you to be concerned about. Just stay in here and you'll be fine."

She started to press him for more, but then reminded herself that slaves didn't ask questions, but simply did as they were told. It galled her, but thanks to her upbringing, it was something she was very good at faking.

The gray-haired man regarded her thoughtfully. "If you need anything, just let me or the captain know."

She gave him a small smile. "Thank you, Hewson."

"I'll let you get settled then."

Teyla watched the older man go, surprised by his kindness. He made her feel as if she were an honored guest instead of payment for a debt.

Letting out a sigh, she set her satchel on the floor beside the dresser. She didn't know why she'd let her mother talk her into bringing the bag. The man who bought her probably wasn't going to allow her to keep anything inside it. She wouldn't miss the change of clothes or small amount of toiletries she'd brought, but the thought of parting with the holographic imager with the photos of her family and friends was almost unbearable. At least she would be able to hang on to it until they got to Arkhon. Unless Slayter took it from her before then.

The thought brought a rush of tears to her eyes and she dropped to her knee beside the bag, suddenly desperate to look at the pictures. She yanked it open and reached for the imager just as someone knocked on the door. Startled, she jerked her head up. Slayter obviously wouldn't knock on the door of his own cabin, which meant it had to be one of the crew. Abruptly, she remembered what Hewson had said about having someone set up a cot for her. Looking at pictures would have to wait.

Teyla reluctantly closed the bag and rose to her feet. "Come in."

At her words, the door slid open. A slight, blond-haired teenage boy stood there, a rollaway cot beside him. He gave her a shy look.

"Sorry to bother you, but the first mate told me to come set this up in the captain's study for you," he said.

"It's no bother. Please, come in."

He ducked his head in a nod, then rolled the cot through the bedroom and into the study. He fumbled with it for a few minutes before finally getting it open. He pushed it closer to the bookcase, then gave her an apologetic look. "Never set one of these things up before. This okay where it is?"

"It's fine." If it wasn't, she was sure Slayter would move it.

The boy stuck his hands in the back pocket of his breeches and shifted from one foot to the other as if not quite sure what to say next. "I'm Olin, by the way."

She smiled. "It's nice to meet you. I'm Teyla."

"I know. I was down in the cargo hold when you came aboard."

Right. "Do you know when we'll be leaving Kallor?"

"We already did."

She blinked. "We did? I didn't even feel us move."

Olin grinned. "That's because Salo's the best pilot this side of a wormhole."

"I thought shooting into space would be more…dramatic."

"We don't actually shoot into space. More like lift off." He frowned. "You've never been on a ship before?"

"No."

He shook his head. "I don't know how you landlubbers do it. Being stuck on one planet all the time would suck."

She laughed. "I never really thought about it before."

Olin grinned again, broader this time. "Take it from me, space is the place to be. Once you start jumping from planet to planet, you won't ever want to stay put on one again." His smile faded, his blue eyes suddenly sad. "Not that you'll get the chance wherever you're going, I guess, will you?"

Her heart ached at the reminder. "Probably not."

He cleared his throat. "I'd, uh, better go. I told the cook I'd give him a hand in the galley."

Teyla opened her mouth to thank him again for setting up the cot, but Olin was already out the door. She sighed. She hadn't expected any of the pirates to feel sorry for her, but the boy definitely seemed uncomfortable with the idea of her being sold as a slave. It was kind of nice to know there was someone on board besides herself who dreaded where they were going.

She shook her head. So much for the promise not to let herself feel even one single second of self-pity. That was all she'd done since she'd stepped foot in this stupid cabin.

Determined not to think about it anymore, Teyla busied herself with looking around Slayter's study. While the holographic map of the Imperial galaxy should have held her interest, especially since she'd never seen one up close before, she found herself wandering over to the bookcase instead. Probably because she loved to read so much. Apparently Slayter did, too.

She ran her gaze over the hundreds of datacubes that were neatly organized on the shelves. She'd never seen so many books in a private library. Not even the rich merchants her father did business with back on Kallor had this many cubes. She wondered what subjects would hold a pirate's interest.

She touched her finger to one of the cubes at random and watched as a small holographic screen popped up above it. Hmm. Spaceship design. She supposed that made sense. She moved her finger from one cube to the next. Besides cubes on weaponry and battle tactics, Slayter had ones on planetary cultures, etiquette and philosophy. There were even two shelves devoted to fictional books. She lifted a brow at that.

Slayter was obviously an educated man, which made her wonder why he'd turned to a life of piracy.

Knowing she probably shouldn't touch his stuff, but unable to help herself, she took one of the cubes from the shelf and picked up the reader from the desk. The device looked old and worn, like he used it a lot. She dropped the cube in the reader and read the extract. It was about a young, untried warrior who must venture alone into enemy territory to infiltrate an evil wizard's empire to save his people. Although it only hinted at the romance between the hero and the beautiful, young witch who reluctantly served the wizard, the story sounded intriguing anyway, and Teyla couldn't resist a peek at the first few pages. To her delight, the book was as exciting as the extract had promised, and before she realized what she was doing, she curled up in one of the two stuffed chairs beside the bookcase to read the rest of it.

She was still there when Slayter walked into the cabin an hour later. In fact, she was so engrossed in the story she didn't even realize he'd come in until he spoke.

"I see you seem to have settled in."

Startled by his deep voice, Teyla lifted her gaze to look up at him. She didn't know if she should be annoyed he had interrupted her, or embarrassed he'd caught her reading one of his treasured books. One look in those amber eyes of his, though, and she forgot all about the story she'd been reading and lost herself in their soul-filled depths instead.

Realizing she was just sitting there gazing up at him, she blushed and got to her feet. "I'm sorry. I didn't mean to help myself to your books."

"No need to apologize," he said. "Books are meant to be read. Besides, I can hardly expect you to sit in here and twiddle your thumbs until we get to Arkhon."

She felt her throat tighten at the mention of the slave market. "How long will it take us to get there?"

He shrugged. "A week. Maybe less."

A week. That meant she had seven precious days of freedom left. The knowledge made her stomach churn, but she forced her expression to remain neutral as she put the cubereader back on the desk.

"You're taking this all very well," Slayter observed from behind her. "Don't you feel the least bit angry with your father for the situation he's put you in?"

She smoothed her hands down the front of her dress as she considered the question. "I can see how you would think I might be," she said without turning around. "But no, I'm not angry with him. My father did what he had to do to take care of the business and his family."

"What about you? Aren't you part of his family, too?" When she didn't say anything, he continued. "When I asked you earlier if you agreed to the deal, you said you had, but now I wonder if your father even gave you a choice."

She didn't answer. Outsiders didn't always agree with the way things were done on her planet and trying to make them understand could be difficult. It was useless to even try. But Slayter seemed to be expecting an answer.

Teyla turned to give the pirate a small smile. "My father didn't force me to come here, Slayter. As the oldest, it's my duty to do whatever is necessary to help my family. By paying off the debt, I've saved my sisters from someday having to do the same."

She waited for him to question her logic, and suspected he probably would have if a knock on the door hadn't interrupted him.

"Enter," Slayter called.

The door slid open and Olin walked in, a serving tray in his hands. Teyla's mouth watered at the delicious aroma coming from the bowls on it, and she licked her lips as he placed the tray down on the table. She hadn't been able to eat much of her lunch before her father had delivered her to the spaceport, and hadn't realized how hungry she was. She hoped one of those bowls was for her.

Slayter glanced at her. "I thought you might be more comfortable eating in here instead of the mess." He gestured to the table. "Sit, please."

Teyla stared at him in amazement, stunned the pirate would even consider her comfort. Abruptly realizing he was still waiting for her to sit down, she slipped into one of the chairs.

As he took the seat across from her, Olin unloaded the tray, setting the bowls and mugs in front of her and Slayter. The bowls looked like they contained some kind of stew, and from the color of the liquid, the mugs were probably filled with ale. She didn't much like the taste of ale, but was so grateful they were giving her something to eat that she didn't complain. Olin's gaze strayed to her as he placed the basket of bread on the table and he gave her a shy grin.

"I made the bread myself," he said. "Hope you like it."

Slayter's mouth twitched. "Thank you, Olin. That'll be all."

Olin gave him a nod, then glanced at her once more before leaving the cabin. Teyla couldn't help but smile as she picked up her spoon.

"They recruit pirates young, I see," she said.

Slayter chuckled. "They usually do."

"How old is he?"

"Fifteen." Slayter helped himself to a slice of bread. "I picked him up on Nennor when he was twelve. He was living on the streets and tried to pick my pocket. I figured I could either try to scare him straight or give him an honest job."

She looked at him dubiously. "With a pirate?"

"I prefer to think of myself as a businessman with flexible ethics."

That was certainly an interesting way to describe what he did. Though if she was honest with herself, she could admit she'd seen her father do some pretty unethical things in the name of business. People in glass airdomes shouldn't toss rocks, she supposed.

From there, the conversation rambled through various subjects, including his ship, how he got his crew together and what kind of work he normally did. She was a little surprised he was so forthcoming. She was also surprised at how easy it was to talk to him.

Then again, maybe it wasn't so surprising. Slayter was a very unique pirate. Intelligent, well-spoken and way more attractive than any pirate had a right to be. She studied him from beneath her lashes as they ate. Uh-huh. He was definitely the most handsome man she'd ever been around.

"Have you ever been to Arkhon before?" she asked, trying to distract herself so she wouldn't stare at him.

Slayter sopped up what was left of his stew with a piece of bread. "Once."

She would have thought he'd go there more since he was a pirate. "What will happen when we get there?"

He hesitated. "I'm not quite sure. I've never sold a slave before, but I imagine it will be the same process as selling anything else there."

Meaning she would be put on the auction block and sold to the highest bidder. "Do you know if buyers look for certain things when they purchase a sex slave?"

He frowned slightly. "I suppose."

"You don't think they'll want to...sample the merchandise before they buy, will they?"

"I'm sure some buyers might, but I don't think the people who run the auction would allow that." Slayter must have seen the relief on her face because he gave her a reassuring smile. "You don't have anything to be concerned about, Teyla. You're a very beautiful woman. Any man can see that."

Considering the situation, the compliment shouldn't have warmed her like it did, but she felt herself blush anyway. "It's just that I don't have very much experience when it comes to sex. I mean, I'm not a virgin, but I haven't been with a lot of men, either. I'm concerned potential buyer will know right away that I'm inexperienced." She looked at him from beneath lowered lashes. "I don't want you to come out on the short end of this exchange."

He shook his head. "I really don't think that's going to be a problem."

She frowned. "Maybe, but the family would be very embarrassed if I didn't earn enough money on the block to cover the debt." She took a deep breath and let it out slowly. "This is very difficult to ask, but do you think you might be able give me some advice on how best to please a man?"

"Advice?" His eyes went a little wide at that, and he cleared his throat. "Uh, actually, sex is more of a...hands-on thing."

"Oh."

Teyla chewed on her lower lip. She couldn't believe she was even contemplating what she was about to do, but the thought that one of her sisters might end up where she was if she didn't earn enough money to cover the debt was enough to give her the courage she needed.

She lifted her gaze to look at Slayter. "Would you be willing to give me hands-on experience then?"

He arched a brow, but didn't say anything. From the expression on his face, though, it was clear he was taken aback by her request.

"I know I probably shouldn't be asking you for favors, but I just want to make sure you receive the money my family owes you." When he still didn't answer, she added softly, "If you don't find me pleasing enough to bed, I understand."

She was afraid to think what that would mean when it came to her value on the auction block. What would happen if no one bid on her at all?

The corner of Slayter's mouth curved. "I find you quite pleasing, Teyla. Perhaps more than I should."

Her pulse quickened. "Then you'll teach me?"

There was a very long pause, then, "Yes, I'll teach you. If that's what you really want."

"It is. Can we start now?"

They only had a few days before they reached Arkhon, and she didn't want to waste any time.

He hesitated, then nodded. "If you'd like."

Slayter might have seemed hesitant when she'd first brought it up, but now that he had agreed, she could see the fire burning in his eyes. Something told her the pirate would be a very thorough teacher. Heat pooled between her thighs at the thought of him showing her all the different ways she could pleasure a man. She might learn more with him in a few days than she probably ever would have with the men on her planet.

Slayter stood and came around to her side of the table. Taking her hand, he gently pulled her to her feet. Teyla had known the pirate was tall when she'd stood in front of him in the cargo hold earlier, but now she realized just how tall he really was. She barely came up to those broad shoulders of his.

She waited for Slayter to say something, but he simply gazed down at her. The smolder in his gold eyes took her breath away and she swayed toward him. Her reaction to being so close to him caught her off guard, but before she could steady herself, he lowered his head and covered her mouth with his.

The kiss took her by surprise and for a moment she didn't know how to respond. She hadn't expected Slayter to do something so intimate. She'd thought they would shed their clothes and get to it. But as his mouth moved slowly and deliciously over hers, she melted against the hard wall of his chest. He slid his hand in her long hair, deepening the kiss with a groan. Teyla parted her lips under his, sighing with pleasure when his tongue invaded her mouth to claim hers. She ran her hands up his chest to clutch his shoulders, afraid if she didn't hold on to something that she would fall. She didn't know a man's kisses could be so intoxicating.

Or that the feel of his hands on her body could set her afire. But as his free hand slid up her midriff to cup her breast through the thin material of her dress, the heat that had pooled between her thighs earlier completely engulfed her. If she responded to him like this when they were fully clothed, how was she going to react when they were both naked?

That was when she remembered the purpose behind what they were doing. She was supposed to be learning how to pleasure Slayter, but instead it was the other way around. She wondered if she should remind him of that, but as he trailed kisses along the curve of her jaw and down her neck, she decided to play the willing student and leave the teaching part to him. Perhaps this was what men wanted in their women. A willing partner in bed.

He slid his hand from her hair to find the tiny hooks on the back of her dress. He undid them deftly, then gently pushed the straps from her shoulders. The dress slid to the floor to pool at her feet, leaving her standing there in only her skimpy bra and panties.

Slayter gazed down at her, caressing every inch of her nearly naked body as thoroughly as if he were using his hands, and Teyla felt herself blush. None of the other men she'd been with had ever looked at her with such hunger before. And she wasn't even naked yet.

Without a word, Slayter slowly ran his forefinger down the thin strap of her bra and along the lacy edge of the cup, just brushing her skin. Teyla caught her breath as she felt her nipple harden beneath the fabric. He moved his hand over her satin covered breast, grazing the taut peak with his thumb

31

before he reached around to unclasp her bra. Her breasts spilled into his hands and he cupped them gently. Taking her nipples between his fingers, he teased the stiff little peaks until they grew even harder. The movement sent tiny ripples of pleasure through her body and Teyla gasped.

"Do you like that?" Slayter asked softly.

"I thought you were supposed to be teaching me how to please you."

"That will come later. Right now, just answer my question. Do you like it when I squeeze your nipples like that?"

"Yes," she breathed. "It feels wonderful."

"Then you should like this even more."

Taking one of her nipples in his mouth, he suckled gently on it. Teyla moaned and arched against him, her hands finding their way into his thick hair to pull him close. It occurred to her that she should probably tell him how much she was enjoying his mouth on her breast, but the way he was swirling his tongue 'round and 'round made it difficult to form a complete thought, much less a coherent sentence. After one more flick of the tongue, Slayter released that nipple to lavish the same attention on its twin before finally lifting his head to gaze down at her. Dear God, he was making her dizzy.

She opened her mouth to tell him how wonderful that had felt, but got distracted when he hooked his thumbs in her panties and slid them down her legs with painstaking slowness. She shivered at his touch, her pulse racing in anticipation.

Slayter rose to his feet and gazed down at her, taking in her modest breasts, slender waist and long legs with obvious appreciation. "I was wrong before when I said you're beautiful. You're perfect."

While Teyla was sure he was exaggerating, the words sent a surge of pleasure through her anyway. Not just because it meant she would earn a sizeable chunk of money on the auction block, either. Knowing a man like Slayter found her so attractive was incredibly arousing. Before she could thank him, though, he captured her lips in another drugging kiss. This time, she wasn't shy or hesitant, but boldly plunged her tongue into his mouth to tangle with his. She assumed a woman should return a man's ardor in equal measure.

Apparently she was right because he groaned and threaded one hand in her hair, tilting her head back. She ran her hands up his chest, following the hard contours of muscle beneath the material of the shirt he wore. Suddenly she had the urge to see if he looked as magnificent underneath his shirt as he felt.

She was just about to go for the buttons when he slipped his hand between their bodies to cup her sex. She gasped against his mouth as he ran a finger along her folds and gently slid it into her pussy.

"You're very wet," he murmured.

"Is that good?" She liked to think a man would want her to be wet, but she wasn't sure.

He chuckled, the sound soft and sexy in her ear. "Very good."

Since she was wet and ready for him, Teyla expected Slayter to move things into the bedroom so he could bury himself inside her, but instead he found her throbbing clit and made lazy, little circles around it with his finger. She hadn't even considered the possibility he might pleasure her. The few men she'd had sex with had been more concerned about their own needs than worrying about if they were making it good for her. Slayter, on the other hand, seemed in no hurry to rush to the finish line, despite the erection straining at the front of his breeches. A very sizeable erection, she couldn't help but notice.

Maybe he thought touching her would somehow make her a better sex slave. Or maybe he got turned-on by making her so hot. She wondered if all men were like that. She hoped so. Whatever the reason, she decided to forget about trying to figure it out and enjoy what he was doing. She sighed and rotated her hips in time with his finger. Almost immediately, she felt a familiar tingle around her clit. While none of the men she'd slept with had ever brought her to orgasm like this, she had pleasured herself countless times in the privacy of her own bedroom, so she knew she was close to climaxing.

Slayter touched her like that for several long, delicious moments. He seemed to know exactly how much pressure to put on her clit, when to speed up and when to slow down. She couldn't be feeling any better if she were doing this to herself.

He captured and held her eyes with his. The power of his gaze was all it took to tip her over the edge, and she clutched his shoulders as her body began to hum in the familiar way that told her she would climax any second now.

"That's it," Slayter said huskily. "Come for me, Teyla."

Teyla couldn't have stopped herself if she wanted to. What he was doing felt too good. Her whole body shuddered with a level of pleasure she'd never experienced at her own hand and if they weren't on a ship full of pirates, she would have cried out. Instead, she rested her head against Slayter's chest and bit her lip to stifle a moan. If his arm hadn't been wrapped around her, she was sure she would have collapsed to the floor.

All she could do afterward was lean against him and catch her breath as the last tremors of her orgasm subsided. She didn't know how that fit in with her education on sex, but right then, she was too grateful to ask. She only hoped whoever bought her could work the same magic with his fingers as Slayter.

"That's your first lesson," he said softly. "A man—a real man—gets turned-on by giving a woman pleasure. So make sure you enjoy yourself in bed, and let him see it."

Cupping her chin, he tilted her face up to give her a long, hard kiss that left her wobbly legs even weaker.

"Have you ever given a man a blowjob?" he asked when he lifted his head.

Teyla shook her head. She'd heard of the sex act before from her girlfriends back home who had performed it, though. From what they said, it was both fun and highly erotic, and she suddenly couldn't wait to get her first lesson from the handsome pirate.

"Get on your knees," he commanded softly.

Teyla did as he instructed, then sat back on her heels and gazed up at him. She was a little surprised by how easily she fell into the submissive role. Despite her willingness to pay off her family's debt, she'd never thought of herself as particularly subservient. She wondered if it was because she was subconsciously preparing for her new life as a sex slave, or whether it was because Slayter was so incredibly dominant. Whatever the reason, being on her knees in front of him made her pussy spasm.

Above her, Slayter unbuttoned his shirt. As it parted to reveal a smooth, muscular chest and washboard abs, all she could do was stare in appreciation. Her imagination hadn't even come close to how gorgeous he was. Why hadn't any of the men on her planet ever looked this gorgeous? Being a pirate obviously did a body good. She was eager to see the rest of him.

Slayter didn't keep her waiting. Tossing his shirt on the floor, he unbuckled his belt and pushed down his breeches to free his thick, hard erection. Soon, he was completely naked. Well, that wasn't quite true. He was wearing a thin chain around his neck with a ring on it. It was a simple design with a single purple gem. From the size, it was obvious it was a woman's ring, and she wondered whom it belonged to. But those thoughts quickly disappeared as she let her gaze roam over his naked body.

She blinked. Dear Sacred Wellsprings of Kallor. He was beautiful. She could only imagine what he was going to feel like inside her. But she wasn't so sure he was going to fit very far into her mouth.

"Wrap your hand around my cock," he said softly.

Heart racing, she obeyed, and was amazed when her hand couldn't fit around him. He really was big.

Slayter's eyes glinted gold as he gazed down at her. "Now take me in your mouth. Just the tip."

Teyla leaned forward and carefully wrapped her lips around the head. He was warm and soft as velvet against her tongue. But hard as a rock at the same time. The contradiction made her whole body tremble.

"That's it," Slayter said. "Now trace your tongue up and down along either side."

She did as he told her, slowly gliding her tongue along the length of his cock, up one side, then down the other, and back again. Above her, Slayter groaned. Hoping that meant she was doing it right, she repeated the move over and over until he slid his hand in her hair and stopped her.

She looked up at him, waiting patiently for his next order. She had the feeling he had been enjoying what she'd been doing, if the look on his face was any indication.

"Now take me into your mouth again, but let my cock slide in deeper this time."

The words alone were enough to almost make her moan with desire. Resisting the urge, she leaned over and took the head into her mouth again. This time, though, she didn't stop there, but let him slide in a little deeper, moving her tongue quickly along the underside as she did so. He hadn't said anything about doing that, but it seemed like the natural thing to do.

Rocking back and forth, she took him a little deeper with each bob of her head until she felt him touch the back of her throat. The sensation surprised her a little at first, and she hesitated. There was no way she could take him any deeper, was there?

From the way Slayter's fingers tightened in her hair, though, it made her think he wanted her to do just that.

Taking a deep breath, she surged forward, letting his length slide in as far as it would go. She had expected to feel like she was choking, but to her surprise, the sensation of his shaft that far down her throat was more arousing than anything she'd ever felt.

She found herself wondering if she could take all of him down her throat. The task seemed impossible, but it was a challenge she was eager to undertake. Grasping the base of his penis firmly in her hand, she took another deep breath and swallowed, taking him as deep as he could go.

Slayter let out a loud groan. Deciding he must be enjoying what she was doing, she drew him into her mouth so she could take him even deeper, only to still when she felt him tighten his hand in her hair again.

Confused, she blinked up at him. "Am I doing it wrong?"

He let out a throaty sound that was somewhere between a chuckle and a groan. "On the contrary, you're doing it exactly right. In fact, I'd say you're a natural."

"Then why did you stop me?"

"Because you're going to me make come sooner than I wish."

Taking her hand, Slayter lifted her to her feet and swung her up in his arms, then carried her across the cabin to set her down on the bed. Teyla's pulse kicked into overdrive as he braced a hand on either side of her head. On top of her like this, his big, muscular body practically engulfed her. The knowledge was heady, and her breathing came a little faster as he settled between her thighs. Her pussy immediately began to throb with anticipation and she let out a sigh as his mouth came down on hers. If being a sex slave was always going to be like this, then she certainly wasn't going to mind her new profession.

Teyla ran her hands up his chiseled chest, intending to bury her fingers in his dark hair and pull him closer, when he abruptly lifted his head. He gazed down at her, his breathing ragged.

"I can't believe I didn't think to ask this before," he rasped. "You are on birth control, right?"

She nodded, but didn't elaborate. Telling him that girls on Kallor went on birth control the moment they reached womanhood to ensure there wouldn't be any unwanted pregnancies that might prevent them from being used as barter would definitely kill the mood.

Slayter breathed a heavy sigh. "Thank God."

Letting out a growl, he closed his mouth over hers again. Instead of entering her right away like she thought he would, Slayter slowly rubbed the head of his cock up and down her slick folds. While his teasing was fun, it was also complete torment and she moaned against his mouth in frustration. He must have figured out what she was trying to tell him because he stopped torturing her and eased his length into her pussy inch by incredible inch.

Teyla gasped as his cock filled her. Granted, she hadn't been with many men, but the ones she'd had sex with had never filled her so fully or completely. It was as if Slayter had been made just for her. She wrapped her arms and legs around him, pulling him in as deep as she could.

"You're so tight, I could come just like this," he said hoarsely.

She felt a surge of pride. Even though he was in charge, knowing she could make him climax simply from being inside her made her feel surprisingly powerful.

She locked her eyes with his. "I want you to come. What can I do to make that happen?"

He bent to give her gentle kiss. "In reality, you wouldn't have to do much of anything. However, you could rotate your hips or reach around with your hands to grab my ass. Or pull me into you repeatedly with your heels. Even squeezing me tightly with your thighs. Anything like that."

She smiled and slowly rotated her hips beneath him. "Like this?"

Slayter groaned in answer, the sound rough and sexy in her ear as he began to pump into her. He took his time, deliberately sliding his cock out of her pussy before plunging deep again and again. He was touching her in places those fumbling boys she'd been with probably didn't even know existed.

She moved her hips faster, wanting more, and more was exactly what Slayter gave her. He thrust into her so hard and so fast it took her breath away. This time, she didn't bother to stifle her screams of ecstasy. Instead, she threw back her head and cried out loud enough for the entire ship to hear. Slayter, on the other hand, was much more disciplined, and buried his face in her neck, letting out a hoarse groan as he came.

It was a long time before he lifted his head, and then it was to capture her lips in a searing kiss.

"I didn't know sex could be like that," she breathed. "It was amazing."

"That it was." His mouth curved. "And your education is just getting started."

Teyla shivered at the promise in his voice. She started to ask what he had in mind, but all that came out was a moan as he kissed her again. It was way more fun to let him show her instead.

Chapter Two

Slayter woke up the next morning to the extremely pleasurable sensation of a woman's warm mouth on his cock. *Teyla.* Last night had been so incredible, he was sure it had been a dream. But not even dreams were this good. Damn, the woman had a talented tongue.

He lifted his head to look at her. Teyla's delicate hand was wrapped around the base of his rapidly hardening shaft and she was swirling her tongue around the head. Watching her was erotic as hell and he couldn't stifle the groan that escaped his lips. She looked up at the sound, her long, dark hair falling over her shoulder to brush his stomach.

"I didn't know you were awake," she said softly.

His mouth quirked. "It's kind of hard to sleep when you're doing that."

Color tinted her cheeks. "I thought I might need some more practice giving you a blowjob. You don't mind, do you?"

Slayter almost laughed. He wanted to tell her she didn't need any more practice doing that or anything else. She was already amazing in bed. She might not have come to him with much experience, but her enthusiasm more than made up for it.

"I don't mind at all. Please go ahead and continue."

Giving him a smile, Teyla bent to slowly run her tongue up the length of his shaft from base to tip. Once there, she wrapped her lips around him and swirled her tongue over the head. Slayter sucked in a breath. *Daaaammn.*

She lifted her head to look at him. "Good?"

He grinned. "Better than good. Don't stop."

Resting a hand on each of his thighs, she bent her head to take him in her mouth again. This time, she didn't swirl her tongue over him, but instead wrapped her lips around his erection and began to slowly move up and down, taking him deeper and deeper with each bob of her head. He let out a ragged groan as the head of his cock touched the back of her throat, then went even further. He'd never been with a woman who could do that so effortlessly.

Just when he thought it couldn't get any better, she took him all the way in and he felt himself slide deep down her throat. *Oh shit.* He didn't think he'd ever felt anything so incredible. He never wanted her to stop. He damn sure wouldn't last long if she kept doing what she was doing, though.

Wrapping his hand in her silky hair, he took charge, guiding her movements more slowly. Teyla let out a soft, sexy moan at his show of dominance, and the sound made his cock throb. Did she even know how hot she made him?

She cupped his balls in her hand, gently massaging them as she licked him. He hadn't mentioned that particular technique last night, but she seemed to instinctively know how to touch him.

Her mouth was warm, her tongue gliding along his length as she moved her head up and down, and it was all he could do not to explode right on the spot. He wondered how she knew he was so close to coming, but she must have because every time he got close, she licked and sucked more slowly, going from taking his cock deep to running her tongue along his hard length to focusing all of her attention on the head. She kept him on the edge for so long he was practically dizzy from it. For a woman who'd never given a man a blowjob until last night, she was damn good at it.

Unable to hold back anymore, Slayter tightened his hand in her hair and urged her head down. "Make me come."

Teyla obediently bobbed her head up and down, swallowing almost all of him, then gliding her mouth back up his shaft. She repeated the motion over and over, faster and faster until he thought he might go crazy from how wonderful it felt.

"Oh yeah, that's it," he rasped. "Make me come, Teyla. Make me come."

She did, slowly drawing his orgasm out of him, and he shot his cum into her mouth with a groan that left him trembling.

Slayter loosened his grip on her hair so she could lift her head. Teyla ran her tongue over her lips, gazing up at him with the sexiest pair of lavender eyes he'd ever seen. Sitting up, he covered her mouth with his in a hard, hot kiss.

"God, you're remarkable," he breathed when he finally came up for air.

"I'm glad I can please you," she said softly.

He grinned. "You certainly did that. And after giving me an orgasm like that, I think it's only right that I return the favor."

Excitement flashed in her eyes, but she quickly hid it. "That's not necessary. You're supposed to be teaching me how to please a man."

Taking her hand, he urged her onto her back. "Perhaps the lesson I want to teach you is how to come over and over again until you scream with pleasure."

He didn't wait for a reply, but started kissing his way down her naked body. He'd just stopped to focus on her perfect, rosy nipples when the ship's intercom interrupted him.

"Captain," the pilot said. "There's something up here I think you're going to be interested in."

Slayter groaned. There was something, or rather someone, right here in his bed who interested him. He couldn't tell the other man that, though. Besides, Salo wouldn't bother him if it wasn't necessary.

"I'll be right there, Salo."

Slayter gently brushed Teyla's hair back from her face. "I have to go up to the bridge. We'll continue this later."

Giving her another slow kiss, he reluctantly got out of bed and pulled on his breeches. Teyla made no move to cover her nakedness with the sheet, but instead lay there on the pillows watching him, her arms stretched out over her head, one leg bent at the knee. Even though her lack of shyness was sexy as hell, he wondered if she did it because she was truly comfortable naked, or whether she thought it was how a good sex slave should behave. Regardless of the reason, it took everything in him not to forget about whatever it was Salo wanted him to see and spend the rest of the day in bed with her. Unfortunately, he had a ship to run.

He grabbed his holster from the desk and strapped to his thigh, then glanced at Teyla. "I'll be back as soon as I can."

"I'll be waiting."

The simple words echoed in his head as he strode down the passageway. While he might have a woman in every spaceport, none of them were bound to be waiting for him when and if he docked on their planet again. He had to admit knowing Teyla would be in his bed when he finished his business on the bridge was rather nice, even if the arrangement was only temporary.

He still couldn't believe she'd asked him to give her lessons on how to please a man. He knew she took her responsibility to pay off her family's debt seriously, but he hadn't realized how much until she'd proposed the idea. Although he didn't have any experience with the sex slave trade, he was pretty sure the scum who went to those types of auctions would purchase her based on her beauty alone, regardless of how much sexual prowess she had or didn't have. Teaching her the tricks of the trade wasn't necessary.

So why hadn't he refused?

Because he wanted her, plain and simple, had probably wanted her from the moment she stepped foot on his ship. So much for not damaging the goods.

Slayter swore under his breath as he walked onto the bridge. He'd think about Teyla later. Right now, he needed to take care of business, and from the frown furrowing both the pilot's and his first officer's brows as the men stared out the view screen, it must be damn important.

"What do we have?" Slayter asked.

Hewson half turned to look at him. "Rommel. Fucking bastard's taking down a luxury yacht."

Slayter ground his jaw at the name. Rommel was a pirate he'd crossed paths with and gotten the better of on more than one occasion. The man hated him, and the feeling was mutual.

He peered out the view screen. Rommel's ship had taken up position to one side of the larger craft and was firing repeatedly at it. While the yacht had some shielding and even a few small cannons, it wasn't a match for the nimble pirate ship, and Rommel disabled it within moments.

"Put up our cloaking shields," Slayter said to Salo.

The dark-haired pirate glanced over his shoulder at Slayter. "We taking the yacht ourselves?"

Slayter's mouth curved. "After we put a few holes in Rommel's hull."

Chuckling, Salo flipped the switch to engage the shields that made the ship invisible.

Slayter crossed his arms over his chest. "Fire when ready."

Rommel couldn't fight an opponent he couldn't see, so it didn't take more than a dozen direct hits with the laser cannons from Slayter's ship to get the other pirate to turn tail and run. Slayter grinned as Rommel's wounded ship disappeared in the darkness of space. Damn, that had felt good. Not only did he have the satisfaction of besting the bastard yet again, but he'd be able to take his booty, too.

As any pirate would say, if you weren't strong enough to keep what you've taken, then it wasn't yours to begin with.

Slayter turned his attention to the luxury yacht. The ship was still floating helplessly where Rommel had left it.

"Life signs?" he asked Salo.

The man typed something into the computer on the control panel in front of him. "I'm showing eight people. The support systems were compromised during the fight, though, so they've only got an hour of air at most."

They'd be easy pickings then. "Round up Valin and Winsen and tell them to meet me in the airlock."

Slayter turned to leave the bridge only to stop in his tracks when he saw Teyla standing in the doorway. He frowned. While he hadn't ordered her to stay in his quarters, he hadn't expected her to show up on the bridge. Clearly, neither had Hewson or Salo. Both men were looking at her in stunned silence.

"Teyla," he said. "Is something wrong?"

She shook her head. "No. I heard the sounds of fighting and wanted to make sure everything was all right."

He nodded. "Everything's fine. We got in a firefight with another pirate who was trying to take possession of a luxury yacht. I'm going to go over with some of the crew and board her."

Slayter didn't owe Teyla an explanation, but he saw no reason to hide the information from her, either. She already knew he was a pirate. Commandeering some wealthy person's yacht was a hell of a lot less reprehensible than selling an innocent woman into slavery.

"What about the people on board?" she asked.

"If they survive, I'll drop them off at the first planet we come to," he said, then added, "I won't harm them if I don't have to."

45

Her face colored and she looked past him to the view screen. "What will you do with the yacht?"

"It would be nice to sell it in one piece, but that would mean hauling it halfway across the galaxy to someplace that didn't recognize it as a stolen ship. So I'll probably just sell it for scrap."

Her brow furrowed at that. She took a step closer to the view screen to get a better look at the yacht. After a moment, she turned back to him.

"The markings on it are Thracian royalty. I've dealt with the Thracians while working for my father, so I know from experience they can be very appreciative to someone who does them a favor. In fact, their extreme sense of honor would demand they pay you the combined value of those on board. A ship like that is bound to be carrying someone important, maybe even someone from the royal family. You'd almost certainly get more money for saving them than you will selling the ship for parts."

Slayter frowned as he considered the suggestion. Pirates didn't usually make deals with the people they stole things from to give those same things back. It was easier to sell them on the open market. Not to mention a hell of a lot less messy. Most people didn't take kindly to paying good money for something that was already theirs.

"Think of it as a salvage and rescue operation," Teyla prompted when he hesitated. "The Thracians don't even have to know you're a pirate. Let them think you're merely a concerned citizen."

Slayter had to fight hard to keep from chuckling. A salvage and rescue operation, huh? He'd always been damn skilled at the salvage part, but the whole rescue thing was outside the realm of his normal business practices.

Even so, he had to admit Teyla had a point. He'd probably only make a few thousand credits from selling the luxury yacht for scrap, and that was after a lot of haggling. If the Thracians were even half as grateful as she thought, then he could easily come out on top, especially considering he'd have to go light-years out of his way to sell the spaceship, which would cut into any profit he made. Thrace was half a day's journey away, if that.

He glanced at Hewson. "Get Valin, Winsen and Deran to patch the worst of the holes on the yacht, then have Conder pump enough oxygen into the thing so we can tow it back to Thrace."

The other man raised a brow in surprise. "Are you sure?"

Slayter let his gaze slide back to Teyla, a small smile curving his lips. "I'm sure."

While his crew patched the holes, Slayter boarded the other ship with Genoone. The communications officer frowned when he heard the plan to return the yacht to its owner, especially when he discovered it was Teyla's idea, however he wisely held his tongue after the scowl Slayter sent his way.

The passengers didn't know Slayter and his crew were pirates, and Slayter didn't volunteer the information. Instead, he took Teyla's advice and simply let them think he was a concerned citizen who had come to their rescue. They were extremely grateful and vowed to forever be in his debt. His mouth twisted wryly at their choice of words. Considering the current position the last man who owed him a debt had put him in, he'd rather have the Imperial credits. The people on the yacht didn't need to know he planned on negotiating their return, though, so he made sure to sound nonchalant when he asked which royal Thracian family owned the yacht.

"So I can escort you safely home, of course," he added with a charming smile.

The passengers were only too happy to supply the information. Ten minutes later he and his crew were on their way to Thrace, the yacht in tow.

"I've been thinking you should handle the negotiations when we get there," he told Teyla when they docked.

She was curled up in the same chair where he'd found her the night before, engrossed in another book, and she looked up at him in surprise. "Me?"

He shrugged. "Why not? You have experience dealing with the Thracian people, so it only makes sense."

Teyla was silent, as if considering whether to agree. Finally, she nodded. "All right. I'll negotiate for you."

Normally, Slayter liked to be in charge, but since Teyla had suggested approaching the Thracians, she might as well be the one to talk to them. If she couldn't handle it or didn't get the kind of money he was looking for, then he'd take over.

Like the passengers on the yacht, the Thracians who greeted them at the port had blue skin that ranged from pale aqua to deep navy. That, combined with their sapphire eyes and indigo hair, made them a race which was both unusual and mesmerizing. They were also extremely polite to outsiders, Slayter learned. When the chamberlain at the royal palace heard why he, Teyla and Deran had come, the man immediately showed them to the Prime's ornate receiving room.

Slayter placed a hand on Teyla's back and leaned close to whisper in her ear. "If you could manage to get enough to pay for a new starboard engine for the ship, I'd be most appreciative when we get back to my cabin."

She slanted him a look, the promise in the silky words hanging in the air between them. From the heat in her lavender eyes, there was no mistaking she knew exactly what he meant. The flare of desire made his cock harden in his breeches, and he had to stifle a groan.

"How much does a new starboard engine cost?" she asked.

"A good one is around eighty thousand credits."

She gave him a smile. "I'll see what I can do."

Any misgivings Slayter had about Teyla's ability to negotiate a good deal for him disappeared the moment she turned that charming smile of hers on the Thracian Prime. Though the elderly man quibbled over the concessions she sweetly pointed out were only Slayter's fair due for saving his yacht and rescuing his niece and her friends from bloodthirsty pirates, in the end he agreed to give her everything she asked for. Not only did she talk the Prime into giving Slayter one-hundred-thousand credits in platinum chips, but she also walked away from the negotiating table with a shiny, new starboard engine and a barrel of Dunagan ale. Slayter was damn impressed. That was a hell of a lot more than he would have gotten out of the Thracian leader.

"You're quite a negotiator," Slayter told her as they made their way back to his ship. "I get the feeling that wasn't your first time at the bargaining table."

Her lips curved. "We Kallorians are known for our ability to negotiate a deal. I just happen to be better at it than most of my people."

Slayter arched a brow. He wondered why her father hadn't let her do the negotiating when he'd come looking for his money the other day. She would have had him agreeing to just about anything. Then again, with that Kallorian sense of duty of hers, something told him she probably would have made the same deal her father had.

"I thought the crew might appreciate the ale," Teyla said, interrupting his thoughts. "I've heard it's very good."

Slayter's mouth twitched, but he didn't say anything. Deran was already grinning from ear to ear at the prospect of drinking the expensive ale. The rest of the crew was just as pleased when they saw the barrel. Even Genoone couldn't hide his approval. The fastest way to a pirate's heart was through his love of alcohol. She'd just made a lot of friends on his crew.

Deciding to leave his men to their ale, Slayter took Teyla's hand and led her to his cabin. Once inside, he pulled her into his arms and kissed her long and thoroughly on the mouth.

"Time to show you my appreciation," he said.

Teyla's pussy quivered at the words. Although that wasn't the main reason she had talked the Thracian leader into throwing in the new starboard engine, she was glad Slayter hadn't forgotten his promise. It might be selfish to want to be on the receiving end, but once she was a sex slave, it was very likely the man who owned her wouldn't worry about her pleasure much.

"Take off your dress," Slayter commanded softly.

She hesitated. It was silly to be shy, especially since he had already seen her naked, but the thought of undressing in front of him made her blush. Reaching behind her, she undid the tiny hooks on the back of her dress. Heart thudding against her ribs, she slowly pushed one strap off her shoulder, then the other before allowing the dress to slide down her body.

"Now your underwear," he ordered.

She did as he instructed, her fingers trembling with excitement as she unhooked her bra, then wiggled her panties over her hips. Oddly enough, even though Slayter was giving the orders, she felt like she was the one in charge, and the feeling of control it gave her was exhilarating. Slayter's molten gaze followed her every move. The heat in his eyes made her pussy throb, and she squeezed her thighs together to ease the ache there.

Tawny eyes caressed her naked body, lingering on her naked breasts for a long, breathtaking moment, before caressing her long legs, and she shivered with anticipation.

Slayter took her hand, but instead of pulling her into his arms for another kiss like she thought he would, he led her across the cabin until she was standing under the coat rack. He tossed the leather duster aside, then gently urging her back against the wall, he took her hands and placed them above her head.

"Don't move," he said.

She obeyed, watching in confusion as he slipped the thin strip of leather that laced the top of his shirt together out of its holes. What was he going to do with that? Realization dawned on her when he expertly wrapped the leather around her wrists, then looped it around one of the pegs above her head. A little tremor of excitement course through her. *Oh.*

Slayter leaned close and put his mouth to her ear. "To show you just how much I appreciate all your hard work at the negotiation table today, I'm going to make love to every inch of your beautiful body. Would you like that?"

The feel of his warm breath on her skin made Teyla quiver almost as much as the erotic image his words conjured up, and she could only let out a breathy, "Mmm."

He pulled back to gaze down at her. "I want to hear you say it."

"Yes," she moaned. "I would like that."

Hands braced against the wall to either side of her, Slayter slowly trailed a path of hot kisses down the curve of her arm. Even though she had no desire to free herself, Teyla couldn't help but wiggle against her bonds a little, just to see how secure they were. They weren't tight, but they weren't loose enough for her to free her hands, either. That knowledge excited her even more and she almost wished Slayter would forget about his promise to make love to her whole body and bury himself in her pussy instead. As he very carefully licked and nibbled on the inside of her elbow, however, she changed her mind. This slow exploration of his might be fun.

Teyla sighed as he pressed light, little kisses along the curve her jaw, parting her lips in anticipation. But instead of covering her mouth with his, Slayter teased her lips with featherlight kisses that made her tingle all the way to the tips of her toes. She squirmed, wanting to grab a handful of hair and pull him down for a real kiss. The fact that she couldn't only made what he was doing that much more arousing, and she moaned as he teasingly traced her lips with his again.

"Kiss me," she begged.

He cupped her chin in his big hand, his mouth hovering just above hers for an excruciating moment before he finally captured her lips in a long, hot kiss. She whimpered when he lifted his head, about to beg him to kiss her again, but the words disappeared as he slowly kissed his way down her neck to pay attention to her breasts.

Palming them gently in his hands, he took one nipple between his thumb and forefinger, then bent his head to close his mouth over the other. Teyla gasped as he suckled on it. Her nipples were even more sensitive than they'd been last night, and she wondered if it was because she was tied up. Was that secretly submissive side she didn't know she had coming out again? Was she all hot and bothered because she knew the pirate could do anything he wanted to her and she'd be powerless to stop him? Maybe. But only because she instinctively knew Slayter wouldn't do anything she didn't want him to do.

And right now, she wanted him to keep doing exactly what he was doing.

Slayter swirled his tongue 'round and 'round her areola with methodical slowness, drawing the bud into his mouth again and again until she was panting for breath. Only then did he move to her other breast so he could do the same to that nipple. In between licks, he nipped gently at it with teeth. The sensation sent tremors through her and she had to bite her lip to keep from squealing.

When he finally lifted his head after several long, delicious moments, she hoped he might treat the first nipple to an encore performance, but he dropped to his knees and slowly kissed his way down her stomach. Her pulse quickened as she realized where he was going. Slayter had not only initiated her to the act of giving oral sex the night before, but receiving it as well. The orgasm he'd given her had been out of this galaxy and she suddenly couldn't wait to feel his mouth on her clit again.

Instead of heading directly there, though, Slayter stopped halfway to make a few teasing circles around her bellybutton with his tongue before moving lower. Teyla caught her breath, surprised at how erotic it had felt, and almost wished he'd spend a little more time on that part of her anatomy. Almost. Her pussy was tingling too much to be ignored.

Although Slayter lifted one of her legs to balance her foot on his shoulder, he didn't put his mouth on her clit immediately, but pressed a gentle kiss to the inside of first one thigh, then the other. His silky hair tickled where it brushed against her skin, and she had to bite her lip as a tremor went through her. Spreading her lips with the fingers of his free hand, he slowly ran his tongue up one side of the slick folds of her pussy, then the other. Teyla moaned every time he came near her clit, but he didn't lick her there. The urge to grab his head and put his tongue exactly where she wanted it was almost too much to take, and she strained at the leather holding her captive. The bindings refused to give even a little, though, and that made the torment even sweeter.

After one more swipe along her lips, Slayter looked up at her, his eyes like liquid fire. "Tell me what you want."

Teyla gazed down at him in confusion for a moment, too dazed by the feel of his tongue on her to even think straight. "I—I want you to lick me."

"Where do you want me to lick you?"

Color suffused her face. He wanted her to say it out loud? She wet her suddenly dry lips. "My clit."

His sensuous lips curved into a satisfied smile, as if he'd won a victory. But as he leaned forward to flick the sensitive nub with his tongue, she decided she was the victor in this little game they were playing.

"You taste so good," he rasped as he made lazy circles 'round and around her clit with his tongue.

Teyla arched against him, her hands balling into fists above her head. "Just like that," she breathed. "Don't stop."

He tightened his grip on her ass cheek, moving his tongue more firmly and deliberately, almost insistently, on her clit. He'd had her on the edge with his teasing since he'd tied her up, so it didn't take long for her to orgasm. The sensation centered directly on her clit, then gradually spread through her entire body until she was trembling all over. Teyla opened her mouth to scream, but as her climax continued to build to a crescendo, the cries were trapped in her throat and she could only writhe against her bonds.

She struggled at the leather holding her prisoner, though whether it was so she could hold him in place or grab him by the hair and drag his mouth away, she wasn't sure. As Slayter lapped at her clit over and over, the pleasure became so intense that she would have collapsed if she hadn't been tied up. Bound like she was, though, she was helpless to do anything except ride out the waves of ecstasy as one orgasm after another coursed through her body.

Slayter didn't stop licking her until he had wrung every bit of pleasure from her body and when he was done, all she could do was lean back against the wall and try to catch her breath. She was barely even aware he'd lowered her leg until he pressed another tender kiss to the inside of each thigh and rose to his feet.

He threaded his hand into her hair, tilting her head back so he could kiss her. He tasted of her juices, sweet and just a little bit musky, and she was amazed at how pleasant the flavor was. He sucked her bottom lip into his mouth, giving it a little tug.

"You drive me crazy, do you know that?" he demanded hoarsely, his breath hot against her cheek. "Your scent. Your taste. Your kiss. I can't get enough of you."

Teyla opened her mouth to tell him he affected her just the same, but his mouth was on hers again. When he finally lifted his head, she was breathless and weak in the knees. She blinked up at him, waiting for him to untie her and take her to bed, but he surprised her by spinning her around so she was facing the wall. Confused, she looked at him over her shoulder, but he slid an arm around her waist, molding her naked body against his fully clothed one. His cock strained against the front of his breeches, hot and hard where it pressed into her ass.

Slayter slid his hand up her stomach to cup her breast, his thumb and forefinger squeezing the stiff nipple he found there while he ran his other hand over her ass in a loving caress. Teyla sighed, only to let out a startled gasp when she felt his hand come down on her cheek a moment later. Then, before she even realized what he was doing, he lifted his hand and brought it down in several more quick smacks. The spanking caught her off guard and she was about to ask what he was doing when she discovered the feel of his hand smacking her ass was creating the most delicious throb between her legs.

He alternated from one cheek to the other, spanking her with an easy rhythm that had her "ooohing" and "aaahing" as much as squealing from the heat spreading across her cheeks, and she almost begged him for more when he stopped to give her ass a firm squeeze. His hand was cool on her red-hot skin, and she moaned. Slayter chuckled, the deep sound sending delightful shivers racing all over her body even as he backed away. She looked over her shoulder at him, wondering what he was doing, and was relieved to see him taking off his clothes.

Naked, he stepped up behind her, pressing his hard, muscular body against hers as he trailed hot kisses down her neck. She let her head fall back against his shoulder with a soft sigh, loving the way his hard cock pressed insistently against her tingling bottom. The spanking he'd given her had been fun, but she liked this even more. She rotated her hips, rubbing her ass against his erection. The husky groan in her ear told her Slayter approved.

Her breath quickened as he cupped her breasts with both hands. Between his fingers on her nipples, his hard shaft grinding against her ass cheeks and his mouth on her neck, there were so many sensations it was difficult to concentrate on any one of them. And Slayter wasn't done yet.

He slid one hand up to gently caress her neck before moving up to lightly trace the outline of her lips with his fingers. She moaned, practically dizzy from his touch. What he was doing felt so incredible she thought she might actually have an orgasm just from that. Before she could find out, however, he pulled his teasing fingers away from her mouth and slowly slid them down between her breasts to the damp curls between her thighs. He slipped his hand between her legs and slid his finger deep inside her wetness.

Teyla inhaled sharply, her pussy instinctively clenching around his finger as he moved it back and forth. He kept his movements slow at first, then gradually picked up speed until she was on the verge of coming. Then he backed off, sliding his finger out of her pussy before she could climax.

She groaned in frustration.

Behind her, Slayter chuckled.

Forgetting for the moment that this was about teaching her how to be a good sex slave, Teyla was about to demand he stop teasing her when she felt Slayter grasp her hips. Giving them a little tug, he pulled her into the perfect position for him slide his cock into her from behind. They both let out a groan of satisfaction as he sank himself as deep inside her as he could go.

She held her breath, waiting for him to thrust, but he didn't. Instead, he leaned close and put his mouth to her ear.

"Ask me to fuck you," he ordered softly.

She automatically opened her mouth to obey, but nothing came out. She wasn't sure if she could say something so naughty.

"Ask me to do it, Teyla," he repeated, his voice husky, almost compelling as he ground his hips in gentle circles. "Or I won't."

Teyla caught her lower lip between her teeth, shuddering at the feel of his shaft pulsing inside her. "Fuck me," she whispered.

His breath stirred her hair. "I didn't hear you. Say it louder."

She ignored the blush that rushed into her cheeks, glad he couldn't see it. "Fuck me," she said, louder this time. "Please fuck me."

Slayter obeyed, his cock gliding in and out of her wet pussy with almost agonizing slowness. He was going to drive her crazy like this.

"Harder," she begged.

"Fuck you harder, you mean?" he asked, pumping into her just as gently.

Her color deepened. "Yes. Fuck me harder!"

He did, the force of his thrusts pushing her forward, and she grabbed onto the hook she was tied to so she could push back. Holding on to her with one hand, he buried the other in her long hair and tugged gently. The primal show of dominance made her tingle all the way down to her toes, reminding her of just how much she liked playing the submissive role. That, combined with Slayter pounding wildly into her, sent her over the edge into oblivion, and she cried out as her orgasm surged through her. As Slayter's groans of release joined her screams to echo around the cabin, she found herself wishing she could be with him like this forever.

Chapter Three

ഇ

Teyla didn't know what was better, the feel of Slayter's strong, muscled arm wrapped around her when she woke up the next morning, or the lingering sensations from last night's sex lessons. Not only were her arms a little sore from being tied up, but her ass still tingled from the spanking he'd given her. Then again, that part might just be her imagination. Or wishful thinking. She'd never been spanked before, so she wasn't sure. Getting her bottom warmed had been a very erotic experience, especially since it had been followed by such incredible sex.

Her lips curved at the memory. Saying it had been "incredible" was an understatement. It had been extraordinary. She'd learned that sex could be very enjoyable, even amazing, the first night on board, but she had no idea it could be so perfect. When Slayter was inside her, it was like she was transported to a world of pure pleasure. Even now, hours later, she swore she could still feel the warmth of his cum in her pussy.

She wondered if sex would be as breathtaking with the man who bought her, but sadly dismissed the thought. As a slave, her pleasure probably wouldn't be part of the equation. It would be about pleasing her master. Even if she was fortunate to have an owner who considered her needs, she couldn't imagine how the sex could ever be as wonderful as it was with Slayter. She might not have a lot of experience on the subject, but instinct told her the ship-shaking good sex she and Slayter had been engaging in had everything to do with the man she was with. It made her wish her father had handed her over to the pirate as payment instead of suggesting he sell her on the auction block. There was no guarantee Slayter would have agreed to the deal, especially since apparently women weren't common on pirate ships, but she certainly would have been happy with the arrangement. Besides being an animal in bed — or wherever else they made love, she thought with a grin — he actually listened to her when she talked, whether what she had to say was as important as suggesting he barter with the Thracians or as simple as what she wanted for dinner. That was rather unusual trait for a man, at least in her experience.

She stifled a snort. What was she doing? This wasn't some romantic fairy tale. Slayter might be polite and attentive and listen to her when she talked, but he wasn't her soul mate no matter how perfectly their bodies fit together. He was only teaching her about sex so she'd fetch him a handsome profit when they reached Arkhon. It was sound business practice. Nothing more.

Maybe, but that didn't mean she couldn't enjoy it. Or pretend they had a future together for a just a little while, she thought as she felt Slayter's arm tighten around her.

He nuzzled her neck. "Good morning."

The trace of scruff on his jaw tickled where it scraped her skin, sending shivers through her. She wrapped her arm around his, intertwining their fingers. "Good morning to you. Did you sleep well?"

He pulled her closer, molding her more firmly to him. "Considering we were up most of the night, very well. I could sleep a few more hours, though."

She laughed as she felt his hard cock press against her ass. "I don't know about that. You seem to be wide awake to me."

He chuckled, the sound soft and erotic in her ear. "You have that effect on me."

Teyla smiled, his words warming her more than they should have. "You do the same to me."

"Is that so? Let me see." He slipped his hand between her legs to run his finger along the lips of her pussy. "Mmm, you're all wet."

Between spending the morning thinking about what they did last night and having his erection snuggly nestled against her now, she didn't wonder why. She smiled at him over her shoulder. "A good slave should always be ready to please her master, correct?"

After all the naughty things she'd said last night, she shouldn't be embarrassed by her forwardness, but she blushed just the same. If Slayter noticed, he didn't mention it. He let out a soft, sexy growl that had her forgetting about how shy she was and instead thrusting out her ass in invitation when he positioned the head of his shaft at the opening of her pussy. She held her breath, half afraid, half hoping he would tease her like he'd done night before, but instead he sheathed himself deep inside her in one smooth motion.

She moaned into the pillow as he reached around and found her clit with his fingers. She rotated her hips as he made leisurely circles around it, matching his thrusts rhythm for rhythm.

Slayter brushed her ear with his lips. "Do you like that?"

"Mm-hmm. Don't stop."

He pressed a kiss to the curve of her shoulder. "I won't. I'm going to keep touching you like this and fucking you like this until I make you come just like I did last night. Would you like that?"

"Yes," she breathed.

She thought he groaned, but she couldn't be sure because he buried his face in the curve of her neck. He kept his thrusts slow and deliberate as he continued making little circles on her clit. Unable to help herself, she reached down to cover his hand with hers, urging him to speed up the pace.

"Mmm," she moaned. "Just like that."

She closed her eyes and thrust her ass back against him, silently begging him to take her harder. He must have understood her silent plea because he moved his finger faster on her clit while at the same time pounding his cock into her pussy as deeply as he could go.

As always, the combination tripped her pleasure trigger, sending her skyrocketing into orbit so fast and so furiously she could only hang on for dear life while her body shuddered in ecstasy. Slayter went over the edge with her, letting out a hoarse groan against her neck as he climaxed.

Afterward, Slayter didn't pull out right away, but stayed buried deep in her pussy as he continued to tenderly move his fingers on her clit. As much as she didn't want him to stop, even that light touch soon got to be too much on her sensitive nub, and she stilled his hand with hers. Rolling over, she looped her arm around his neck and pulled him close for a slow kiss.

He brushed her hair back with gentle fingers. "I could stay here with you all day."

Her pussy spasmed at the prospect of spending hours on end doing what they just did. "Then why don't you?"

He let out a heavy sigh. "Because I have a ship to run and a crew that's bound to come looking for me if I don't make an appearance."

Of course. In the afterglow of their lovemaking, she'd completely forgotten where they were. She tried to hide her disappointment behind a small smile, but it mustn't have worked because he reached out to caress her cheek.

"You're more than welcome to come with me while I make my rounds, if you want."

She blinked, surprised by the invitation. "Really? You wouldn't mind?"

He flashed her a grin. "Of course not. It'll give me a chance to give you a proper tour of the ship."

Teyla's heart did a little backflip.

"Unless you'd rather stay here and read," he added.

"No!" she said quickly. "I'd much rather see the ship."

Actually, she wasn't all that interested in the ship. She just wanted to spend time with Slayter. Which went against all common sense, of course, especially since in a few days time, she'd never see the handsome pirate again. But maybe that was exactly why she did want to accompany him. It was like stolen time.

Teyla didn't want to keep Slayter waiting, so she hurried through her morning routine in the bathroom, then dressed as quickly as she could. When she walked into his study a little while later, it was to find him at his computer. He looked up at her entrance.

"Ready?" he asked.

She nodded, as eager to take the tour of the ship with him as she would be if he were taking her out on a date.

They stopped to get something to eat in the mess before beginning their excursion. Since it didn't look like any dining room she'd ever been in, however, Teyla supposed it should probably be considered part of the tour. She was both surprised and pleased that they had the place to themselves.

"The crew's been up for hours already," Slayter said when she remarked on it.

She sipped her tea thoughtfully, wondering if the men would be curious as to why their captain hadn't eaten breakfast with them. Did they suspect she and Slayter were sleeping together? She wanted to ask him, but couldn't figure out how to broach the subject.

As Slayter showed her around a little while later, Teyla had to admit she didn't pay much attention to the ship or its components. She was too caught up in the man himself to listen to what he was saying. Even though she couldn't remember where the engine room was or which direction was aft and which was fore, the one thing she learned was that

Slayter not only loved his ship, but that he cared very much about its crew. They were like a great big family to him.

Oddly enough, the men didn't treat her like an outsider. To a man, they were polite and gracious, pointing out things they thought she might be interested in when she and Slayter stopped by. Even Genoone didn't have a curt word or a harsh glare for her. She suspected the ale she'd gotten for them was partly responsible for their attitude adjustment. Having Slayter beside her almost certainly had a lot to do with it, too.

"I think the only place you haven't really seen yet is the bridge," Slayter said as they walked along yet another passageway. "That's where the magic really happens."

Teyla wanted to tell him that all the magic happened in his bedroom, at least as far as she was concerned, but she only smiled.

She and Slayter were just about to step onto the bridge when the ship suddenly bucked under them. Teyla stumbled, automatically reaching out to steady herself, but Slayter caught her before she could fall.

He swore under his breath. "What the hell was that, Salo?"

The pilot didn't even bother to glance over his shoulder. "A cloaked ship just locked onto our foredeck, Captain. They're trying to board us!"

Teyla's eyes went wide. She looked at Slayter. "But you're the pirates. Who would try to board your ship?"

He clenched his jaw. "Other pirates. They must have heard about the platinum chips we picked up in Thrace. It's the only thing we have that would make someone ballsy enough to attack us."

"Captain, they're trying to get in the main airlock," Salo shouted. "They're coming in the loading dock on C-deck, too."

"Shit," Slayter muttered.

Teyla opened her mouth to ask what they were going to do when the interior of the ship went dark. A moment later, emergency lights bathed the bridge in a red glow. A split second after that, an alarm went off.

"They've gotten into the life-support system," Salo reported over the shrill sound. "The power's going down and I'm losing control of the helm."

Slayter swore again as he yanked his pistol from the holster on his thigh. "Do what you can to get back manual control. I need to get Teyla back to my cabin."

He didn't wait for a reply, but grabbed her hand in his free one and quickly led her down the passageway the same way they'd come.

She had to run to keep up with him, taking two steps to every one of his long strides. "I can help," she shouted over the noise. "Just tell me what to do."

Slayter threw her a quick glance over his shoulder. "I want you in my cabin where it's safe."

"But I know how to shoot a gun!" she insisted.

Slayter ignored her as he led her down a set of stairs and along another passageway. They just rounded the corner at the far end of it when they ran into Genoone and Olin. Both of them had their weapons drawn and would have continued past her and Slayter if he hadn't stopped them.

"Take Teyla back to my cabin and stay with her," he ordered. "I need to get to the main airlock."

Genoone's mouth tightened at the command, clearly not happy to be put on babysitting duty, but he didn't argue. Instead, he gave Slayter a curt nod and took her arm.

As he and Olin hustled her down the passageway, Teyla threw a worried glance over her shoulder to see Slayter running toward the main airlock. Her heart had been pounding with fear ever since Salo announced they were being boarded, but it wasn't until now that she realized she wasn't afraid for herself, but for Slayter. The thought of something happening to him terrified her so much she could barely breathe. It didn't make her feel any better when she heard the sound of laser fire coming from the direction he'd gone.

Heart in her throat, she looked over her shoulder again, expecting to see the intruders coming after them, but the passageway was empty. She bit her lip, wondering if she should tell Genoone and Olin that she could make it to Slayter's cabin on her own when she heard a loud grinding noise ahead of them. In front of her, Genoone skidded to a halt.

"What...?" she began just as Olin stopped short behind her, but the rest of the words ended in a startled cry as the hatch at the end of the passageway blew open and black-clad men bearing weapons stormed onto the ship. At the sight of her, Genoone and Olin standing there, they immediately started firing.

Genoone darted into the connecting passageway on the left, then stuck his laser rifle around the corner to fire at the enemy pirates while Olin grabbed her hand and pulled her into the passageway on the right. She ignored the urge to protect the teenager and instead crouched down behind him, pressing herself against the wall.

Olin didn't start shooting, though. Confused, she looked up to see him holding his hand to his side, a stunned expression on his face. Oh no. He'd been shot.

The wound didn't bleed, but instead hissed and steamed, as the fire from the laser burned his skin. She'd never seen anything like it before, but she knew it had to be bad.

Olin gritted his teeth against the pain, ragged determination in his blue eyes even as he dropped to one knee.

"Run," he told her, his voice so low she could barely hear it. "Genoone and I will hold them off so you can get back to the bridge."

Tears stung Teyla's eyes. The knowledge that the fifteen-year-old boy was determined to protect her when he was almost assuredly going to die a hideous and painful death himself stunned her. She wasn't anything but payment for a debt, meant for the auction blocks of Arkhon, and yet he was willing to give his life for her.

Well, she'd be damned if she was going to let him do it. He had as much right to live as she did. Blinking back the tears, she reached down and grabbed the laser rifle out of his weak hand. Ignoring his feeble attempts to stop her, she stepped around him and poked her head around the corner. While the handful of pirates lying motionless on the floor of the passageway was no longer a threat, the dozen men still shooting at her and Genoone were. Tightening her grip on the laser rifle, she aimed it in their direction and pulled the trigger.

Thanks to the mandatory weapons training everyone on her planet received, she had handled a gun before, and while she hadn't ever had to use one to defend herself, she knew how to fire the thing. More importantly, she could hit what she was aiming at. Unfortunately, whenever a man went down, there were two more to take his place. They kept coming and coming, slowly working their way down the passageway toward her and Genoone. Twenty more feet and the pirates would reach the intersection protecting them.

On the other side of the passageway, the red-headed man ducked behind the wall for a much-needed breather, only to do a double take when he saw it was Teyla doing the shooting and not Olin.

"Olin's been shot," she shouted as she darted behind the wall for cover.

Shock flickered in Genoone's eyes, along with something that looked like concern, though she couldn't be sure. "How bad is he?"

She glanced down at Olin. He was pale as a ghost and lying as motionless as the pirates in the passageway. For one horrified moment, she was afraid he might be dead, but then she saw his chest slowly rise and fall. He wasn't going to last much longer without medical attention.

She looked back at Genoone. He was shooting at the enemy pirates again and she had to shout over the sound of the laser fire.

"Not good. If we don't get him to the medlab soon, he's not going to make it."

Genoone glanced at her. "Go ahead and take him. I'll hold off these bastards until you can send reinforcements."

Teyla darted around the corner to get off a few quick shots, then took cover again. "The medlab's two decks down. There's no way I can drag him that far. You'll have to take him."

Genoone's eyes went wide. "And leave you here alone? The captain would have my hide if I did that."

"And Olin will die if you don't," she insisted. "I can take care of myself. Go."

He stared at her, indecision in his gray eyes. "Are you sure you can hold them off?"

She nodded, hoping she looked more confident than she felt. "Yes. Go!"

With a swiftness she didn't think the big man possessed, Genoone darted across the hallway while she fired at the intruders. Dropping his rifle, he picked up Olin, cradling the teenager in his arms. Teyla heard the boy groan. That was a good sign at least.

"I'll be back with reinforcements as soon as I can," Genoone told her. "Good luck."

Giving her a nod, he ran down the passageway toward the stairs, Olin in his arms.

Teyla took a deep breath, then chanced a quick peek around the corner. There were still plenty of pirates left and from the triumphant look on their faces, they had figured out she was alone. They probably thought she'd drop her weapon and run. They didn't know her very well.

She crouched down, keeping most of her body behind the wall for protection, then fired at them, squeezing the trigger as fast as her finger would go. The ferocity of her attack must have surprised the pirates because the ones she didn't hit immediately ran back to the hatch they had come through without bothering to return fire.

While her frenzied shooting forced them to retreat, it also had other unintended consequences. Within seconds, her rifle began to beep, warning her that the power charge was low. Unfortunately, the pirates must have heard it too, because they left the safety of the airlock and headed in her direction again just as her rifle died with a sputter.

Dammit!

Heart pounding, she spun around to grab the rifle Genoone had left behind. By the time she got back into position and started to fire, however, the pirates were halfway down the passageway.

She tried to force them to retreat just as she'd done before, but they were so close she couldn't get more than a few shots off before having to duck for cover or else risk getting hit with laser fire. Not that it mattered much anyway since Genoone's rifle had already begun beeping to alert her that it, too, was low on power.

She leaned back against the wall, panting for breath as she tried to figure out what to do. She could stay here and keep shooting for as long as she could and pray she could take out the rest of the pirates, or she could run and hope she made it to safety before they caught up with her.

Teyla darted a glance around the corner again. There must have been fifteen dead pirates scattered along the hall, with at least twice that many coming her way. If they had attacked the other parts of the ship with this many men, then Slayter and his crew had almost certainly been overrun, too, or soon would be. The thought of him getting hurt—or worse—was almost more than she could take.

Not that she was probably going to be around to see what happened to him since her rifle was out of power. The pirates would be on her in seconds.

Getting to her feet, she turned and ran down the passageway. The pirates followed, their booted feet echoing on the floor behind her. Her breath coming fast and hard, she turned down the next passageway, and bumped into something very solid and very unexpected. Gasping, she automatically took a step back, afraid one of the pirates had somehow gotten ahead of her, but instead she found herself gazing up into a familiar pair of amber eyes. *Slayter.*

Teyla probably would have thrown herself into his arms right then if the pirates who had attacked the ship hadn't come around the corner. The men immediately froze, shock clear on their faces. They had clearly expected to find a defenseless woman with a burned-out laser rifle. Instead they walked into a pissed-off captain with a half dozen of his own crewmen backing him up.

Slayter grabbed her arm and pulled her behind him, firing point-blank at the enemy pirates before the men could move. His crew did the same. The intruders tried to return fire as they scrambled back down the passageway to the hatch they had come through, but Slayter and his men followed them relentlessly, taking them down one by one. Slayter probably would have followed them into the airlock, but the com on his ear hissed and he paused to listen while the rest of his crew moved past him to secure the hatch.

Teyla couldn't hear much of what was being said over the alarm that was still blaring besides Slayter demanding to know what the hell was taking so long to get life-support back up, but whatever the person on the other end of the link said, it mustn't have been what he wanted to hear because his face turned to flint. He muttered something curt in reply, before closing the link.

Turning to her, he put his hands on her shoulders, his eyes intent as he gently turned her this way and that. "Are you okay?"

She nodded. "Yes. But Olin got shot. Genoone took him to the medlab."

Slayter frowned. "I know." He looked around at the bodies littering the passageway, then back at her. "Come on."

Teyla almost protested, thinking he was taking her to his cabin. She would much rather check on Olin. Which was why she was relieved when she realized Slayter was heading in the direction of the medlab.

She quickly followed him into the room, expecting to see Bantly, the ship's medtech, desperately trying to save Olin, but instead the man was frantically running from one makeshift bed to another. Considering the number of pirates who had attacked the ship, she knew she shouldn't be surprised, but she was shocked to see how many of Slayter's crew had been injured.

"How bad is it?" Slayter asked as the blond-haired medtech leaned over one of the beds.

"Bad." Bantly threw Slayter a glance over his shoulder. "Two of the men didn't make it and I have eight more who are barely hanging on. I put the worst of them in the nutrient pods, but I'm still not sure if they'll make it."

Teyla looked around, taking in the sac-like healing pods. When Slayter had explained their purpose on the tour of the medlab earlier, she hadn't imagined she would ever see them in use. The men inside lay unmoving, floating in a nutrient-rich bath of liquid that gave them their best chance to survive.

She wanted to ask the medtech about Olin, but then she spotted Genoone beside one of the pods, and knew from the grim look on the communication officer's face that the boy was inside. Heart heavy, she slowly walked over to look through the small window. Olin's eyes were closed, his face pale, but he was alive.

Slayter came over to peer through the window. A frown creased his brow. "Did Bantly say if Olin would make it?" he asked Genoone.

"Maybe," was all the redheaded man said, but Teyla could tell from his gruff voice that neither Genoone nor the medtech were holding out much hope the boy would survive. Tears stung her eyes.

Beside her, Slayter's face hardened to stone. He opened the link on his com. "Do we have our sensors up yet?" he asked whoever was on the other end. The man must have given him the answer he was looking for because he nodded. "Good enough. Do you have any life signs on that damn ship still stuck on us?" A pause as he listened. "Get a team of men assembled at the main hatch." Then, "No, I'm taking them over. I want the team briefed before I get there. There will be no mercy offered and no quarter taken. They need to learn what happens when they attack a real pirate ship."

Teyla felt a shiver run through her at the murderous look in his eyes. Slayter had every right to be angry with the men who had attacked his ship and killed and injured his crew, but that didn't make it any easier to know he was going to walk onto that ship and execute every single person he found. It only reminded her that despite all his good qualities, Slayter was still a pirate himself. He made his living with violence, weapons and a merciless heart.

Yet none of that changed how terrified she was for him.

She impulsively reached out to grab his arm as he turned to go. "Be careful."

His gazed down at her for a long moment, his expression softening. Then, without a word, he gave her a nod and walked out.

Chapter Four

က

The pirate ship latched onto the hull was like a damn parasite, but it didn't take long for Slayter and the team of men he took with him to deal with the pirates on board. There hadn't been many of the vermin left and most of them had been falling all over themselves to negotiate for surrender rather than continue the fight. True to his word, though, Slayter hadn't wanted any of that. If they thought they could attack his ship, breach the hull, and injure and kill his men, then barter their way out of it once their plan failed, they soon learned otherwise. He and his crew had put down every single one of them like the sick animals they were. It had been harsh, but necessary. Life in his line of work was hard enough. If he gained a reputation as being soft and an easy mark, it would only be harder, and that would get even more of his crew killed. When word got around the pirate underworld—and Slayter would make damn sure it did— another ship would think twice before attacking him or his again.

When they were done, Slayter and his men dragged the bodies of the enemy pirates off his ship and piled them with the rest in the hold of the other spacecraft, then left without touching a single piece of cargo. He wouldn't have it said he had profited from the pirates' attack. Someone would find their ship and be able to piece together what had happened.

Leaving his men to set the other ship adrift, Slayter headed down to check on the members of his crew who had been injured. The moment he stepped inside the medlab, though, he stopped. The smell of the place always got to him. He didn't know if it was the medicinal odor of the nutrient bath or the ever-present disinfectant, but it was almost more than he could stand, and he had to steel himself before going further.

As he waited to get a grip on his senses, he spotted Teyla slowly moving from bed to bed, talking softly to those men who were patiently waiting for their turn in the healing pods. Even though they were obviously in tremendous pain, whatever she said seemed to ease them somewhat. One or two of them even managed a weak smile.

Teyla's compassion didn't extend only to the men who were conscious, though. When she left them, she stopped at each healing pods and spoke a few words of encouragement. The men couldn't hear her in the medically induced comas they were in, but even so, it was an incredibly kind gesture coming from a woman who would soon be on the auction block.

"She was amazing, you know."

Slayter turned to see Genoone standing beside him. The man watched Teyla as she pressed her hand to the glass window of Olin's pod.

"When Olin got shot, she never hesitated, just picked up his rifle and started shooting at those bastards," the man continued, admiration in his voice. "She insisted I bring him here while she stayed to fight because it gave Olin the best chance at survival. She's got more brass than any woman I've ever met. Hell, more than some men, too. Those assholes would have killed me and Olin both if she hadn't been there."

Slayter didn't say anything. When he'd first discovered Genoone had left Teyla to fend for herself, he'd been mad as hell and filled with so much fear he had barely been able to think straight. But then he'd seen how badly Olin had been hurt and he knew Genoone hadn't had a choice. He still couldn't believe Teyla had held off the pirates on her own so the two men could make it to the medlab safely. What she'd done had taken guts. Every time Slayter thought of what might have happened to her, he wanted to kill those scumbags all over again.

Slayter ground his jaw as he thought back to the attack. He had known something was wrong the moment he'd arrived at the main airlock. Although the hatch was open, the other pirates hadn't been trying to board his ship. They had been shooting and ducking back. He'd known in his gut it had all been a ruse to draw the defenders away from the main point of attack. But there wasn't a hell of a lot he could do about it since the ship's internal com had gone out along with the external sensors and life-support systems. Unable to do much more than guess where the pirates might actually be attacking, he'd hauled ass down to the C-deck loading dock only to find nothing there, either. After that, he and his men had raced from one likely entry point to the next, shouting the whole time for engineering to get the damn sensors up and working.

It had been pure luck that had taken him past the medlab at the exact moment Genoone carried Olin in. Slayter had stopped him only long enough to ask where Teyla was before he took off down the passageway again, this time toward the evacuation bay — and Teyla. He should have realized that was where the pirates would try to board the ship. It was the perfect place to attack because it wasn't designed as an entrance. People who went out that door didn't come back.

Slayter was so relieved to see Teyla alive and unharmed he'd almost grabbed her in his arms right there in front of his men. His relief was quickly replaced by fear for her again when he realized she wouldn't have been running like her life depended on it if the threat was gone. The thought that someone would come onto his ship and take what was his, attack his crew, endanger his woman — it had made him seethe with a level of fury he'd never felt before in his life.

It was only after he'd taken out that rage on the pirates who had attacked his ship and stood here now with Genoone watching Teyla tend to his injured crewmen in the medlab, that he realized he had subconsciously called her his woman. Where the hell had that idiotic idea sprung from? Teyla was a beautiful and amazing woman who was not only courageous, talented and business savvy, she was also a natural-born enchantress in the bedroom as well. The one thing she wasn't, was his woman. She was payment for a debt and she'd be the first to remind him of that.

As he watched her stand vigilantly beside Olin's pod, though, he had to ask himself if a woman who was nothing more than payment for a debt would have done what she had done—for the ship, for his men, for him.

Slayter mentally shook himself from his musings. That kind of introspection was not only pointless, but dangerous, too. It could make a man think about things he shouldn't, want things he couldn't have.

Leaving Genoone's side, he walked over to Teyla. A look of relief washed over her face at the sight of him.

"You're back."

He nodded.

"Are the other pirates...?"

"Yes," he said simply. "How's Olin?"

"The same." She shook her head. "I keep seeing him lying there in that passageway, his face in agony. He could barely stay conscious and yet he still tried to protect me. He told me to run, but I couldn't leave him."

"So Genoone told me. What you did was very brave, Teyla."

Her face colored. "I only did what anyone would have done."

Slayter considered arguing the point on that, but didn't. As humble as Teyla was, she wouldn't agree anyway. Instead, he told her he'd be back in a little while, then went to check on the rest of his injured crewmen.

Teyla was still by Olin's pod when he returned, her smooth brow lined with worry.

"Why don't we go to the mess and get something to eat?" he suggested.

She shook her head. "I don't want to leave Olin."

"Olin's in good hands, Teyla. There's nothing we can do but wait and let the nanos do their job." Slayter slipped his arm around her waist. "Bantly will call me if there's any change. Come on."

She hesitated, indecision in her lavender eyes. Finally, she nodded. "Okay. But only if we come back and check on him right away."

Slayter nodded. "We can do that."

Since it was time for the evening meal, Slayter wasn't surprised to find the rest of the crew at the table in the mess. None of the usual jokes and laughter filled the room like it normally did, and the men only gave him and Teyla a somber greeting as they sat down. It was the first time she had been in the same room with all his men together since coming aboard the ship, and Slayter couldn't help but notice the distinct change in how they looked at her now. He didn't know whether it was because she had gotten them the barrel of Dunagan ale back on Thrace or had stood up to the pirates who attacked the ship, but they definitely had a new respect for her.

"Genoone told us about you did after Olin got shot," Deran said around a mouthful of bread. "Where did you learn to handle a weapon like that?"

Teyla accepted a slice of bread from the basket Genoone held out. "Kallor doesn't have an organized military force, so everyone is trained on the use of weapons. I went to the local militia hall with my parents and sisters twice a year to practice."

Slayter wasn't surprised to hear that. He'd read a lot about Kallor's culture and history before getting involved with Teyla's father. What did surprise him, though, was how her story got his crewmen discussing what life had been like on

76

their own home worlds. He learned more personal information about them tonight than he had in all the years he'd been aboard ship with them.

After leaving the mess, he and Teyla stopped by the medlab to check on Olin and the other members of his crew again. They smiled as soon as they saw her, clearly pleased she had stopped by before turning in for the night. Unfortunately, there was still no change in Olin, but Bantly assured him and Teyla that the boy was responding well to the nanos, as were the other men in the healing pods.

Slayter got the feeling Teyla would have stayed there all night to help tend to the men, but thankfully the medtech talked her into going back to the cabin and getting some sleep. She looked exhausted.

He was damn tired, too, he realized as they walked into his cabin a little while later. With a sigh, he pulled off his boots and stripped off his clothes.

"I'm going to take a shower," he told Teyla.

Any other night he would have asked her to join him, but after the day's events, he wasn't in the mood and he suspected neither was she.

Once in the tiled enclosure, he turned on the spray full force and stepped underneath it, resting a hand on the wall as he let the warm water run down his body. He wished it had the power the wash away the memory of what had happened that day along with the dirt and sweat, but when he closed his eyes, all he could see was Teyla running from the attacking pirates and he was reminded again of how close she had come to getting killed. The thought made his gut clench.

Slayter was so lost in the images playing over and over in his head that he didn't realize Teyla had stepped into the shower with him until he felt a gentle pair of hands on his shoulders.

"I thought you might like some company," she said, pressing a kiss between his shoulder blades.

He closed his eyes as she made slow circular motions on his shoulders with her fingers. "That feels good."

Actually, "good" didn't even begin to cover it. Her touch was magical and he could only groan as she slowly moved her hands down the muscles of his back, then up to his shoulders again. The tension gradually started to leave his body.

She continued the massage, focusing on every knot in his back and shoulders as if she knew exactly where they were. He leaned against the wall of the shower, letting her fingers melt the stress of the day away. God, she had amazing hands.

While the massage had his muscles so relaxed he was practically sagging against the wall, it had the reverse effect on a certain other part of his anatomy. Slayter opened his eyes to look down at his rapidly stiffening cock. So much for not being in the mood. Perhaps making love to Teyla was exactly what he needed. Perhaps it was what they both needed.

Turning around, he took Teyla in his arms and without a word, kissed her on the mouth. Her arms went around his neck, her fingers threading into his wet hair as she parted her lips and gave him a taste of her tongue.

He urged her back against the wall with a muffled groan, his hands gliding up her taut tummy to cup her perfect breasts. They were slick from the shower and her nipples slipped teasingly through his fingers as he gave them a squeeze. She whimpered against his mouth, arching into him, and he buried his face in the curve of her neck to trail kisses up to her ear. He swirled his tongue inside, unable to resist, chuckling when she let out a breathy moan. The feel of her wet, naked body against his made his cock throb and he groaned again. He'd thought he would be able to take things slow, but now he wasn't so sure.

Gazing deeply into her eyes, Slayter cupped her pussy in his hand, then gently slipped a finger inside. She was hot and wet and ready for him, and he let out a low growl of appreciation as he moved in and out of her wetness. Teyla rotated her hips in time with the fast, steady rhythm of the movement, grinding against his hand. Slayter felt his erection harden to new and painful proportions, and he closed his eyes.

Sliding out, he lifted his hand and sucked his finger into his mouth to hungrily lick her juices from it. She tasted just as sweet and intoxicating as she had last night.

He couldn't wait any longer. He wanted, *needed*, to be inside her.

Grasping her ass in both hands, he lifted her up against the wall and sheathed himself inside her in one forceful motion.

Teyla gasped, her legs going around him to squeeze him tightly. The move pulled his cock even deeper into her pussy, and for a moment, Slayter thought he might come right then. He reminded himself again about taking it slow and easy, but she felt too damn good wrapped around him for that. Tightening his grip on her ass, he starting fucking her hard and fast.

She grabbed his head, tilting it back so she could kiss him. "Harder," she demanded breathlessly against his mouth. "Fuck me harder!"

Slayter obeyed, the force of his thrusts slamming her back against the wall, and still Teyla begged him for more. He gripped her ass more firmly and pumped into her even faster. That must have been exactly what she was looking for because she dragged her mouth away from his and cried out her pleasure.

"That's right," he rasped. "Come for me, baby."

She did, her screams echoing over and over in the small space and drowning out his own hoarse groans of release as he exploded inside her. The urgency of their lovemaking and the feelings that came with it shocked him. He'd never felt as close to a woman as he did to her. It was as if in that moment, their souls had somehow become one.

The significance of what that might mean was too dangerous to even contemplate and Slayter concentrated on regaining his breath instead. When he got it under control, he released Teyla, letting her slide down his body until her feet touched the floor. He slipped his fingers beneath her chin and tilted her face up his. Her beautiful lavender eyes were so full of emotion he expected her to say the three little words that could change everything between them. He held his breath, not sure what he feared more, hearing the words or not hearing them.

She didn't say anything though, and the moment passed. He finally lowered his head to kiss her long and lingeringly on the mouth, then turned off the water, swung her up in his arms and stepped out of the shower.

Grabbing a towel from the rack, he slowly and methodically dried her off, afraid if he didn't do something, he'd start analyzing the confusing bevy of emotions he was feeling. When he was done, he picked her up in his arms again and carried her over to the bed. Setting her down, he climbed in beside her and pulled her close. She rested her head on his shoulder with a contented sigh. He gazed up at the ceiling, listening to her breathing and wondering if she might fall asleep.

But instead, Teyla ran her finger over the delicate ring on the chain he wore around his neck. It was then that he noticed the gem set into it was the exact color of her eyes. He was about to comment on it, but she spoke first.

"You never take this off. Not even in the shower," she observed softly. "It must be very special to you."

"It is."

She was silent for a moment, her finger still absently playing with the ring, tracing the purple gemstone set in it. "The woman whom it belonged to must have been very special to you as well."

"She was," he said quietly. "It was my mother's. It was passed down from mother to daughter or son for generations in her family. She gave it to me before she died."

Teyla lifted her head to look at him in surprise. "Slayter, I'm sorry. I didn't realize."

He gently brushed her hair back from her face. "Don't be sorry." The corner of his mouth curved. "It was a long time ago."

"How old were you when she died?"

"Ten."

"That must have been hard on you and your father."

Slayter put his arm behind his head. He'd never been the sharing type of guy before, especially about where he came from, but for some reason, it was easy to open up to Teyla. "It was hard on me. My father took off for planets unknown when I was five. Haven't seen him since."

She nibbled on her lower lip. "Who took you in after your mother passed?"

"I lived on the streets for a few years until I got a job on a pirate ship."

She frowned. "Isn't that a little young to be a pirate?"

His mouth quirked. "I was mature for my age. Luckily, Hewson was a crewman on the ship. He took me under his wing, watched out for me and taught me the ropes."

"Just like you did for Olin," she said softly.

Slayter cupped her cheek, wishing he could take away the pain he saw reflected in her eyes. He couldn't believe how close she'd gotten to the boy in such a short time. "Olin will be okay, Teyla. You'll see. In a few days, the kid will be good as new."

The smile she gave him was sad, as if she didn't quite believe that. He wasn't sure he believed it himself. He couldn't let her see that, though. He pulled her down for a tender kiss, then wrapped both arms around her, hugging her close. He thought she might want to talk some more, but after a while her breathing became slow and even, and he knew she'd fallen asleep.

Slayter stared up at the ceiling, his thoughts once again turning to the unfamiliar emotions he'd felt earlier. The sex they'd just shared hadn't been "training" to make her a better slave. It had been about finding comfort in the arms of someone he cared about.

The fact he found that consolation in the arms of a woman he barely knew, one he planned to sell off to the highest bidder in a few days, seemed a contradiction. But the feelings wreaking havoc on his heart right now didn't lie. As crazy as it was, he was falling for Teyla. Hell, he'd already fallen. Hard.

He swore under his breath. He needed to get a grip on reality, and fast. He didn't even know if what he was feeling was real or the result of a long, hard day. God knew, he wasn't qualified to judge the subtleties of the male-female dynamic. Pirates weren't exactly known for their stable, meaningful relationships, after all. While he might be feeling what he thought he was feeling for Teyla, it was just as likely he simply enjoyed being in the company of a beautiful woman. A woman who just happened to be more practical and honor bound than anyone he had ever met. Hell, for all he knew, she was being nice to him because she thought it was part of her training. She'd as good as said it was her obligation to make herself as valuable as possible on the auction block. Their apparent sexual chemistry might be no more than a desire on her part to make sure she was talented enough to earn the money her father owed him. She might be lying beside him even now because she thought it was part of her duty.

For some ridiculous reason, that thought hurt like hell.

Slayter sighed. He needed to stop this. Teyla would only be on his ship and in his bed for a few more days. Distancing himself now would be the smart thing to do. But as he lay there waiting for sleep to come, he couldn't stop thinking about how nice it would be to have her fall asleep in his arms like this at the end of every crazy day.

Chapter Five

∽

Teyla's heart beat a little faster when Slayter told her the next morning that they wouldn't be going to Arkhon.

"At least not for another day or so," he added as he strapped his holster to his thigh.

She tried hard not to let her disappointment show. For a moment, she'd thought Slayter had decided to forgive her family's debt and keep her for his own. But that was just foolish.

"Since Fennec, Layton and Yarbry won't be able to take a turn in the healing pods for a while, I'm going to drop them off on Verane so they can get medical treatment," Slayter continued.

Teyla nodded, but didn't say anything. She couldn't believe she hadn't even considered that might be the reason for their detour.

Hurriedly getting dressed, she sat down to a quick breakfast with Slayter, then went off to check on Olin. Although he hadn't woken up yet, Bantly said his vital signs were stronger. That was reassuring, at least.

Teyla was still in the medlab when they docked on Verane later that afternoon. Slayter came in with a doctor and four other men a few minutes later. She waited anxiously while the doctor checked on Olin and the other crew members who were in the healing pods. He nodded approvingly, assuring them everything possible was being done for the men, although he did recommend Bantly add a few extra nutrients to the bath to promote quicker healing and prevent infection. Between the medication he prescribed and the medical treatment for the three men they left on the planet,

Slayter spent a good portion of the platinum chips the Thracian Prime had given him. He didn't seem to care about the money, though. Teyla suspected he would have spent every penny he had on them if he had to.

Getting Fennec, Layton and Yarbry to agree to leave the ship long enough to receive medical care, though, turned out to be a battle in itself. They had no desire to be left behind and only relented after Slayter swore by some kind of pirate's oath that he would return for them in less than seven days.

Teyla assumed they would be going straight to Arkhon after leaving Verane, but Slayter gave the order to set course for a planet called Haan. When she gave him a curious look, he explained that the two crewmen who'd been killed during the attack were from Haan, and that they would be taking them there for burial. She was a little surprised at that. She hadn't thought rough, tough pirates would be so religious and sentimental. Apparently she'd been wrong. It turned out she was wrong about a lot things when it came to pirates.

During the trip, Teyla spent most of her time in the medlab helping Bantly tend to Olin and the other wounded. Olin still hadn't regained consciousness, which worried her, but the tech assured her the teenager was doing much better.

When she wasn't in the medlab, she was making love with Slayter. The sex they had ran the gamut from slow and gentle to wild and urgent. While Slayter was just as attentive and wonderful in bed as he'd always been, she couldn't help but notice he seemed preoccupied whenever they weren't in the throes of passion. She wondered if he blamed himself for the attack on the ship and the two crewmen's deaths. She wanted to tell him it wasn't his fault, but she got the feeling he wasn't in the mood to talk about it.

Although Teyla wished they were going to Haan under better circumstances, she was grateful for the reprieve. While she was firm in her decision to honor her father's deal, that didn't mean she wasn't more than a little scared at the prospect of being sold into slavery. More importantly, however, going to Haan gave her the chance to spend more time with Slayter and the crew. As amazing as it sounded, she was going to miss the newfound camaraderie with the men and her life aboard the ship.

Mostly, though, she was going to miss Slayter.

She had never expected to feel anything for the pirate her father had bartered her away to. When she'd first suggested Slayter train her in the ways of pleasuring a man, she had assumed she would have sex with him, gain some valuable experience, then leave the ship and never think of him again.

That wasn't going to happen, though.

Somewhere in between that first kiss and the glorious nights she'd spent in his bed afterward, she had come to think of him as more than simply a pirate. Of all the bandits in the galaxy, her father had traded her off to the most intelligent, decent and captivating rogue she was likely to ever find. It was no wonder she'd fallen in love with him.

Her breath caught in her throat at the thought. Holy Mother of Kallor. She'd just admitted to herself that she was in love with Slayter. It was almost ironic. She was in love with a pirate who was going to sell her into slavery.

She only wished they could have met under different circumstances. As a teenage girl, she'd fantasized more than once about a man like Slayter sweeping her off her feet and falling in love with her, then whisking her away to live among the stars with him. But that wasn't going to happen. Slayter was a pirate with expenses and obligations little different than her father's, and she was the woman who would earn him enough money on the slavery block to take care of those expenses for a long time. There was an even bigger issue, though. Slayter didn't feel anything for her.

Relationships like theirs didn't have happy endings, even in the silly romance stories she liked to read.

Tears stung her eyes and she blinked them away. Stop it, she told herself. She could be as miserable as she wanted when they got to Arkhon. For now, she would enjoy her time with Slayter. It was the Kallorian way to live in the moment.

They arrived on Haan in the early morning hours the following day. Slayter dressed in silence, putting on the finest shirt and breeches she'd seen him wear. Teyla chewed on her lip, watching as he shrugged into his coat.

"I realize I didn't know Donnel or Feeny very well, but do you think I could come to the service so I could pay my respects?" she asked.

Slayter looked surprised by the request, but after a moment, he gave her a small smile. "Of course. Donnel and Feeny would like that. So would the rest of the crew."

The service for the two crewmen was extremely moving and Teyla had tears in her eyes the whole time. When they'd first arrived at the church, she hadn't been sure what kind of reception Slayter and the pirates would get from the men's families, considering they had died on his ship, but to a person, they were kind and gracious. They even thanked Slayter for bringing the men home. Several of the men's male relatives were curious as to why Slayter's ship had been attacked, however.

Slayter told them what little he knew, that a group of pirates had boarded his ship presumably looking for the credits they'd gotten for a recent job.

"You would do wise to be watch your back out there," one of the men said. "Word is that someone instigated the attack, maybe even paid the bastards to do it."

Slayter frowned. "Who?"

The man shrugged. "Some pirate you poached from."

"Poached from?" Slayter's brows knit together in confusion, then he swore. "Rommel. You have to be shitting me. That bastard paid someone to attack my ship because I stole his take, fair and square?"

The man shook his head. "I never said it was him. You should be careful, though. If Rommel did do it, and I'm not saying he did, he won't be satisfied with simply killing two of your men. He's going to want retribution. The man doesn't live by the code."

Teyla's blood ran cold at the words. She didn't know much about the other pirate or the code they were referring to, but she'd heard enough to know the man and Slayter had been enemies for a long time.

Beside her, Slayter's jaw tightened. "I'll watch my back," he told the other man. "And when I run into Rommel again, you can be sure he'll pay the price for what he did."

Slayter said little on the way back to the spaceport. Teyla wanted to ask him about the pirate Rommel and whether Slayter thought the man would attack his ship again, but he didn't seem to want to talk.

"We'll be landing on Arkhon tomorrow morning," he said when they were alone in his cabin.

Teyla's heart seized in her chest at the thought of leaving him, and she was glad she had her back to him. If Slayter knew she was upset, then he might feel guilty, and she didn't want that. None of this was his fault. It was just how things were meant to be. Tomorrow would bring what it would and there was nothing either of them could do about it. At least they had this last night together. And she meant to enjoy every minute of it.

Forcing a smile to her lips, she turned and put her arms around his neck. "Then that means I have tonight to show you how much I've learned."

She didn't wait for him to answer, but instead pulled him down for a long, deep, intoxicating kiss. Slayter slid his hand into her hair with a groan, his tongue urgently seeking out hers and tangling with it.

Tearing his mouth away, he kissed his way down her neck to the curve of her shoulder as he reached around to undo the hooks on her dress. He slipped the straps off her shoulders, pushing the garment down until it landed in a puddle of silk at her feet and she was left in nothing but her lacy bra and matching panties. He took a step back, slowly looking her up and down before bending his head to kiss her again.

His mouth was hot and even more demanding on hers than before and Teyla parted her lips with a moan as he plunged his tongue into her mouth to take sweet possession of hers. Slayter's hands glided up her back to find the clasp of her bra. Unhooking it, he slid the straps off her shoulders and down her arms, freeing her breasts from their confines. Teyla waited anxiously for him to cup them in his hands, but instead he hooked his fingers inside her panties and slowly pushed them down. As he got to his feet, he ran his hands up her bare legs and over her hips to bury his hands in her hair and close his mouth over hers once more.

Teyla grabbed the front of his shirt, pulling him closer. Her nipples tingled where they brushed against the material, and she eagerly undid the buttons so she could push it off his shoulders. She would have reached for the fastenings on his breeches next, but he swung her up in his arms and gently set her down on the bed.

Slayter gazed down at her, his molten gold eyes caressing her naked body with a passion that made her breath catch. No matter how many other men saw her naked, she would never forget the way the handsome pirate looked at her.

The thought brought a stab of pain with it that was so intense tears suddenly clogged her throat. She swallowed hard, wondering how she was going to keep from losing her composure. Dammit. She didn't want to spend her last night with Slayter crying, and was relieved when he finally stripped off the rest of his clothes so she could focus on his magnificent body instead of how much she was hurting inside.

Tossing his breeches on the floor, Slayter climbed onto the bed and settled himself between her legs. Bracing himself on his forearms, he nibbled lightly on her lips as he teasingly rubbed the head of his cock up and down her pussy. The sensation made her forget her dismal thoughts, and she lost herself in how good what he was doing felt.

Teyla gasped when he finally entered her, wrapping her arms and legs around him to pull him in even deeper. Slayter mumbled something she couldn't hear, but before she could ask what it was, he bent his head to claim her lips in another scorching kiss. She moaned against his mouth and tightened her arms around him, automatically lifting her hips to meet his when he gently began to thrust.

Unlike the other times they'd made love, Teyla didn't beg him to go faster or take her harder. This time, she wanted the pleasure to last all night.

It was as if Slayter wanted the same thing because he kept his thrusts slow and steady, sliding out until only the tip of his shaft was inside her before sliding back in to completely bury his length in her pussy again. Then he held himself there, pressing so firmly and so deeply she swore she was going to climax just from the fullness of him.

He repeated the same sequence of mind-blowing moves over and over until she was practically dizzy from it. Just when it seemed she would go insane with ecstasy, Slayter suddenly rolled over onto his back, taking her with him so she was now the one on top. Breathless, Teyla could only sit there and gaze down at him.

"Ride me," he commanded huskily, the hands on her hips urging her to move even as he spoke.

Teyla didn't need him to tell her twice. Placing her hands on his chest, she made slow, rhythmic circles on his cock. In this position, she could grind her clit against him perfectly, and she caught her bottom lip between her teeth.

She teased herself, grinding against him until she was close to coming, then switching to an up-and-down movement that still felt amazing, but allowed her to hold off on climaxing.

Slayter lay back and let her do whatever she wanted, a smoldering look in his eyes that was almost enough to make her orgasm just from the intensity of it.

She prayed the pleasure would last forever, but soon the sensations became too strong and she rotated her hips faster and faster until she felt herself start to come. Then she went even faster. Ecstasy consumed her and she cried out.

When she finally regained her senses, she opened her eyes to find Slayter looking up at her with a hungry expression in his gold eyes. There was something else reflected in their molten depths as well, some emotion she was afraid to put a name to, but it made her catch her breath all the same. Could Slayter actually feel something for her? The idea was too crazy to even contemplate. Not that she could have analyzed it right then anyway, because at that moment, he sat up and closed his mouth over hers. She wrapped her arms around him, surrendering to him with a throaty purr.

"Who told you to stop moving?" he growled, capturing her lips again.

That was when she realized he hadn't come yet.

She started rotating her hips again, this time intent on making him groan in pleasure. In spite of how tempting it was to move up and down on him wildly, Teyla controlled herself, wanting this to be the best night of his life.

Murmuring something unintelligible, Slayter tore his mouth away from hers to trail blazing-hot kisses over her jaw and down her neck. His stubble scraped against her tender skin and she shivered as he slowly kissed his way back up to the curve of her jaw before reclaiming her lips once again.

Groaning, he slid his hands down her back to grasp her ass. Firmly holding on to both cheeks, he guided her up and down on his cock in a slow, sexy rhythm. It felt so good Teyla knew she would be able to come soon, but she didn't want to do that. She wanted him to come first.

She reached behind her and grabbed his hands, pulling them away from her ass and pinning them down to the bed. Teyla enjoyed the look of surprise that flashed across his face.

"I'm supposed to be showing you what I've learned, remember?" she said softly.

A smile curved his mouth. "By all means. Please do."

In this position, she was able to rub her breasts against his muscular chest while she gyrated on his cock. She kept his shaft deep inside her as she clenched her pussy around him, wanting it to be as tight and hot as possible for him.

Only when she felt his hips begin to thrust uncontrollably upward did she start moving up and down on him. Even then, she moved as slowly as she could, keeping her pussy clenched tightly around him, letting him slide almost all the way out before sheathing him deep inside her again.

She teased him mercilessly, lifting her pussy off him every time he tried to thrust into her. He got the idea soon enough, lying back to let her do all the work.

When he began to come, she squeezed his cock even tighter, milking the hot cum from him even as she shuddered and trembled uncontrollably with her own release. The orgasm that washed over her was so powerful and so beautiful that it brought tears to her eyes and she was glad when he sat up to wrap his arms around her. This time she didn't try to stop the tears, but wrapped her arms just as tightly around him and rested her cheek against the top of his head, letting them roll silently down her cheeks.

Teyla wasn't sure how many times she and Slayter made love after that. She demonstrated every skill he'd taught her, as well as a few more she thought up on her own. Whenever they came down from one intoxicating high, they would do it all over again. It was as if neither of them could get enough of the other.

They had just fallen into an exhausted slumber sometime after dawn when Teyla felt the ship touch down. Her lips curved into a sad smile. It was funny how she had become so attuned to the sensations of the ship in such a short period of time.

She pushed herself up on one elbow and looked down at Slayter. Though he was asleep, a slight frown marred his handsome features. Fighting the urge to kiss it away, she tore her gaze away from him with a muffled sob and carefully slipped out of the bed. As desperately as she wanted to spend the few precious hours left in his arms, she wasn't sure she'd be strong enough to walk away from him when the time came if she did.

She couldn't stay in the cabin, though. She didn't want to waste the hour or two of freedom she had left, either. She should go check on Olin, then take one more look around the ship. Perhaps she might even ask Genoone to go outside with her so she could walk around the spaceport while she was still a free woman because that was almost certainly one of the things she wouldn't be allowed to do after today.

Chapter Six

ॐ

Slayter jerked awake, his heart pounding, his gut telling him that something was very wrong. He looked over at Teyla's side of the bed only to realize it was empty. He ran his hand over the sheets. They were cold.

Uncontrollable terror seizing him, he jumped out of bed and threw on his clothes. It was irrational to panic like this. She was probably having breakfast or checking on Olin. Then why was there a voice in his head screaming at him to find her?

He went to the mess first, but found it empty. He ran to the medlab next, but no one was there except the medtech. Bantly looked up from the computer monitor curiously.

"Have you seen Teyla?" Slayter asked.

"She was here about thirty minutes ago. She looked in on Olin, then left."

"Do you know where she went?"

"She didn't say."

Slayter swore under his breath. Turning on his heel, he raced up to the bridge. Hewson and Salo were there, but Teyla was nowhere in sight.

"Where's Teyla?" he demanded, the question coming out sharper than he'd intended.

His first mate frowned. "Take it easy. She's out with Genoone, strolling through the market. She didn't run away, if that's what you're concerned about."

Slayter clenched his jaw. "I didn't think she had."

"Then why do you looked so worried?" the older man asked quietly.

That was just it. Slayter didn't know what the hell had gotten him so riled up. It certainly wasn't like Teyla was going to go and put herself on the auction block. His lip curled. No, that distasteful task would be up to him.

Realizing his first mate was still waiting for an answer, Slayter walked out rather than face the older man's penetrating and all-too-knowing hazel eyes.

Angry with himself as much as with the situation, Slayter strode down the passageway toward the medlab. It was as if events had taken control of his life these past few days and he was simply along for the ride. Teyla was payment for a debt, which was completely aboveboard and legal on almost every planet in the galaxy. He had every right to do what he was doing. He needed the money to run his ship and pay his crew.

Then why did he feel like he was making a huge mistake?

When he walked into the medlab, it was to find Bantly frantically disconnecting wires and tubes on Olin's pod. Sure the boy was dead, Slayter rushed across the room, only to sag with relief when he saw a heartbeat on the monitor.

He moved closer. "What's wrong?"

"Nothing," Bantly said. "He's coming out of his medically induced coma."

"Is that good?" Slayter asked.

The medtech pushed a button on the side of the pod to lift Olin out of the water. "That's very good."

Slayter wasn't so sure. Olin emerged wet and slimy from nutrient bath, like some sort of strange rebirth. The thick, viscous liquid blocked his nose and mouth, and Bantly worked quickly to clear both as a fit of coughing racked Olin's thin body. After clearing both airways, the medtech attached an oxygen tube, then wiped the boy clean.

"When will he wake up?" Slayter asked after the medtech had transferred Olin to a bed.

Bantly shrugged. "It's hard to tell. It could be a few minutes or it could a few hours."

Though he had a million things he probably should be doing, Slayter commandeered a chair from a nearby desk and sat down beside Olin's bed. He wanted to be there when the boy woke up, regardless of when that was.

To Slayter's relief, Olin's eyes fluttered open a few minutes later. He looked around in confusion for a moment, as if trying to figure out where he was.

"It's okay. You're in the medlab," Slayter said.

The boy's brow furrowed, then his eyes widened. "Oh God, Teyla! Is she okay?"

"She's fine," Slayter assured him. "What about you? How do you feel?"

Olin grimaced. "Like I went twelve rounds with a Baklonian ornyx."

Slayter chuckled.

Olin looked around in confusion again. "We're not moving. Where are we?"

"We're on Arkhon."

Olin frowned. "Arkhon? But I thought..."

"You thought what?" Slayter asked when the boy's voice trailed off.

"I thought with everything that happened...everything Teyla did for us...that you'd change your mind about selling her into slavery."

Slayter sighed. If only Olin knew. "I don't like the idea of putting Teyla on the auction block any more than you do, but it's complicated."

Olin sat up, feebly pushing away Slayter's hand when he tried to urge him back down. "Let me up," he said, his voice halfway between timid and angry. "It's not complicated to me. Teyla's one of us, Captain. She ate with us, negotiated for us, fought alongside us. If you don't want to sell her, then don't."

The boy had no idea how hard this was for him. "I understand what you're saying, Olin, I honestly do, but I have

95

a responsibility to you and the other members of this crew. Teyla represents the money you were supposed to get paid for that job we did for Dunai on Zenoral 5. I might be able to forget about the money, but I can't ask you or the rest of the crew to do that."

"I don't care about the money I was supposed to get paid," Olin protested. "Neither does the rest of the crew. Ask them, they'll tell you!"

"I don't have the right to ask them, Olin."

Or did he? Maybe Olin made more sense than he gave him credit for. Maybe he needed to hear it from someone else, someone who wasn't jaded by this profession yet. Maybe it was as simple as telling the crew he'd changed him mind about putting Teyla on the slave block and that he would have to find another way to pay them the money they were due.

Slayter swore silently. What the hell was he thinking? This was real life, not some damn fairy tale. This wasn't going to have a happy ending. Not for Olin. Not for Teyla. And certainly not for him. He was deluding himself if he thought it could.

"Captain, please. She saved my life." Tears shone in Olin's eyes. "Hewson, tell him. Tell him he can't put Teyla on the slave block."

Slayter looked over his shoulder to see his first mate standing behind him. How much had the older man heard?

Hewson gave Olin a placating smile. "Why don't you get some rest? We can talk about all this later."

Thankful for the interruption, Slayter stood and walked out of the medlab. To his annoyance, his first mate followed.

"You know the boy's right," Hewson said once they were in the passageway.

Slayter scowled. "Olin knew Teyla would be leaving. He was foolish to let himself get so close to her."

"He's not the only one, apparently."

Sometimes Hewson was too damn perceptive for his own good. Slayter narrowed his gaze at the older man. "What the hell is that supposed to mean?"

Hewson shrugged. "I'm simply saying that women like Teyla don't come into a man's life every day. Especially if that man's a pirate."

Slayter folded his arms over his chest. "Maybe not. But that doesn't change anything."

The other man regarded him thoughtfully. "Can you stand there and watch them drag her up on the auction block so men can bid on her? Can you live with knowing some sadistic bastard might buy her and use her for his depraved amusement? Maybe beat her now and then just for the fun of it?"

Slayter clenched his jaw, his gut wrenching at the image. He'd kill any man who did that. He opened his mouth the answer, but a commotion in the passageway behind them interrupted him. He turned to see Deran and Winsen dragging the half-conscious Genoone toward the medlab. There was blood pouring down his face from a gash along the top of his head, though he barely seemed to register the mess as he tried to focus his eyes on Slayter.

"What the hell happened?" Slayter demanded as he followed them into the medlab.

"I don't know," Deran said. "He staggered into the cargo hold like this."

Slayter's heart beat faster. "Was Teyla with him?"

Both Deran and Winsen shook their heads.

Ice cold fear settled into the pit of his stomach. Slayter grabbed his communications officer's sagging head, lifting it so he could look into the man's unfocused eyes.

"Genoone, what happened to Teyla? Where is she?"

Genoone's gaze sharpened a little at the sound of Slayter's voice, but he didn't answer right away, and Slayter had to fight the urge to shake the injured man.

"They...took her..."

"Who took her?" Slayter demanded.

"Three men...they jumped us...at the market... I tried to stop them, but they surprised me. Hit me before I even saw them."

Bantly hurried over to wave a light in Genoone's eyes. "Captain, he's got a pretty bad concussion. I need to get him in a bed."

"In a minute," Slayter said. "Genoone, do you know who took Teyla? Or where they went?"

Genoone nodded. "Yes. I recognized one of them." The words were slurred, but his voice was strong. "It was that damn scar-faced first mate of Rommel's. I've seen him before."

Slayter's heart dropped through the deck. *Shit.* He glanced at Hewson. "Tell Salo to get on the nav-program and find out where the hell that bastard's ship is headed."

"He took her to the auction house," Genoone said.

"Are you sure?" Slayter asked.

"I'm sure. I heard them say Rommel was going to sell her out from under you the same way you sold that Thracian yacht out from under him."

Fuck.

Slayter looked from Hewson to the other two crewmen. "Meet me on the loading dock in five minutes, armed and ready. We're going to get Teyla back."

"I'm coming too," Olin said from the other side of the room as Hewson and the other two men raced out of the medlab.

Slayter swore under his breath. He'd almost forgotten about the boy. He looked over to find Olin already half out of bed.

"No, you're not," Slayter told him. "You're staying right where you are, and that's an order."

Olin opened his mouth to argue, then closed it again at the warning look Slayter gave him. Satisfied the boy would stay put, Slayter left the medlab and ran down the passageway.

He made it barely ten feet when he heard booted feet behind him. Furious that Olin had disobeyed a direct order, he was about to stop and turn around when Genoone caught up with him.

"I'm coming with you, Captain, whether you like it or not," he said as he followed Slayter down the steps. His voice sounded surprisingly firm for a man with a concussion. "I told Teyla I'd keep her safe out there and I'm not coming back here until she is."

Slayter ground his jaw. Damn, but sometimes the Belkin could be pigheaded. When the redheaded man put his mind to something he did it, and nothing short of a tranquilizer was going to stop him. Not that Slayter wanted to. He was going to need all the backup he could get.

Hewson, Deran, and Winsen were already on the loading dock waiting for him, along with Valin, Conder and Salo.

"You know weapons aren't allowed outside of Arkhon's port," Hewson said as they hurried down the gangway. "There will be hell to pay if we go charging into the auction house carrying them."

"I don't give a damn," Slayter said. "I'm not going to let that asshole Rommel take the most precious thing I have and sell her into slavery."

He tried hard not to remember he'd been going to do the exact same thing ten minutes ago.

"Can he do that?" Deran asked as they pushed their way through the crowded streets inside the port. "Sell Teyla, I mean. Doesn't he have to show proof of ownership or something?"

Slayter threw the man a quick glance. "No. Teyla came with me willingly as payment for her father's debt. There's nothing in writing. Not that it matters, though. The auction house here isn't exactly big on how people get to the block. They only worry about what happens once they're there. Most of the slaves they sell have been kidnapped from somewhere or someone." He sidestepped a slow-moving vendor with a cart of sweet cakes. "It might slow the auction down a bit if she claimed she already belongs to someone else, but I doubt Rommel will let her do any of the talking."

"Then how are we going to get her back?" Genoone asked.

Slayter clenched his jaw. "I'm going in there and putting a hole through his head, then taking back what's mine."

"That's a wonderful plan," his first mate yelled as he skirted a hovercar parked near the exit of the port. "But it doesn't explain how we're going to get out of the port toting these weapons. The alarm will go up the moment we walk through the gates."

The alarm actually went off before they even got out of the gates thanks to the detectors just inside the perimeter. As soon as the alarm sounded, the two security guards posted at the exit immediately stormed into the street to bar their way, rifles at the ready.

Slayter knew it would be pointless to try to reason with the guards, so he fired his weapon instead, hitting both men in the center of their chests before they could a shot off.

Around them, the port erupted into chaos, screams echoing in the air as people ran for cover. Slayter headed for the exit, taking advantage of the confusion.

Hewson caught his arm. "You shot them?"

"I only stunned them. They'll be fine."

"I'm sure that's the information dozens of screaming witnesses are yelling into their coms right this minute." The older man swore. "If you thought it was going to be tough to get into the auction house before, it will be impossible now.

Hell, we probably won't even make it to that part of town. They'll have a hundred guards out looking for us."

"They won't be looking for me," Slayter told him calmly. "They'll be looking for you and the rest of the crew."

Hewson frowned. "What are you talking about?"

"They'll be looking for a raving group of pirates waving their weapons around and firing indiscriminately. That will be you and the rest of the crew." He motioned down the street in the opposite direction. "You'll be going that way while Genoone, Deran and I go to the auction house."

"So that's your plan, huh?" Hewson said. "We run off and get shot while you go off and save the girl single-handedly?"

"Not quite single-handedly. Genoone and Deran will be with me. And as far you getting shot, don't. It's not part of the plan."

Sighing, the first mate motioned down the street with his pistol. "You heard the captain. Let's go be a distraction."

Slayter didn't watch them go. Instead, he slipped his pistol under his coat and took off down the street toward the auction house, Genoone and Deran at his heels. He moved quickly, but not fast enough to attract attention. Not that he needed to worry about it. The street was full of people running in the same direction as he and his men, eager to get away from the gunfire down at the port.

In the street, militia hovercrafts went zipping in the direction he and his men had just come from. Slayter hoped Hewson and the others were careful. He would do anything to get Teyla back, but at the same time he didn't want any of his men killed or thrown in prison. Although from his crew's newfound attitude where Teyla was concerned, they'd probably think it was a small price to pay for her safety.

Slayter ground his jaw as he thought of Teyla. He never should have brought her here. He should have turned his ship around days ago and taken her home. When he got her back, that was exactly what he was going to do. This whole slave thing was wrong from the beginning, even before he realized what an amazing woman she was.

First he had to find her, though. Which might be more difficult than he thought considering the auction house was immense. He was still trying to figure out a way around that issue when laser fire made him duck.

Slayter instinctively dived behind one of the ornate columns along the square in front of the auction house and pulled his pistol while Genoone and Deran did the same on the other side of the walkway. Slayter peered around the edge of the column, wondering how the hell the guards had figured out he and his men had been part of the group creating the ruckus down at the port when he spotted four pirates positioned in front of the building covering the entrance. Rommel's men. Clearly, they hadn't adhered to the no-weapons rule, either. Since there weren't any guards around, Slayter assumed Rommel's men had either already taken care of them or that they were down at the port looking for Hewson and the rest of his crew.

As far as Slayter was concerned, that meant there were fewer obstacles for him to get through.

He caught Genoone's eye, then did the same with Deran. "Keep them busy."

Slayter didn't wait for a reply, but instead took off running across the open square. Genoone and Deran covered him, shooting at the four pirates guarding the entrance. That didn't keep Slayter from having to go through one hell of a crossfire to get there. He made it, but not without a few burn marks to show for it.

He burst through the glass doors, skidding to a halt when he saw the three huge guards standing behind the counter. They didn't even hesitate to see if Slayter was an innocent bystander trying to get away from the melee outside, but immediately fired at him.

Slayter threw himself toward them and hit the ground rolling, laser fire zipping over his head. It was risky, but with nowhere to take cover, he didn't have much of a choice. The move must have caught the guards unaware because they stopped shooting momentarily to duck behind the counter. Slayter used the momentum from his roll to launch himself over the counter, coming down on the three men. They went sprawling, Slayter on top of them.

The guards were all bigger than he was, but he had surprise and determination on his side. They were standing between him and Teyla, which meant they had to go.

Tightening his grip on his pistol, he rammed it into one man's jaw, then head-butted another, breaking the man's nose.

While that neutralized two of the men, it gave the third guard time to take a shot at him, and Slayter had yank his head back to keep from getting it blown off. He lunged at the man, forcing his arm back, then lifted his own pistol and fired it point blank into the guard's gut. The man spasmed once, then went still.

It was only after Slayter dragged himself to his feet that he realized his weapon was still set to stun. The guard was lucky guy, he thought as he changed the setting from stun to kill and ran toward the inner doors, eager to find Teyla. He only imagined how terrified she must be. The thought of her being put up for display on the block and bid on like a piece of livestock made his blood turn to fire in his veins. He needed to get to her. Now!

The moment he rushed through the tall, wooden doors and saw the huge concourse inside, however, he knew he was in trouble. While it was full of people, including more guards, luckily none of them noticed the gun in his hand. Wanting to keep it that way, at least for the time being, he quickly tucked the weapon in his belt so his coat would cover it.

Slayter looked around at the numerous doors lining the concourse, wondering which room to look in first. How the hell was he going to figure out which one she was in?

Deciding to start at one end and go from there, he jerked open the door closest to him and walked into the room. There were a dozen naked men lined up on the stage, while more than thirty men and women in fancy clothes inspected every part of them.

Swearing under his breath, Slayter ducked out of the room and tried the next. The auction in this one sold men as well, though they were clothed and all had dark crimson skin, indicating they came from the planet of Carnorra, in the Hotheth system.

The third room he looked in wasn't auctioning people at all, but horticulture. The prospective buyers inside were busy inspecting a collection of colorful, long-stalked plants that emitted strange mewling sounds and wavered slowly back and forth.

He rushed out to the concourse again, his heart pounding. This was insane. There was no way he could check every auction room. Teyla would be long gone by the time he found the right one, if she wasn't already. He needed to find a better way than running aimlessly from room to room.

Slayter's eyes narrowed as he spotted a small man wearing an official-looking uniform and carrying a fancy compad. He definitely looked like he could help.

Trying to look as casual as he could, Slayter walked over and positioned himself in front of the man.

The man looked up from his compad questioningly. "Can I help you, sir?"

"I hope so." Slayter slid his pistol out of his belt just enough for the man to get a good look at it.

The man's eyes went wide. "Sir, there's no need for that! I carry nothing of value on my person."

"But you have something of value in that head of yours," Slayter growled. "Either there or in that compad. I want it now, or I'll put a hole in both of them."

The man glanced at the guard on the other side of the room, clearly debating whether he could get his attention before Slayter could pull the trigger. He must have decided against it because he nodded.

"What exactly do you want?"

Slayter took his arm and pulled him off to the side so they were off the main thoroughfare. "I'm looking for a woman."

The man lifted his chin, his eyes taking on a haughty look behind his glasses. "Sir, I believe you have the wrong establishment. We are an auction house, not a brothel."

Slayter swore in frustration. "I know that, you moron. I'm not looking for a prostitute. I'm looking for a woman being auctioned off."

"Oh. Now I see. You wish to buy a woman." The officious little man gave him a knowing smirk. "Well, we certainly have a lot of those to choose from."

Slayter clenched his jaw. If he didn't need the man's help so badly, he'd shoot him and be done with it. He grabbed the man and shoved him against the wall, then pressed his pistol hard into the man's gut.

"I'm looking for someone from my ship. She was kidnapped and brought here to be sold."

The man frowned. "Is she a member of your crew?"

"No, she's not a member of my crew. She's my...."

Slayter hesitated, not sure exactly how to describe Teyla. What word did a man use to describe someone who had become more precious to him than his own life?

"She's your...?" prompted the man when Slayter didn't answer.

"My woman. She's my woman." The words came out in a rush—like he was taking some crazy word association test.

"Ahhh." The man nodded. "Now I really do see. Someone took a woman you care for very much and is attempting to sell her at this auction house, and now you'll do anything to get her back. Am I right?"

Slayter scowled. "Didn't I just say that?"

"Not precisely, but I'm very quick at picking up on things like that, you see."

God, the man was irritating. Slayter's hand tightened on his weapon, pressing it harder against the man's stomach. "Can you help me find her, or do I need to shoot you in the head and ask someone else?"

"Now that I know what you're looking for, I'll be pleased to assist you." The man glanced down pointedly at the gun. "If you could remove the weapon from my stomach?"

Slayter stepped back a little, but not far enough for the man could slip past him. The man didn't try to escape, though. He merely adjusted his glasses and typed something into his compad.

"I assume your female companion was abducted recently, or that you have reason to believe she is to be auctioned off sometime soon?" the man asked, his fingers dancing rapidly over the touchscreen.

Slayer nodded. "The man kidnapped her less than an hour ago. They couldn't have been more than twenty minutes ahead of me."

The man typed something else into his computer. "And I assume this woman of yours is very beautiful?"

"Yes."

The man looked at him over the rim of his glasses. "Do you think the person who took her might try to sell her as a sex slave then?"

"Yes," Slayter answered without hesitation. He didn't mention he'd planned to do the same thing just that morning. That was then, and this was now. He wasn't going to sell Teyla, and neither was anyone else.

"You're in luck then," the man said. "There's only one room selling female sex slaves today. The auction has already started, though, so we'll have to hurry. Come with me."

The man led him down the main concourse, turning right, then left, then right again. As he followed, Slayter realized he'd been crazy to think he would have been able to find Teyla on his own. He just prayed he hadn't wasted too much time already.

The man with the compad stopped in front of an ornate door where two burly guards were posted. Slayter tensed, but the man motioned with his hand and one of the guards immediately opened the door.

It was filled to capacity with people and Slayter had a hard time seeing around the men and women blocking his view.

"If she hasn't been sold yet, this is the where she will be," the man said. "If she's already on the block, then I can't imagine how you're going to get her back, but I wish you the best. Good day."

Slayter would have thanked the man for his help, but at that moment a flash of long, dark hair and shapely legs on the dais in the front of the room caught his attention. He watched in horror as the woman he loved was led up onto the auction block. His gut clenched. Dammit to hell, he was too late.

Chapter Seven

𝕰𝕺

Teyla hadn't stopped fighting since Rommel's men had grabbed her in the market. Unfortunately, the little bit of hand-to-hand combat training she'd had back home hadn't done much good and the two pirates had easily overpowered her. Once their cohorts had dealt with Genoone, it was easy for them to tie her up and throw her in a hovercraft.

At first she thought they were simply everyday, run-of-the-mill thugs, but then they addressed the man who'd been waiting for them in the hovercraft as Rommel. Her blood ran cold at the name and it was all she could not to cower when he turned those cruel, dark eyes of his on her.

"This will teach that thieving bastard Slayter not to take what doesn't belong to him," he said in a gruff voice. "Let's see if he likes a taste of his own medicine."

Teyla immediately remembered the warning the men on Haan had given Slayter. Apparently they'd been right about Rommel seeking revenge. What better way to do it than to take her away from Slayter?

As they drove through town, she wanted to ask where they were going, but didn't think Rommel would tell her anyway. She found out soon enough when they stopped at the side entrance of a large, imposing building and dragged her inside.

A ripple of fear coursed through her as one of the pirates yanked her out of the hovercraft. "Where are we?" she demanded.

"The auction house." Rommel sneered. "I can't think of a better way to get back at Slayter than by selling his woman to be a sex slave."

Teyla trembled again, this time with fury. She'd been willing to be sold into slavery to repay her family's debt, but there was no way she was going to let this bastard sell her just to get back at Slayter. She was nobody's pawn.

When she told Rommel as much, though, he only laughed. "You don't have any say on the subject, bitch. And by the time Slayter finds out you're missing, you'll already be another man's whore."

The insult made her even more furious and she struggled to free herself from the scar-faced man holding her. When he tightened his grip on her arms, she lashed out with her feet, but Rommel easily sidestepped her kick.

"You are a spunky one, aren't you?" he said. "It almost makes me want to fuck you myself. Unfortunately, the only sex slave auction of the day starts in ten minutes, so I'll have to pass. But don't worry. I'm sure you'll get well fucked before the day is out."

He slanted a look at his men. "Four of you stay here and guard the entrance. If Slayter shows up, make sure he doesn't get inside. I don't want him spoiling the fun."

Teyla thought she detected a hint of fear on the pirates' faces. Rommel and his men seemed almost petrified of what Slayter would do if he caught up with them. From what she'd seen after the attack on Slayter's ship, she supposed she couldn't blame them. Slayter could be scary as hell when he wanted to.

Despite how afraid she was, her heart soared at the thought of Slayter coming to rescue her. He wasn't the kind of man to let some small-time pirate like Rommel take what was rightfully his. Not before he got his payment, at least.

Teyla swallowed hard at that last part. Even though she knew it was silly and sentimental, she found herself wishing Slayter would come for her because he cared for her and not because she represented the money her family owed. But

Slayter was a pirate and she was simply payment for a debt, end of story.

She glanced toward the street, hoping to see Slayter striding up the walkway, but she didn't see anything other than finely dressed men and women as Rommel and his men dragged her into the auction house. If Rommel's men had killed Genoone, there would be no way for Slayter to even know what had happened to her. Tears stung her eyes at the thought of the red-haired communications officer. She should never have asked him to take her outside.

They went down a long hallway to a small room. Rommel stopped to talk to whoever was in charge, but Teyla barely paid attention to what was being said. Her attention was focused on the women in the room. Half naked and bound, they looked wide-eyed and terrified. It was the defeated set of their shoulders that troubled her the most, though. Would she look as beaten down as they did before all was said and done?

Teyla jumped as someone sliced through the rope binding her wrists. She turned to see one of the guards standing behind her, a subservient-looking blonde woman at his side.

"You are to take off your clothes and wear this for the auction, like the rest of the women," she said softly, handing Teyla a skimpy bra and short skirt.

Teyla looked down at the clothing for a moment, then around at the other women waiting to be auctioned off. She'd been so busy looking at their demeanor she hadn't noticed what they were wearing. Now that she did, she saw the outfit barely covered them.

She held the clothes out to the other woman. "I'm not going to parade around in this for those pigs out there." She glared at Rommel. "Or the ones in here."

Rage flared in the pirate's eyes and he grabbed her arm cruelly. "Look, bitch, I don't care if you wear this or not. I'd as soon put you out there naked, but the auctioneer insists that having a woman wear a little bit of clothing brings a much higher price. Some shit about leaving something to the imagination. It doesn't make much sense to me, but I'm willing to go along with it if it makes me a few extra Imperial credits. Now, either you put it on or I'll put it on you myself." He pulled her close. "Which is it going to be?"

The thought of Rommel's hands on her naked body made her feel sick. "I'll put it on."

His lip curled. "I thought so."

He gave her a shove, then crossed his arms over his chest, clearly going to stand there and watch. Teyla clenched her jaw. She might have to put on the detestful outfit, but she didn't have to give him a show while she did it. Hands clenched into fists, she turned her back to him and the other men in the room. Taking off her clothes while holding on to the ones the woman had given her was trickier than she'd thought, though, and it took her a few minutes to manage it. The bra left the tops of her breasts exposed, barely covering her nipples. The skirt wasn't much better. Although it was long enough to cover her ass, the filmy material was all but transparent, leaving her pussy practically bare.

Face flaming, she turned around to face Rommel. The way the pirate looked her up and down made her skin crawl, and she would have covered herself if the guard hadn't yanked her arms behind her back and bound her wrists.

Teyla resisted when the man led her across the room, but it did little good, and in the end, she gave up. She had prepared herself for this moment ever since her father had given her over to Slayter. She just hadn't thought it would be so humiliating.

She tried not to look at the men and women waiting to bid on her as the guard led her onto the dais and secured her to one of the pillars. That strategy worked up until the prospective buyers came over to take a closer look. Every time one of them cupped her breasts or squeezed her ass, she felt like spitting in their faces.

111

It didn't help that Rommel stood off to the side, a smirk on his face. She glared at him with the full force of her hatred, but that only seemed to amuse him even more.

Finally, she just ignored everyone and everything in the room and thought of Slayter. She remembered how he'd made love to her the night before, and pictured about how handsome he'd looked lying there in bed that morning. The memory brought tears to her eyes and she cursed herself for not waking him up before she'd left. She hadn't even gotten the chance to say goodbye.

"And now, ladies and gentleman, we've come to the last slave being offered for today."

Teyla jerked out of her musings at the auctioneer's words. She looked around and realized all the other women had been sold while she'd been lost in thought. She was the only one left.

Behind her, a guard disengaged the energy beam securing her bound wrists to the post, then led her up to the auction block in front of the dais. She stepped up on it obediently, standing there while he engaged the energy beam that secured her bound wrists to the pillar behind her.

She stared straight ahead over the heads of the men and women in the crowd, not wanting to see which one among them bid on her, when a commotion in the back of the room drew her attention. She watched as someone pushed through the crowd in an effort to get to the front of the room. Her heart stopped as she caught a glimpse of dark hair and broad shoulders, afraid to hope. Her eyes were playing tricks on her. There was no way it could be Slayter. But as the man finally succeeded in shoving his way through to the front of the room, she saw that her eyes hadn't been playing tricks on her at all. It was Slayter, all six-foot-four leather-clad feet of him, and he looked mad enough to spit laser fire.

As he strode into the open space in front of the auction block, half a dozen of Rommel's men stepped forward and leveled their weapons at him.

Teyla caught her breath, terrified they would shoot, especially since Slayter was already reaching under his coat for what had to be a pistol even as Genoone and Deran burst into the room brandishing weapons of their own. Relief flowed through her at the sight of the red-haired man. She'd been so afraid Rommel's men had killed him.

None of the men managed to get a shot off, however, thanks to the guards and their laser rifles, which were pointed at Slayter, Rommel and their men.

"Drop your weapons now!" one of the guards ordered. "All of you!"

Slayter and Rommel both hesitated, but then finally nodded at their men to obey. As soon as they did, two of the guards hurried forward to collect their guns.

The auctioneer rose to his full height behind the podium, his brows drawing together. "Weapons are strictly prohibited outside the gates of the spaceport. I could have you all executed. What is the meaning of this?"

"This woman belongs to me." Slayter gave Rommel a scathing look. "This bastard kidnapped her from the market down by the spaceport."

"He's lying!" Rommel protested.

Teyla craned her neck to look at the gray-haired auctioneer. "He's telling the truth," she shouted. "My father gave me to Slayter as payment for a debt so he could sell me at auction."

The auctioneer frowned at Slayter. "Is this true? Did her father give her to you as payment for a debt?"

Slayter gave the man a curt nod, his mouth tight. "It is."

"And you have something in writing to back up your story, I presume?"

"No," Slayter said. "It was a gentleman's agreement and she came with me willingly."

The auctioneer let out a heavy sigh. "Well, that certainly complicates matters. Without proof, I have no way to know if you're telling the truth or not. House rules dictate that a sale must be made once merchandise is placed upon the block."

Teyla furrowed her brow. If Slayter couldn't prove ownership, did that mean Rommel would get to keep the money from the sale since he was the one who had brought her there? She couldn't let that happen.

She looked at the auctioneer again. "But I can corroborate Slayter's story. Isn't that just as good as having something in writing?"

The man gave her an apologetic smile. "I'm afraid not, my dear. Slaves have no voice within the walls of the auction house."

Rommel slanted Slayter a malevolent look. "I could just kill him. That would make the issue less complicated, wouldn't it?"

Teyla's heart crept into her throat when she saw the thoughtful glint that came into the auctioneer's eyes at the pirate's words. Surely, the man wasn't going to take Rommel's suggestion seriously.

The auctioneer nodded his head. "That would indeed resolve the matter. It has been a long time since anyone has chosen such means to resolve a dispute, but a duel is completely within the rules, as long as you both agree."

The man looked at Slayter. Teyla held her breath as she waited for his answer. He had to see she wasn't worth losing his life over. But to her chagrin, he nodded.

"I agree."

The auctioneer inclined his head. "Very well. If everyone else would clear a space."

He motioned with his hand and the crowd gathered around Slayter and Rommel stepped back, giving them room.

Teyla stared at the two pirates in stunned disbelief. She'd heard dueling still existed in parts of the galaxy, but she never dreamed she would actually see one, much less be the prize the two combatants fought over.

"It can't be much of a duel without weapons, can it?" Slayter pointed out as he took off his coat and handed it to Genoone.

"He's right," Rommel agreed. "Unless you intend us to fight hand to hand."

The auctioneer gave them a placating smile. "House rules expressly forbid any personnel other than the guards to carry weapons of any kind in the auction rooms. You can imagine how that would cause concerns in the heat of a bidding war. However, we do pride ourselves on providing an unsurpassed purchasing experience, so I'll bend the rules a little just this once." He motioned to one of the guards. "Two shock rods, if you would, Lieutenant."

The man gave him a nod, then relieved two other guards of the six-inch-long batons they carried at their waist. At a touch of the button, a three-foot-long beam of energy sprang out from each of the rods. Teyla's eyes went wide. She'd seen a guard prod one of the slaves with the exact same thing earlier when the woman hadn't moved fast enough for his liking. From the cry of pain she'd let out, the energy beams could cause some real damage.

"Standard house rules apply, gentleman," the auctioneer said. "The duel will continue until one of you drops his claim, loses his weapon, or is otherwise unable to continue. You may begin when ready. And please, mind the paying customers and the merchandise."

Teyla couldn't seem to breathe as she watched Slayter and Rommel circle each other warily in the space in front of her. Slayter was bigger and taller than the other pirate, but she worried Rommel wouldn't fight fair. If he said or did something to distract Slayter, the duel could be over before it started.

Slayter was the first to attack. He lunged at Rommel, bringing his shock rod down in an arc at the other man's head. Rommel immediately blocked the blow. He might be smaller than Slayter, but he was surprisingly fast, and Teyla gasped as he spun out of the way.

Below her, the two men swung the shock rods at each other over and over. Most of the time, they ducked each other's strikes or smacked their weapons against each other with a sizzle and pop of electricity, but every so often, their attacks hit home. When that happened, they grunted in pain, and if the blow caught them on the exposed skin of their arms, an immediate welt showed up, evidence of how painful the energy beams could be. Teyla cringed every time Rommel struck Slayter, not wanting to watch, but afraid to look away.

While Slayter and Rommel both appeared to get in an equal number of blows with their shock rods, Slayter seemed to be able to handle the pain better than the other pirate. Teyla almost cheered as Rommel visibly swayed on his feet when Slayter connected with his shock rod yet again.

That was when Rommel must have decided Teyla would make a good shield because he moved as close to the auction block as he could without actually climbing on top of it with her.

Slayter immediately froze. He glowered at Rommel. "Stop hiding behind her like a coward and come out here and fight me like a man."

Rommel laughed. "What you call cowardice, I call quick thinking."

Without warning, the pirate lunged past Teyla to get to Slayter. Slayter stepped back, avoiding the blow, but Rommel's shock rod grazed the exposed skin on Teyla's midriff. She let out a cry of pain as tears stung her eyes. Damn, that hurt. How had Slayter taken dozens of shocks with that thing?

Slayter's gold eyes blazed. "You sonofabitch!"

116

"Come at me again, Cardona, and she might get zapped a few more times. Completely by accident, of course." Rommel grinned. "Why don't you just drop your weapon and forfeit now."

Slayter didn't move, but Teyla could see from the look in his eyes that he was considering Rommel's demand. The room seemed to be holding its collective breath right along with her. Jaw tight, Slayter lowered his shock rod.

"Slayter, no," Teyla moaned. "Don't let him do this to you. The money from whoever bids on me is rightfully yours."

Slayter lifted his head to lock eyes with hers, and the look she saw in them made her think he was about to do something very stupid. Or very brave.

She only had time to shake her head before Rommel let out a bellow and thrust his shock rod at Slayter as if he intended to shove the energy beam through his heart.

Teyla screamed, sure the shock rod would burn a hole right through Slayter's chest, but he moved faster than she would have thought possible, sidestepping the blow just in time so that the energy beam slid harmlessly under his arm.

She sagged with relief against the pillar only to gasp when Slayter lowered his arm to trap the energy beam between his chest and biceps. It popped and sizzled, filling the room with the sound, but while the pain must have been intense, Slayter didn't even blink.

Rommel tried to yank his weapon free, but Slayter was too strong. Holding the shock rod immobile, he grabbed Rommel's forearm in a tight grip and twisted it violently to the right, wrenching the weapon out of the pirate's hand. It flew across the room, sliding dangerously close to the crowd of onlookers, who quickly backpedaled in an effort to get away from the thing.

Without a word, Slayter released Rommel, then walked around the auction block Teyla was standing on, bringing his shock rod down on the other man's head and slashing it across his face. Rommel flew backward with a strangled cry to land in a heap on the floor.

Teyla craned her neck to see Rommel holding up one hand in surrender, an angry, red welt on his ugly face, hatred and defeat in his black eyes.

The auctioneer cleared his throat. "I believe the issue of ownership has been resolved."

Giving Rommel a scornful look, Slayter shut off the energy beam emanating from the shock rod and turned to Teyla. Behind him, Rommel scrambled to his feet and threw himself at Slayter, a short dagger appearing in his hand, aimed at her lover's unprotected back.

"Slayter, watch out!" she cried.

But Slayter must have been expecting the underhanded move because he spun around and grabbed the pirate's wrist, twisting it sharply. Rommel howled in pain, the dagger that had been mere inches from Slayter's chest moments before falling uselessly to the floor.

"You sneaky piece of shit," Slayter snarled. "I should take that knife and shove it up your —"

"That won't be necessary." The auctioneer glanced at the guard who had distributed the shock rods before. "Lieutenant, if you would be so kind?"

Without a word, the guard lifted his pistol and shot Rommel in the head.

Slayter released his hold on the pirate, a stunned expression on his face as Rommel crumpled to the floor. Slayter wasn't the only one taken aback by what had just happened, Teyla noticed. Everyone in the room was staring down at Rommel's lifeless body in stunned disbelief.

"I distinctly remember saying that weapons were expressly forbidden in the auction room," the auctioneer said. "Rules must be followed."

He motioned to two of the guards, waiting patiently while they unceremoniously picked the dead pirate's body and carried it from the room before continuing.

"Since we have resolved the issue of ownership, we can now resume with the auction."

Slayter turned to her, his tawny eyes filled with that same emotion she'd seen the night before. "There isn't going to be an auction."

Teyla's brow furrowed in confusion. "There isn't?"

"No," he said. "I'm taking you home."

She blinked. "I—I don't understand."

He reached up to gently cup her cheek. "You deserve to be a man's equal, Teyla, not his slave."

She felt her pulse quicken. "B-but what about the debt my father owes you?"

"It's been paid in full. Even if it wasn't, I could never sell you. Not after realizing how I feel about you."

She held her breath, afraid to hope. "What are you saying?"

"I'm saying that I love you, Teyla." He smiled up at her. "I love you more than I ever thought it was possible to love someone."

The words, so heartfelt and without hesitation, made her feel warm all over, and if she hadn't been secured to a damn pillar, she would have jumped off the auction block right into his arms. She couldn't do that, but she could still tell him how she felt in return. She opened her mouth, but the auctioneer's booming voice cut in.

"I'm sorry to interrupt such an emotional moment, but I need to clarify one minor point. There is most definitely going to be an auction, sir."

Slayter dropped his hand, his brows drawing together as he fixed his gaze on the man. "You don't understand. I don't want to sell her anymore."

The auctioneer's mouth curved. "That's very romantic, it really is. But unfortunately for you, once merchandise has been placed on the auction block, it must be sold. It's in the rules."

"I don't give a damn about the rules," Slayter snapped.

"Well, we do. Rules are the very foundation of our business. Imagine if owners pulled their merchandise off the block whenever they felt like. It would ruin our reputation." The auctioneer waved his hand. "Let us commence with the bidding. Do I hear five-hundred credits?"

Slayter took a threatening step toward the podium, his expression hard. "I said she's not for sale and that's final."

Half a dozen guards immediately stepped between him and the auctioneer, their rifles leveled at Slayter.

The auctioneer's mouth tightened. "Sir, as the owner of the merchandise, you have every right to be present during bidding, but if you attempt to prevent the sale of this woman, I'll have you dragged out of here. If you resist, you will be shot."

Teyla's heart squeezed in her chest. To come all this way, to find the man of her dreams and fall in love, then have it all taken away because of some damn bureaucratic rules. There had to be something they could do, some way to make the auctioneer change his mind.

She looked at Slayter, silently willing him to come up with a solution. From the fury on his face, though, she feared he was about to do something that would only likely get him killed. As if that wasn't bad enough, Genoone and Deran looked like they were ready to join him in whatever insanity he had planned.

The auctioneer picked up his gavel and held it poised above the podium, seemingly oblivious to the threat. Instead of picking up where he'd left off, though, he lifted a brow at Slayter.

"Since you seem to have some desire to retain possession of this lovely woman, I assume you'd like to open the bidding?"

Slayter frowned. "I can buy her myself?"

"Of course. Obviously, it's not regularly done, but this is a free and open auction. Anyone may bid on the merchandise. However, I'm afraid I'll have to ask you to use cash or the equivalent if you don't have a credit account established with our establishment."

"I don't."

"Then what is your opening bid?"

Slayter dug through the pockets of his breeches, as well as the ones in his coat. "One-hundred-and-thirty-two credits."

Teyla held her breath. That wasn't anywhere close to the five hundred the auctioneer had tried to open the bidding with before. She only hoped the crowd had been moved by Slayter's declaration of love and wouldn't outbid him.

"Two-hundred credits!"

Teyla scanned the sea of faces, trying to figure out which man had spoken, and saw a tall, thin blond-haired man step forward. Her blood froze in her veins as she recognized him. He had lingered near her during the inspection period before the auction, running his fingers up and down her arm and telling her how much he would enjoy bruising such fair skin.

He gave her a mocking grin. "Glare at me all you want, girl, but I'm no fool. It would be a crime to let beauty such as yours go for such a pittance." He glanced at Slayter. "If he doesn't have the money to afford you, then he doesn't deserve you."

Teyla saw Slayter's jaw clench, and for a moment she was afraid he was going to launch himself at the man. Genoone and Deran must have thought so, too, because they were frantically searching their pockets. Beside them, the rest of his crew was doing the same. Teyla hadn't even seen the other men come into the room and could only watch in disbelief as they shoved what money they had on them into Slayter's hand.

Slayter quickly counted it. "Four-hundred-and-seventy credits."

The blond-haired man snorted. "This is a mockery. The woman is clearly worth a hundred times that figure, a thousand times even. Let's be done with this travesty now. I bid two-thousand credits."

Teyla wanted nothing more than to slap the smug look off the man's face. Since her bonds made that impossible, she settled for glaring at him instead. Tears of frustration stung her eyes and she blinked them back. The idea of being sold to this bastard when Slayter was right there was almost too much. If he thought she was ever going to let him touch her, he was insane. She'd kill him first.

Slayter looked like he wanted to do the same thing. He turned to the auctioneer. "Would you accept my ship for collateral?"

"Since you don't have an account with us, I'm afraid not," the man said. "We can only accept cash or something with recognizable and immediate cash value."

Taking a deep breath, Slayter reached into his shirt and pulled out his mother's ring. He undid the clasp on the chain, then strode up to the podium and handed it to the auctioneer. "How much is this worth?"

Teyla's eyes went wide. "Slayter, no! That ring means too much to you."

Slayter walked over and tenderly cupped her cheek in his hand. "It doesn't mean nearly as much to me as you do, sweetheart." He swallowed hard. "Teyla, you're the best thing I've ever stumbled upon in my miserable pirate life, and I'm not going to lose you. My mother would be the first to tell me to give it up to buy your freedom."

Behind the podium, the auctioneer cleared his throat. "According to the appraiser, the ring is worth four-thousand credits."

Teyla gasped. "That gem is Kallorite, Slayter. The setting is platinum. They're offering you half of what's it worth. I'm begging you, please don't do it. There has to be another way."

Slayter shook his head. "If there is, I can't think of it. And I'm not taking the risk." He looked at the auctioneer. "Add the ring to the money I already bid."

"Very well. That brings the current bid to four-thousand, four-hundred-and-seventy credits. Do I hear another bid for this beautiful woman who inspires such passionate in the men around her?"

The blond-haired man strode forward, clearly intending to bid more, only to fall face first onto the floor thanks to Genoone, who stuck out his foot just enough to trip him. The man lay sprawled there, as if waiting for someone to help him up. Slayter did the honors, grabbing the man's arm and hauling him to his feet.

The man eyed Slayter in confusion for a moment, then shrugged off his hand. Straightening his clothes, he sidestepped Slayter and looked at the auctioneer.

"I believe you dropped this, Mr. Lattenmore," Slayter said.

At the name, the blond man turned to give Slayter a startled look. His eyes widened at the sight of the leather folio Slayter held up.

"How did you...?" The man's voice trailed off as he reached into the inner pocket of his overcoat and fumbled around urgently.

"This is yours, isn't it, Mr. Lattenmore?" Slayter flipped open the folio, scanning the identification card inside. "Mr. Jok Lattenmore of Mellone Manor in Strant City on the planet Kahoon. It has your picture right here, as well as all the rest of your personal information, so I suppose it must be yours. Wouldn't want to lose something like this."

Red-faced, the man stepped forward to snatch the folio out of Slayter's hand. "You picked my pocket, you thief!"

Slayter gave him an affronted look. "I did no such thing. It fell out of your pocket when you tripped. Everyone saw it." Folding his arms across him broad chest, he looked around the room at the crowd. "Isn't that right?"

To Teyla's surprise, everyone nodded in agreement. She hadn't seen the folio fall out of the man's pocket, and wondered what game Slayter was playing.

"I can certainly understand why you'd be upset about it, though," Slayter continued conversationally. "Someone gets their hands on that folio and within moments, they can learn everything about you they'd ever want to know, especially if they had something malicious planned for you."

"Malicious?" The man's eyes narrowed. "Are you threatening me?" He took a step back and looked wildly around the room. "Everyone, did you hear what he said? He threatened me!"

Slayter smiled, the movement nothing but a slight, almost sinister twist of the lips. "I'd never do such a thing. In my line of work as a freelance merchant of flexible ethics, however, I've come in contact with a lot of unscrupulous men you'd certainly have to be concerned about. Men who, if they were wronged, would have no problem tracking you down to what I'm sure is a very palatial home, breaking in during the middle of the night and committing untold atrocities upon every person living there, then leaving you cold and dead after hours of torture." He shrugged. "It happens all the time, or so I'm told."

Though his voice was calm, Teyla saw the fury burning in Slayter's eyes. It was the same look she'd seen there after those other pirates had attacked his ship and butchered his men. She knew right then that if Lattenmore bought her and took her back to his palatial home, Slayter would have no compunction about doing exactly what he had just described. This time, though, it didn't bother her, but instead comforted her.

"I'm not saying anything like that is in store for such a fine gentleman as yourself, of course." Slayter stepped closer to tower over the man, his grin broadening. "I'm just giving you the benefit of my vast experience with people of dubious moral character. You wouldn't want to wrong a person like that."

Lattenmore flinched as if Slayter had struck him, quickly taking a step back.

"Though I'm sure you've never given anyone reason to be that vengeful or remorseless, have you?" Slayter said. "Never caused them such pain that they'd rather die than go on living. Never separated two life mates from each other for just a few credits, for example."

Lattenmore took another step back, throwing a desperate glance at the auctioneer. "Aren't you going to do something about this?"

The auctioneer looked down at the blond-haired man from atop his podium. "House rules clearly state that if you die prior to taking possession of the merchandise you've bid on, your final bid will be honored. Be assured that if you die prior to leaving the hall, Mr. Lattenmore, we'll ensure your purchase is safely transported to your home of record."

"What?" The man frowned, then shook his head. "That's not what I mean! He's threatening to kill me when I return home. What are you going to do about that?"

"Mr. Lattenmore, implied threats of bodily injury are not expressly forbidden under house rules. In fact, it's a frequently employed bidding tactic. If you'd like to lodge a formal complaint after the auction has closed, then I will certainly assist you. If it were me, though, I'd return the threat in like kind. Call his bluff, as it were. I've seen that tactic used to great success. Though I suggest you put a little menace in your voice if you want it to be effective."

Lattenmore eyed Slayter warily, as if considering whether he should take the auctioneer's advice or not. He either decided Slayter wasn't buffing, or that he couldn't successfully pull off a believable counter threat because he blanched and turned away.

"Mr. Lattenmore, the bid of four thousand, four hundred and seventy is to you," the auctioneer said. "Do you have a counterbid?"

Lattenmore looked down at the floor, his brow furrowed. After a moment, he shook his head. "I withdraw my bid and defer to the other bidder."

The auctioneer raised a brow. "All previous bids, or just your most recent bid?"

"All previous bids," Lattenmore said quickly.

He didn't wait for the auctioneer to ask him anything else, but instead gave Slayter a wide berth as he hurried from the room.

The auctioneer smiled. "Now, are there any other bidders at the current low price?"

Slayter swept the crowd with a withering gaze. There were no further bids.

"Going once, going twice, going three times." The auctioneer banged his gavel on the podium with a flick of the wrist. "Sold to the threatening yet passionate gentleman in the front row."

At his nod, one of the guards immediately hurried over to release Teyla from her bonds. Once she was free, she jumped down from the pedestal and ran to Slayter. He caught her in his arms, pulling her close for a long, passionate kiss that left her breathless.

"I can't believe you did that for me," she said. "You not only forgave my family's debt, but gave up your mother's ring. How could you do all that for me?"

Slayter smoothed her hair back with a gentle hand. "How could I not? I love you, Teyla." He bent to press tender kiss to her lips. "Come on. I'll take you home."

"Home?" She took a step back to gaze up at him. "Slayter, I don't want to go home. Not home to Kallor, anyway. I want to go home with you. To your ship."

Slayter's brow furrowed. "You do?"

"Of course." She reached up to cup his cheek. "Slayter, I love you. I would have told you before, but the auctioneer interrupted me."

Slayter kissed her again, long and hard. "How did I get so lucky?"

"I'm the lucky one," she insisted.

Teyla would have given him another kiss, but Genoone tapped Slayter on the shoulder.

"I hate to interrupt," he said, "but I think the auctioneer is waiting to get paid. And in case you haven't noticed, they really seem to be sticklers about following the rules."

Slayter chuckled. "I almost forgot that part."

Grabbing his coat from Genoone, he helped Teyla put it on, then took her hand and led her over to the podium.

The gray-haired men smiled kindly at them. "In all my years doing this job, I don't think I've ever seen a more exciting round of bidding. That will be one-hundred-and-thirty-two credits, if you please."

Slayter frowned. "My bid was four thousand, four hundred seventy."

"Yes, well, since the other bidder withdrew all of his previous bids, your first bid of one-hundred-and-thirty-two credits is the winning bid."

"He doesn't have to give you the ring then?" Teyla asked.

"No." The man held out the piece of jewelry. "Congratulations and good luck to you. I hope your purchase brings you years and years of entertainment."

Slipping the chain over his neck, Slayter tucked the ring inside his shirt, then took Teyla's hand. He gave her a smile. "I'm sure it will."

They started for the door when the auctioneer's voice stopped them.

"Gentlemen, a moment."

Thinking the man meant Slayter and his crew, she turned. Slayter did the same. But the auctioneer wasn't looking at them. Instead, he was focused on Rommel's men, a hard look on his face.

"There's that little matter of the shooting down at the spaceport to clear up, not to mention the assault on three of the guards in the lobby. There are very serious consequences for what you did."

Glancing at Slayter, the auctioneer gave him a wink. Curious what that was about, Teyla turned to ask Slayter, but he was already leading her out of the room.

"Now, who's the best negotiator?" he asked, slipping his arm around her as they walked down the passageway. "I got you for only one-hundred-and-thirty-two credits."

Teyla couldn't help but laugh. "If I had been doing the talking, the auctioneer would have paid you to take me."

Slayter only chuckled.

Chapter Eight

ဢ

"That's so romantic!"

Teyla smiled at her youngest sister's words. She had called her family on the compvid to tell them the good news the moment Slayter had let her out of bed. To say they'd been surprised to hear from her was putting it mildly. Her mother had burst into tears at the sight of her and hadn't stopped crying since. That had been thirty minutes ago.

"It was very romantic," Teyla agreed.

"That's all well and good, dear, but tell me truthfully," her mother said. "Slayter hasn't decided to keep you just as a sex slave himself, has he?"

Teyla laughed. "No, he isn't keeping me as a sex slave, Mother. He's making me his wife. Slayter is the most caring and loving man I could have ever hoped to meet. I love him and he loves me."

In the background, her father let out a snort. "I hope he doesn't think he's going to get money out of me now just because he wouldn't sell you."

Teyla's mouth tightened. She couldn't believe that was all her father was concerned about. He could at least act pleased she was getting married.

"No, Father, he doesn't. I told you, Slayter considers the debt paid in full." She gave him a sweet smile. "You might want to be careful, though. Now that I'm doing the negotiating for him, profits will be going through the roof. We might just make enough money to buy a controlling interest in your company."

In the bedroom, Slayter chuckled. The deep, sexy sound made heat pool between her thighs, and Teyla stifled a moan. Eager to get back to bed for more of the toe-curling sex he'd treated her to when they'd gotten back from Arkhon, she gave her parents and sisters a grin.

"I have to go. I'll call again as soon as we get close to Kallor."

"Wait!" her youngest sister begged. "Show us your ring again."

Laughing, Teyla held up her left hand to show off the platinum and Kallorite ring. Slayter had given it to her the moment they'd stepped into his cabin, but only after getting down on one knee and asking if she would make him the happiest pirate in the galaxy and marry him.

When she went back into the bedroom, she found Slayter lying back on the pillows where she'd left him, one arm behind his head. Teyla slipped off the robe she'd put on while talking to her family, then crawled into bed beside him.

"You know," she said. "I wasn't kidding about buying a controlling interest in my father's company. Silicate processing is very lucrative. Now that the ore processor has been purchased, there's almost no overhead. Then again, Dunagan ale is also a very hot commodity right now. What do you think about buying a distillery?"

Slayter shifted on the bed to lean over her. A grin tugging at his mouth. "I think that all work and no play makes for a dull sex slave."

Teyla laughed and opened her mouth to reply, but all that came out was a moan as he covered her mouth with his. They could talk about business later.

SCARLET TEAR

B.J. McCall

80

Chapter One

Answering an urgent summons, Captain Wytt Sann marched into the private quarters of Prince Xxan Thrane on the Merck Space Station. Wytt fisted his right hand over his heart and waited for the prince to acknowledge him.

As the commander of the Anti-Pirate Defense Force, the prince used the Merck station as his base of operation. Prince Xxan turned away from the massive communication center dominating the room and rose to his feet. The prince was taller than Wytt. His long brown hair was tied at the nape and fell almost to his waist.

"Wytt."

Although the prince was dressed casually in the loose sand-colored pants and shirt common to Sark, the ring on the prince's left hand marked him as one of the most powerful men in the Aktarian Federation. The ring's three stones representing the planets of Aktares, Sark and Glacid flashed as the prince strode toward him.

"It's good to see you."

Bowing his head, Wytt responded, "Your Highness."

The prince extended his hand. "At ease, my friend."

Wytt shook the prince's hand.

"You're looking fit," the prince said.

"I've spent the last four weeks at the academy training with the cadets. I haven't been so physically challenged in years."

"Remember when we entered the academy? We were ready to conquer the universe."

Wytt had been the prince's roommate. Despite the differences in their social status, they'd become lifelong friends.

"I'm glad you're here, Wytt. I have need of your skills and what I'm going to ask of you is very dangerous."

The prince's encrypted transmission summoning Wytt to Merck had piqued his curiosity. Wytt rubbed his hands together. As he'd advanced in rank, his job had become more involved with the planning of the mission than the execution of it.

Wytt followed Prince Xxan into a room adjacent to his office, a space meant for relaxation with thick carpet, muted colors and comfortable-looking sofas and chairs. A wall of *permashield* provided an incredible view of Aktares. Beyond the ringed planet and to its left, the steady golden light of Sark glowed in the dark void. Deeper in the starry void was Glacid, the ice planet.

"I'd never tire of this view," Wytt said.

"It humbles me," the prince said. "It's been a long day for both of us. Join me for a glass of wine."

After the prince was seated, Wytt eased into a chair. On the table before them was a carafe of wine and two glasses. Next to the carafe was an electronic tablet.

The prince poured two glasses. "The wine is from the Armath region."

Thanking the prince, Wytt accepted a glass of the fine Sarkian wine. He sipped. "Excellent. Nothing better than an Armathian grape."

"You've heard of the pirate, Kirxx?"

Wytt nodded. "I know my brother died trying to capture him."

The prince's gaze narrowed. "Hadr was a fine soldier."

"My mother still hopes. Without his body, she refuses to accept his death."

"I am sorry for your mother's pain, but the details of Hadr's last mission remain classified."

"Your Highness, I meant no disrespect. My family is honored to serve the Federation."

"Show me your sword hand."

The request surprised Wytt. Except for the Elite, a military unit assigned to the prince's father and his family, few were skilled with the *falx*, a Sarkian sword. The calluses on his open palm bore proof of his dedication to the ancient art.

"I practice daily, but I'll never be as skilled as Hadr."

Each time Wytt wrapped his hand about the hilt of Hadr's sword, Wytt felt a connection to his brother.

"Excellent," the prince said. "We must spar. It's been a long time since I've had a good opponent."

The prince was one of the best swordsmen in the Federation. "I'd be honored."

"Do you still play *zap*?"

The game invented in Sark had become popular throughout the universe. "Every week."

The prince picked up the tablet and handed it to Wytt. "My staff has compiled an extensive dossier on Kirxx. The pirate is a skilled *zap* player."

Wytt's heart pounded. He'd finally get to avenge his brother's death. "My mission is to capture Kirxx?"

"Your mission is to impersonate him."

Chapter Two

ை

Wytt read through the dossier while the prince answered several important communications. Wondering what the prince had in mind, Wytt turned off the tablet and waited for the prince to join him.

The prince finished his call and resumed his seat. "An invitation to participate in Rangar's annual *zap* tournament on Osesar was discovered on Kirxx's ship. Do you believe you could convince someone you are Kirxx?"

"Rangar invited Kirxx? His sworn enemy?"

The prince nodded. "To our knowledge, Kirxx and Rangar have never met face-to-face. It's a dangerous mission, Wytt. Can you do it?"

The challenge of the prince's question stirred Wytt's imagination. Was it possible to enter the den of thieves and fool them? "Osesar security is excellent. If Rangar has invited Kirxx to participate, he must have an *Ident* pattern on file."

"Kirxx was captured three weeks ago," the prince said. "Our lab has made a special pair of eye lenses so you'll pass the *Ident* screening and, like you, Kirxx is of mixed blood."

"Sark and Aktarian?"

"Yes. If Osesar security is using any race typing, you'll pass."

Faking one's identity with documents was easy. *Ident* lenses were expensive and required advanced technology, but faking thousands of years of evolution was impossible. A simple test of one's saliva, blood or skin identified a Sark from an Aktarian. Glacidians were amazingly unique. Crossbreeds were a minority.

"When is the competition?"

"In thirty days."

"As Kirxx, I should be granted permission to land on Osesar. I might get close to Rangar, but I doubt I'll be able to take him out."

"Killing Rangar isn't your mission. Your mission is to maintain your cover and compete as Kirxx."

"What of Kirxx's crew?"

"Rangar is a cautious man and he has guaranteed each competitor's safe passage, but they must come alone and unarmed."

"I'd rather go it alone than have to worry about a knife in the back from one of Kirxx's friends. If the mission objective isn't to kill Rangar, what is it?"

"Win the competition and bring the prize back to Merck."

"You want me to win?"

The prince picked up a control device. "Perhaps this will inspire you."

A holographic image of a woman filled the space before Wytt. A glittering silver cloak covered her from neck to toe. Mesmerizing silver-gray eyes dominated her face. Her pink lips were slightly parted and sensual. Given her pale skin and near white-blonde hair, the woman's heritage was unmistakable.

"She's Glacidian. Who is she?"

"We have no idea. We've ran every database. She doesn't exist."

"But how?"

"How did a young Glacidian female fall into Rangar's hands and become a pirate's prize? That's what my mother wants to know. You can imagine her reaction when she saw this."

The prince's mother was Queen Tayra of Glacid. "I'd bet Her Highness was ready to lead a division to Osesar?"

"A fleet, but fortunately the queen is a reasonable woman. She's giving my plan a chance before confronting the Jagir Conclave. As long as Rangar remains in the Jagir system, the Federation can't touch him without the Conclave's permission. So far they've refused. This contest will provide an opportunity to infiltrate Osesar security."

Wytt stared, fascinated, as the woman raised her arms, lifting the cloak. Except for a pair of silver sandals and a narrow belt of white Jagir crystals riding low on her hips, the woman was naked. Slender in build, her legs were long, her hips sweetly curved and her firm breasts tipped with tempting pink nipples.

Regal as the queen who wanted her rescued, the blonde was a vision of Glacidian perfection with a fortune wrapped around her hips.

Wytt had always considered Prince Xxan's younger sister the most beautiful female he'd ever seen, but this woman rivaled the princess.

"What are the rules for Rangar's competition?"

"A series of heats. Winner moves on to the next round until the field is narrowed to the final two. Rangar is fanatical about *zap* and holds this tournament of pirates for personal amusement."

Wytt's gaze slid over the beautiful blonde. "He certainly knows how to entice one to compete."

"She is exquisite. If I could pass for Kirxx, I'd compete."

Exquisite didn't begin to describe her. The thought of winning her stimulated Wytt's competitive juices and his libido, but Queen Tayra expected him to rescue the Glacidian beauty, not seduce her. Honor had guided his life and he'd complete the mission.

"She's only part of the prize. Watch."

The woman turned and dropped the cloak. Dangling from the strand of crystals, a teardrop-shaped, blood-red stone rested right above the sweet crack of her curvaceous ass. The image froze.

Wytt couldn't believe his eyes. "Is that? Is that what I think it is?"

"A rare scarlet tear?"

For the first time since the prince had begun the holographic message, Wytt turned away from the image of the woman. "It can't be."

Scarlet tears were reserved for the Glacidian diplomatic corps, presented as gifts on official state visits.

"I've had this communication analyzed. If the stone isn't genuine, it's an amazing reproduction."

"But it must be a copy."

"Now you know the real mission. Win this contest, Wytt, and bring the stone to me and the woman to safety."

How had a notorious pirate obtained a scarlet tear? "What if the stone is real?"

"Then perhaps the Jagir Conclave will rethink their relationship with Rangar."

Wytt had wanted action and this was a mission of a lifetime; a valuable stone and a mysterious beauty. Wytt released an audible breath.

"I know what you're thinking, old friend. What I'm asking of you is more than I have a right to ask."

"You have every right to ask and I can't wait to get started. Do you have a training facility available?"

"Yes. I've gathered my best *zap* players to help you hone your skills."

Playing *zap* required speed and muscular strength to defeat an opponent plus quick reflexes to avoid being struck by laser whips. "Good. I'll begin tomorrow."

"We have learned that Rangar purchased a custom-made *falx*."

Few were skilled with the ancient sword. "Not the usual weapon of a pirate."

"According to our intel, he practices daily. It would be wise to anticipate a challenge from Rangar."

Wytt sipped his wine. "How is it that these pirates are skilled with the *falx*?"

"Rangar boasts that his grandfather was a member of the Elite. As for Kirxx, our knowledge of the man is limited. Despite all the information we've gathered, most of the pirate's life remains a mystery."

"He's revealed nothing?"

"He's unable to speak. His ship was under attack and he received a serious blow to the head. A memory tap might kill him. The physicians give little hope he'll be able to provide information before the competition."

"His real identity is unknown?"

A genetic map existed for every child born in the last three centuries on Aktares, but the databases of Sark and Glacid were incomplete.

"The process is underway to trace his lineage. We know that, like you, he is of Sark and Aktarian blood. It's only a matter of time before we know his true identity."

On Sark, crossbreeds weren't readily accepted. Wytt had struggled with his heritage all his life and the knowledge that Kirxx had turned against the Federation and become a pirate reflected poorly on all crossbreeds. Once Kirxx's true identity became public, a Sarkian family would suffer.

"I pray his is not a Sann relative."

Chapter Three

৯১

Ceyla rose from her bath and plucked a thick robe from the warming rack. Usually her baths were relaxing and private, but today she had an unwanted intrusion. Rangar had chosen to join her.

Sprawled on a chaise, the pirate appeared calm, but Ceyla noticed his sword hand was clenched. Since the pirate king preferred an audience while practicing with the *falx*, Ceyla had often attended Rangar's sparing sessions. The fitted black pants and knee-high boots he wore were his usual practice attire. His bare chest gleamed with sweat and tendrils of black hair stuck to his forehead.

Rangar had transported her from her rural home to Osesar City and had moved her into a chamber next to his private suite. Since her arrival, she'd dined at his table every evening, but they were rarely alone.

Ceyla waited for the pirate king to speak.

"That's what I've always liked about you, Ceyla. You're not like the other women. You know how to hold your tongue and not nag a man to death."

An outsider since she could remember, Ceyla longed to join in with the joyful chatter of the young women her age. Since she was a child, the color of her skin, hair and eyes marked her as different and rarely was she allowed interaction with others. Even Mada, the gentle golden-skinned woman who had reared her, loved the hot sun, but Ceyla's pale skin blistered easily. As a child she'd had to watch from the window while the other children played half-naked in midday heat.

"Remove the robe so I may look upon my prize."

Resenting his demand, Ceyla lifted her chin and slipped the robe from her shoulders, letting it slide down her arms to the floor.

"I like that about you too. That pride of yours isn't a product of Mada's training. The woman flinches at the slightest sound, but you carry yourself like a queen."

Mada had often chided her for holding herself apart, but Ceyla had fought back with the only weapon she had, pride. Being aloof and mysterious was better than becoming an object of ridicule.

On Osesar, looking different wasn't an asset. When Rangar had chosen her as the prize for the special competition, she had become even more of an outsider. Even as a child she knew Osesar wasn't her home and its residents weren't her people.

Rangar's gaze slid over her, settling on her sex. "Kneel before me."

On Osesar, Rangar ruled. Fulfilling her expected role, Ceyla dropped to her knees. Although chaste, she understood the gleam in his eyes. Women fought to win a place in the pirate king's bed and Mada, having experienced the privilege more than a decade ago, declared him a wonderful lover. Most thought him handsome.

The streaks of gray in his shoulder-length hair did not detract from his looks. Of mixed blood, Rangar acknowledged only his Jagir heritage. It was said his grandfather came from a faraway planet and his mother wasn't from royal blood as he claimed, but those speculations were spoken in hushed voices.

Rangar's eyes were dark, almost black, and his body fit for a man twice Ceyla's age. The muscles in his arms bunched as he shifted to a sitting position. His powerful legs bracketed her. Although his hands were strong, he gently cupped her face.

"You do not shiver in anticipation."

His lips touched hers briefly, but Ceyla remained unmoved. Despite his gentleness, warming Rangar's bed held no appeal.

Rangar lifted his head and looked into her eyes. "It is said ice flows in your veins, but even one like you has a weakness."

He pressed his lips to the tiny nodule at the base of her left ear, another physical trait that marked her as an oddity. He flicked his tongue over the node and desire, hot and intense, slid through her. The closer to her annual cycle, the more sensitive the node became.

He lifted his head and smiled. "That made you shiver."

Ceyla covered the node with her hand. Manipulation of the nodule brought intense pleasure. Never had a male touched her so intimately.

"How does it feel? I've heard it's like hot fire in your blood."

The sensation was like a cool burn. Her body shivered and her nipples tingled as if she were cold, but inside her blood burned, running hot in her veins. But explaining the feeling to Rangar would only encourage him. "It's pleasant."

"Pleasant!" He grabbed her by the hair, twisting hard. He licked the tiny nodule at the base of her ear, then suckled. Heat flashed through her veins and her pussy throbbed, the sensation so intense it bordered on pain.

He lifted his head and looked her in the eye. "Did that make your pussy cream?"

She nodded.

"I want to lick that cream."

The thought of Rangar's mouth on her made her shiver, in fear rather than excitement.

He smiled and cupped her chin. "You can't help what you are. I've seen what happens during your cycle."

"You've seen?"

"That's why you and Mada visited my country home last year. I watched through an optic viewer."

Just the thought of Rangar spying on her made her ill.

"I've watched you writhe in delicious agony, shivering as if you were freezing and hearing your cries that your blood was on fire. Watching you bring yourself to climax again and again was pure agony."

Mada didn't know why she was so tormented during her cycles. Did Rangar know? "Why do I suffer, year after year?"

He laughed. "I'm the one who has suffered. Owning you, but not being able to have you. You've tempted me, Ceyla. You still do, but I've saved that sweet cunt of yours, knowing one day it would serve me well. That day has finally arrived."

"So nothing can be done to end my torment?"

"Kirxx will end your torment, then he will suffer."

"Kirxx? I don't understand."

"That's why you're the perfect prize." Rangar released her chin and palmed her breast. "When Kirxx wins my prize, he won't be able to resist you."

When Kirxx wins? Rangar wanted his rival to win?

Rangar stroked her breast. "And I will have my revenge on that Sarkian dog."

Rangar's dislike of Kirxx was common knowledge. Although she was never included in the conversations between Mada and her friends, Ceyla listened and learned.

While Rangar's new mistress was on a shopping trip to the Jagir capital city, Kirxx had seduced her. Young and handsome, Kirxx had publicly challenged Rangar. Not one to forget or forgive an insult, the pirate king had sold the girl into slavery. For weeks, Mada and her friends had speculated on Rangar's revenge and Kirxx's fate, but not one of them had guessed Ceyla would play a role in settling the score.

"It is whispered that Kirxx wants to be king."

"The gossip of foolish women." Although Rangar dismissed her words, his hand tightened on her breast. "What do you hear?"

"The worries of your women," she whispered, the lie sliding easily from her lips. It was whispered that Kirxx had finesse in the bedroom that Rangar lacked. "They fear losing the one they love."

His grip eased and a slight smile curved his lips. "They have nothing to fear. He will never be king. My plan is infallible. If you follow my instruction, Kirxx will meet his fate."

Ceyla's hopes of escaping Osesar soared. Becoming Kirxx's slave might well serve her purpose. "Must I leave you and go with him?"

Rangar stroked her breast, caressing and squeezing her flesh. "Your sweet cunt is my weapon. Once Kirxx has you, he'll think of little else. Right now all I can think about is fucking you."

When Rangar had told her she was the prize of his *zap* tournament, Ceyla had accepted her fate. Unable to change her destiny, she plotted her future away from Osesar. Once off-planet, she'd escape her new master. Somewhere in the universe her people existed and she intended to find them and solve the mystery of her birth.

"For you, I am prepared to sacrifice myself," she said. "Even to one such as Kirxx."

Her words pleased Rangar. He smiled and thumbed her nipple to a tight peak. Although she had no desire to respond to Rangar's touch, her body betrayed her. The time of her annual cycle had arrived and within a few days her natural urges would overpower her. The other young women on Osesar weren't cursed with her cycles, which drove her to near madness. Mada couldn't explain why she was so different from the other women.

"Unlace me."

Ceyla reached for the laces of Rangar's trousers and untied them with unsteady fingers. His cock sprang free, poking its bulbous head toward her. Ceyla had seen men in various states of nakedness, but she hadn't seen an erect penis mere inches from her face. She stared, curious about the thick appendage that had been an ongoing subject of Mada's gossip.

"Look at Kirxx's cock like that and you'll have him at your mercy."

Ceyla looked away, but Rangar grasped her chin. "Touch me."

She reached out, her fingertips barely brushing his warm flesh.

"I must save that sweet cunt of yours for Kirxx, but there are other methods of pleasure. Things you can do with your soft hands and lush mouth."

Although she'd never been with a man, she'd seen the amorous couples in the gardens beneath her bedroom window. Recalling the images of writhing bodies in various states of undress on the stone benches and soft grass, Ceyla felt her cheeks blush with heat. The last few days had provided an interesting education. Had Rangar orchestrated those events?

"Your lack of experience is refreshing."

Covering her hand with his, Rangar placed it firmly on his cock. The heat and the hardness of his flesh surprised her. He moved her hand up and down his length, teaching her how to please him. The clench of his jaw and his quick intake of a breath told Ceyla she controlled his pleasure.

Control meant power and Ceyla grasped it eagerly with both hands. Using the pad of her thumbs, she stroked the underside of his cock from base to tip. His moans encouraged her. Measuring her strokes, she maintained a tight grasp on his hot flesh. His breathing became quick and harsh.

"Faster."

With fierce determination, she increased the tempo until the muscles in her arms burned. His strangled cry came as thick cream spurted from his cock. She released him.

Chest heaving, Rangar sucked in several deep breaths. "I still want to fuck you."

Realizing she had to understand a man's needs to control her fate, Ceyla bowed her head. "I did not please you?"

Placing a fingertip beneath her chin, Rangar raised her head. "You did well. Too bad that sweet virginal cunt of yours must be given to Kirxx. He doesn't deserve it, but giving you to him serves my purpose."

"Then you must teach me how to satisfy a pirate."

His dark eyes blazed. "With your kind, pleasure comes naturally. A foolish man can get a nasty burn."

She'd often questioned her heritage, but Mada offered no answers. "What is my kind?"

Ignoring her question, he unfastened his boots. Picking up her robe, Ceyla stood. Rangar caught a handful of material and pulled the robe from her grasp. His gaze raked her from head to toe, settling on the triangle of curls between her legs.

"I didn't give you permission to dress. Never hide your beauty from my gaze."

After removing his boots, the pirate stood and stripped off his trousers. He stepped into the tiled shower and turned on the water. Despite his muscled frame, he moved gracefully, completely at ease with his nakedness. Partially erect, his cock stood out from a nest of dark curls.

He stepped out of the shower and ordered her to dry him. Having no choice, Ceyla plucked a towel from the warming rack. When she rubbed the soft fabric over his genitals, his cock stretched.

"You will remain at my side during the competition, but between the heats you will walk down the staircase and around the playing field. I want the competitors to get a good close look at the stone and the audience to get a long look at you. That should whet all their appetites. My bordellos will make a fortune."

She toweled his belly. "Mada said the stone is very valuable."

"It is. But you're going to help me get it back. Within a week, I want that stone in my hand and you back on Osesar."

Fear ripped through Ceyla. "How will I be of help?"

"Kirxx will win and leave Osesar with his prizes, you and the stone."

"How do you know Kirxx will be victorious?"

"Let's just say I've worked the odds in his favor."

After drying his broad chest, she tossed the damp towel aside. "What if he chooses to remain on Osesar?"

"Only a fool would remain in a pirate haven with a valuable stone. He wouldn't last six hours."

"But a pirate such as Kirxx surely has a crew?"

"If a pirate wishes to compete, he must arrive alone and unarmed. Competitors are confined to special quarters during the contest. Outsiders cannot bring weapons to Osesar."

A pirate with an armed crew might well decide to challenge Rangar's rule. That meant she and Kirxx would be alone. One-on-one she'd have better odds of escaping.

"Why do you want Kirxx to win?"

"I have my reasons."

He snaked an arm around her waist and pulled her close. A new and oddly delicious fire licked through her as their bodies touched. As her cycle drew nearer, her needs grew stronger and the fiery flashes happened more often.

The hard ridge of his cock pressed against her belly. "Your job is to keep him occupied."

"What if Kirxx doesn't want me?"

"He's half Sark. It's in his genes to want you. My Sarkian blood is minor, but you speak to it."

If she wanted to escape from Rangar's amorous clutches, she had to keep him talking. "You plan to follow us and steal the stone?"

"Of course. The stone is mine." He rubbed against her and groaned.

"Mada said the prize must be untouched."

He grabbed her ass, digging his fingers into her flesh so deep it hurt. "I decide your fate."

Becoming Rangar's woman wasn't part of his plan. He wanted her with Kirxx, but why? Rangar was holding back information that Ceyla knew was important.

"I do not believe it is purely coincidental that the timing of the tournament coincides with my cycle, but instead it is the genius of the pirate king of Osesar."

"Your mind is quick. Not the best asset in a woman, but I still want to fuck you."

"Why toss away all your plans for a short moment of pleasure any lover might provide?"

His gaze narrowed, then he released her. He looked down at his swollen cock and laughed. "If you have the same effect on Kirxx, my plan will succeed. Never again will he take what isn't his. The bastard deserves the fate I have planned for him."

"How can I help you?"

He shoved his hand between her legs. "This is my weapon."

Rangar pushed a long finger inside her. "You're so beautiful, cold and aloof, but inside you're fiery hot. You make a man burn for you. You have no idea what that combination does to a man."

Ceyla reeled from the skin-to-skin contact. His stroking finger made her burn with need. Her pussy pulsed, aching for release. When he added a second finger, she bit her lip to keep from moaning. She didn't desire Rangar, but her body betrayed her.

Rangar's eyes widened and his breathing changed. He swore and yanked out his fingers. "You're a temptress."

His reaction confused her. One moment he was passionate, the next he was angry. "Did I do something wrong?"

"Just a minor ice burn." He cupped her face. "It's Kirxx I want you to burn."

"I'm not sure I understand."

"Don't worry. He will. He'll understand how I exacted my revenge."

"Tell me your plan."

His nostrils flared. "Step away. Just breathing your scent makes me horny."

Ceyla stepped far enough away that Rangar couldn't reach out and touch her.

His erection was still thick and full. "Great Gods, I want to fuck you."

"If I have the same effect on Kirxx, I am far more useful fucking him."

"Hearing you say the word drives me crazy." Rangar gritted his teeth and raked his fingers through his long hair. "Cover yourself before I forget why I chose you as the prize."

Ceyla scooped up her robe and slipped it on. Rangar stepped into the shower and cursed as he turned on the cold spray. After several minutes, he turned off the water and wrapped a towel about his waist.

"There's a case on your bed, fetch it."

Ceyla rushed into her sleeping chamber, scooped up the rectangular box and took it to Rangar.

He opened the box and removed a collar made of black Jagir crystals. He placed the collar around her neck, clasping it in the back.

"Do not remove this collar. It's not only an exquisite piece of jewelry, it's also a tracking device. During the tournament, I will attach a leash to the collar and at the end of the competition I will hand the leash to Kirxx, awarding him the prize."

"What if Kirxx removes it or discards it?"

"It's too valuable for him to discard. As long as it remains on his ship, we can track it. But I will need your help."

"What do you want me to do?"

She feared Rangar would order her to kill Kirxx. Although she held no affection for any pirate, she sought her freedom, not another's death.

"I want you to let him claim his prize. Fuck him until he's exhausted. While he sleeps, take the scarlet tear and eject from his ship in the life pod. I'll be tracking you and will reclaim the pod. You'll be safe and sound in my ship within hours."

"I've never been in a ship and have no knowledge of how to operate a life pod."

"But you have a talent for memorizing complicated procedures. Mada tells me you have a superior memory and a talent for fixing and programming appliances and vehicles."

"I have reprogrammed her food facility and her communication unit and I've replaced the cells and chips in her personal transport, but those are simple. Mada doesn't have the patience to follow the instructions."

"I'll download an instruction manual to your reader with the necessary sections marked. Kirxx may not allow you to take your reader onboard, so you must memorize the procedure."

Her heart thumped hard in her chest. Rangar was handing her the key to her freedom. The only thing she'd place in the ejection pod was the tracking collar. "I will study hard."

He gripped her chin. "Repeat my instructions."

"I take the stone and eject in the life pod."

His eyes narrowed. "Try again."

"I will bed Kirxx until he's exhausted. While he sleeps, I will take the scarlet tear and the collar. Then I will eject in the life pod and wait for you to locate me."

His grip tightened. "Disappoint me and you will suffer. Return a virgin and you'll beg me to end your agony."

Chapter Four

❦

Wytt joined the parade of competitors entering the arena Rangar had built for his annual competitions. The inebriated crowd of pirates, mercenaries and disreputable folks from several galaxies roared and stamped their feet as sixteen men dressed in nothing but colorful trunks strode onto the field of play in the center of the stadium. At the opposite end of the arena, a long open staircase led to a dais with a large, ornate chair. A narrow balcony ran the length of the arena on both sides. Seated along the two balconies above the rowdy audience were Rangar's celebrity guests.

The parade continued until all players were standing on the diamond-shaped *zap* field. The skimpily clad competitors were bombarded with several vessels of *kvass*. A vessel hit the shoulder of a tall Jagiri next to Wytt, splashing the brew over them and onto the grass field.

"I'm glad Rangar doesn't allow weapons," Wytt commented as he dodged another vessel. He spoke in the pirate lingo, a combination of Sark and Jagiri, the language common to the inhabitants of Osesar. The planet had once thrived as a mining settlement, but the mines were closed. The population had dwindled to a few hundred people. Then the pirates came and laid claim to Osesar.

The bald-headed Jagiri turned toward Wytt and glared.

"You're Kirxx." The Jagiri's lip lifted in a muted snarl and his yellow eyes narrowed. "I've heard about you. They say you're good, but just so you know, the stone is mine."

So far no one had challenged Wytt's identity. Fortunately, like Kirxx, Wytt spoke several languages and responded in Jagiri. "And you are?"

"Hatip, the Jagiri champion."

Had Rangar stacked the deck? "And I thought the competition was opened only to pirates," Wytt shot back.

Hatip smiled, revealing a mouthful of overly large teeth, but his eyes were cold. "Who says I'm not a pirate?"

"A pirate and a champion. I'm impressed."

While several of the competitors flexed their muscles and posed for Jagiri camera crews, Wytt scanned the arena, memorizing points of entry and exits, details he might find useful. To complete his mission, he had to convince the audience and Rangar he was Kirxx while defeating a strong group of competitors. If he failed, he needed a secondary plan. Steal the stone, abduct the girl and escape a stronghold of pirates and the Jagiri Security Force. Plan one, winning the competition, seemed the easier course.

"What of the woman?" Wytt asked.

"She's skinny and pale. After I'm through with her, you can purchase her at the slave market. She'll be priced to sell."

"What of the stone? If it's real, who will have the credits to buy it?"

Again Hatip smiled. "It's real. I'll dangle it before the Federation."

"Why the Federation?"

The smile disappeared. "Don't fuck with me, Sarkian dog. I know the scarlet tears are created exclusively for the Glacidian diplomats. The Glads will pay to get it back."

The dimming of the lights and the beat of drums brought a hush to the rowdy crowd. The competitors turned to face the spotlighted dais. The crowd cheered when Rangar, resplendent in an open-to-the-waist, silver-colored shirt tucked in clinging black trousers that emphasized the pirate's manhood to what should be an embarrassing level, raised his arms in welcome. Beneath the bright lights, the pirate's shirt sparkled.

No one upstaged Rangar.

"Welcome to Osesar and the tenth annual *Zap* Tournament. For those of you who are visiting Osesar for the first time, I am Rangar, your host."

As the crowd roared, Rangar bowed. No one dared throw vessels of *kvass* now. Although Rangar had a reputation as a very dangerous man and controlled Osesar with an iron fist, he set himself apart from most pirates by conducting himself before the camera in a civil manner.

The pirate swept his arm in a wide arch. "I present the competitors."

Drums and trumpets sounded. As pre-directed, the competitors took turns walking to the center of the field. When Rangar introduced Kirxx, Wytt fisted his hand and raised his arm. A deafening roar greeted the popular Kirxx.

Upon his arrival on Osesar, Wytt had received celebrity treatment and security had whisked him through a private competitors' entrance. Away from the public, Jagiri security officers had scanned his eye and taken a skin scrap. His apprehension quickly disappeared when a competition official arrived and escorted him to his assigned quarters.

After all the introductions were completed, a cloaked and hooded figure joined Rangar on the dais and stood before him. "Gentlemen, this is Ceyla."

Removing the hood, the young woman looked up at Rangar. Beneath the lights her hair looked white and her silver cloak shimmered beneath the lights.

"Ceyla, the competitors and our guests would like to see the prize."

Rangar unfasten the cloak and the audience leaned forward in anticipation. As the pirate lifted the edges, a low murmur flowed through the crowd. With a quick flick of his hand, Rangar removed the cloak.

A collective gasp from the audience joined those of the competitors. Suspended on a thin belt of crystals, the scarlet tear rested on the small of Ceyla's bare back.

Naked except for a black collar and the crystal belt, the stunning Ceyla accepted a silver cup from Rangar. All eyes on the Glacidian beauty, the rowdy crowd remained hushed as she walked down the stairs and approached the competitors on the field.

Following tradition, each player drew a disc from the cup. Once palmed, the disc activated and locked in the heat number. When Ceyla held out the cup to Wytt, his breath caught. The competition hologram sent out by Rangar hadn't prepared him for Ceyla up close and in the flesh. Her gaze held his as he palmed a disc. If only they were able to converse, but the rules forbade the competitors to speak while drawing lots.

After the discs were chosen, Ceyla returned to the dais and Rangar announced the participants in the first round of heats beginning within the hour. His gaze on Ceyla, Wytt raised his hand as the pirate king called his name. He'd face one of Rangar's lieutenants in the third heat.

The crowd cheered and Ceyla's gaze locked with Wytt's. To his surprise, she smiled. Heart pounding, he bowed. When he raised his head, she'd turned her attention to Rangar. At least she hadn't looked through him as she had the other competitors.

* * * * *

After a short entertainment of dancing female slaves, the overhead lights were dimmed to pale orange orbs and the floor lights flashed in a red and blue pattern. In the center of the arena's grounds was the diamond-shaped *zap* playing field. As the first two competitors were spotlighted, the audience roared.

Sitting on a white pillow at Rangar's feet, Ceyla watched the game. To score, each player had to touch his designated diamond-shaped plate at the far end of the field while preventing the other player from touching his plate. The physical contact between players was brutal, but the bloody game derived its name from the snakelike laser whips that moved in random patterns over the field.

Ceyla noticed the players wore illuminated bands around their necks, wrists and ankles. "Why do they wear bands?"

"When the tip of the whip comes in contact with bare skin, the player receives a *zap* and the skin is cut. The players' bodies are scanned and the bands put in place so the laser whips won't strike the head, face, hands or feet. Their genitals are protected by special trunks."

Ceyla winced as a player took a strike. "It looks painful."

"He feels the sting of the whip, but the strike isn't deep enough to really injure him. The crowd loves a bloody game."

Ceyla bit her lower lip as the player took two more strikes. The Fant's chest and thigh bled profusely. Although the Fant people came from a distant Jagir moon, the competitor had a small group of supporters in the crowd.

The Fant's opponent touched the plate at the pointed end of the diamond-shaped field. The plate lit up and the crowd cheered. "Did the Jagiri just score?"

"Each player is assigned a plate," Rangar said. "When they touch their plate, it lights up and a point is scored. Contact with the tip of a *zap* whip is a half-point deduction. The first player to score ten points wins the match."

The first bloody heat ended quickly.

Ceyla leaned against Rangar's leg. "The Fant didn't have a chance against the Jagiri."

Rangar caressed her bare shoulder.

"The Fant's father still owes me tribute. I wanted his ass kicked."

"I thought the heat selection was random."

Instead of responding to her statement, Rangar stood and announced the second heat. Players pitted against one another rose from the competitors' box near the base of the stairs leading to the dais and walked to the center of the field.

During the second heat, Ceyla glanced at the competitors' box where Kirxx waited. In anticipation of competing he wore his long brown hair in a tight queue. Instead of the dissipated face common to the pirates of Osesar, Kirxx's reflected strength and health. He turned and looked up at her. His brown eyes were clear and alert.

Lined up with fifteen nearly naked men of all shapes and sizes from all over the galaxy, the handsome pirate had stood out. She'd hoped one of the invited competitors would have resembled her in skin color and ethnic heritage, but none looked like her. Kirxx remained her only option for escape.

The second heat ended. Kirxx and his challenger, Bagor, walked onto the field. Kirxx bowed to Rangar and then to her. His heated gaze met hers and Ceyla's heart thumped in her chest. The pirate wanted her. Unlike Bagor, his eyes weren't cold and brutal. Thankfully, Rangar intended Kirxx to win.

During the heat, Ceyla keep an eye on the scoreboard. When Kirxx fell a point behind his challenger, Ceyla began to worry. If Bagor scored again, he'd win. "I thought Kirxx was supposed to win."

"Bagor is a good player, but he's beginning to lag. Kirxx hasn't hit his stride."

"He's holding back?"

"He knows he can take Bagor if he allows him to tire. Watch and learn."

Bagor lunged to his left to avoid a laser whip and Kirxx tackled him. The two sweat-drenched men rolled on the bloody ground, grappling for purchase. Ceyla gasped when Bagor appeared to gain the upper hand by throwing his body over Kirxx and placing him in a chokehold. Bagor screamed in pain as the whips struck him across the back and on the thigh. Bagor released Kirxx.

Scrambling away from Bagor, Kirxx took a step, then dove toward his designated plate. He thrust out his hand, slamming it down on the plate and scored a point. The laser strikes had cost Bagor a point.

Streaked with blood, the players looked like savages. Yet Ceyla couldn't take her eyes off Kirxx. She gasped when he took a strike on the upper thigh and arm. He'd lost a point. To win, Kirxx needed to score twice and avoid contact with the whips.

Rangar glanced at her and grinned. "Don't worry. His wounds will be sealed by the medic after the match."

The two men faced off, and at the sound of the bell, the laser whips snapped around them. Bagor dove for Kirxx's knees. In an unanticipated move that wowed the crowd, Kirxx jumped up and landed a foot on Bagor's back. Using his competitor as a springboard, Kirxx leaped forward and scored.

Still on his belly, Bagor took another laser to the arm and the leg, losing another point.

Rising slowly to his feet, Bagor moved into position at the center line. The bell rang and the whips cracked. Bagor charged and Kirxx ducked and swiveled to his right. Before Bagor managed to turn, Kirxx took two quick steps and dove forward. Arm extended, the pirate's splayed hand made contact. He'd won. The crowd demonstrated their approval by applauding and stamping their feet.

After bowing to his opponent, Kirxx raised his arm in triumph and the crowd roared. As he left the arena, the pirate looked up and Ceyla acknowledged him with a slight nod of her head.

Chapter Five

෨

A medic sealed Wytt's laser wounds and certified him as fit to continue in the competition. Wytt returned to his assigned quarters and stepped into a hot-water shower to wash away the sweat and blood. Built at the convergence of a river and a massive landlocked lake, Osesar City offered the on-planet luxury of an abundance of water.

Shortly after Wytt stepped out of the shower, a messenger arrived and delivered an invitation to an evening reception at the Fortress, Rangar's private home. Since Kirxx was reputed to prefer comfortable Sarkian style of dress, Wytt wore a sand-colored loose shirt and pants with sandals.

Walking around the arena, Wytt noted the number of exits, security stations and guards. Eventually, he worked his way back to the arena to watch the final three heats. Tomorrow, he'd face one of the winners. During the contest, he observed Ceyla and Rangar. The competition promised a virgin prize, but the pirate king touched Ceyla with the ease of a lover.

According to Kirxx's dossier, the pirate had seduced Rangar's woman. Had Rangar invited Kirxx to compete to show the pirate world he didn't care or to seek revenge? Was Ceyla a slave or a willing participant? Was she in love with Rangar?

If she attended the reception, perhaps he'd have the opportunity to speak with her and find out the answers.

Glancing toward the dais, Wytt locked gazes with the Glacidian beauty. He hadn't seen another Glad since arriving on Osesar. Even Queen Tayra's in-depth investigation of the

Glacidian birth records hadn't produced a single clue to Ceyla's identity or how she'd become a pirate's prize.

At the end of the final heat, Rangar invited the winners to line up along the field. Ceyla approached the players and congratulated each with a kiss on both cheeks. When her lips brushed his skin, Wytt seized the opportunity to speak to her in Glacidian.

His voice a bare whisper, he asked her family name.

Her gaze met his briefly and she responded in the pirate lingo. Once unique to the Osesar, the pirates were spreading the language throughout several galaxies.

"I do not understand."

As her lips touched his opposite cheek, he said, "I speak the language of your people."

He heard the sharp intake of her breath before she moved to the next contestant. As she kissed the angular jaw of the Vidarian standing beside him, Ceyla's gaze met Wytt's.

"Who are my people?"

Speaking in the pirate lingo, Wytt addressed the Vidarian. "It is said that women of the planet Glacid are the most beautiful in the universe. Don't you agree?"

As expected, the Vidarian defended his race and Ceyla heard the interchange.

"You haven't had a Vidarian lass tremble beneath you, Sark."

Her gaze met his several times as she strolled around the playing field to display the scarlet tear to a gaping crowd. Her silvery eyes were filled with uncertainty and suspicion. He'd piqued her curiosity.

Ceyla completed her slow circle and joined Rangar on the dais. The pirate king addressed the audience.

"Tonight we celebrate. The pleasures of Osesar, and there are many, await you."

The answering roar shook the building.

"Spend your spoils. Enjoy the beauties of Osesar. I'll see all of you tomorrow for more exciting action."

No matter who won or lost, Rangar made a profit.

Following protocol, Wytt left the field with the players. A few hours later, security officers escorted the players to a private reception in the great room of Rangar's two-story home. The pirate king maintained tight security. Wytt noted the guards posted at several places along the roofline and five observation orbs buzzing around the building. Little wonder Rangar's home was called the Fortress.

Passing a phalanx of applauding fans, the players filed into the great room. Two huge screens, placed high on the walls, replayed the day's heats.

Long tables laden with food ran along one side and young women in sheer gowns served drinks. Wytt filled a plate and picked a chair to wait for Rangar's entrance. While he ate slices of succulent Jagiri boar, Wytt listened and observed.

"My money is on Hatip."

The speaker wore rings on his fingers and the official robes of a Jagiri council member. His companion, a popular Vidarian singer, agreed. The two spotted Hatip and rushed toward him. The rich, famous and foolish liked to rub elbows with pirates and Rangar's great room was filled with celebrities and politicians.

If any of Kirxx's friends or enemies were attending the reception, they hadn't approached Wytt. The pirate's dossier offered little information on friends, but listed many rivals and enemies. Apparently, none of Kirxx's fans were among the guests.

Wytt had consumed his meal and had his glass refilled with an excellent Aktarian wine by the time Rangar and Ceyla made an entrance. The pirate king had changed to a black shirt trimmed in silver beads with matching adornments in his long hair. Rangar dressed with a flair, but Ceyla stole the show.

The Glacidian beauty wore her pale hair up in a braided knot and a long black gown. The material clung to her curves, and when she moved, it was if dark liquid slid over her body. Tiny beaded straps clasped at the base of the neck held the gown in place and two long beaded strands fell along the bare curve of her spine. He'd observed her naked curves at every given opportunity during the competition, yet Wytt found the clinging gown alluring and mysterious. He enjoyed the chase and the slow unveiling of a woman's body far more than blatant nudity.

Although Rangar had addressed the guests, Wytt hadn't heard a thing he'd said. His attention, his thoughts, his wants were centered on the Glacidian beauty walking toward him.

Her smile and her delicate, but sensual, scent reached him before she did. He hadn't moved. She'd come to him, but as friend or enemy remained another mystery to unravel.

Speaking in Glacidian, he complimented her beauty.

"I do not understand," she responded in pirate lingo.

"Your beauty stuns me," he repeated in the language she understood.

Her eyes narrowed. "But I look nothing like the others."

"Even among the beauties of Glacid, you remain remarkable."

"Where is this Glacid?"

"In the Aktarian System."

"Is that where you are from?"

Wytt nodded. "The Aktarian System has three inhabited planets, Glacid, Aktares and Sark. I was born on Sark. The leader of Sark, the Lord Chancellor, is married to the Queen of Glacid, a love match."

Her eyes widened in disbelief. "A woman rules Glacid?"

"Queen Tayra is beloved by her people and respected throughout the Aktarian System for humanitarian work. I've seen no other Glads in Osesar."

"There are no others like me. I am an oddity."

"You are magnificent. I intend to win this competition and take you to Glacid, a place where the sun will not burn your skin and where the cities are made of ice."

He caught the sharp intake of her breath. "Cities made of ice? You would take me there?"

"I will. I will take you to Cryss, the great city of ice."

"But first you must win the tournament."

Wytt took her hand and lifted it. "I will win. The prize is far too precious to lose."

He pressed his lips to her wrist, felt the race of her pulse and inhaled her alluring scent. Heat flashed through his body, desire tightened his balls and his heart thundered.

Again, Wytt heard the sharp intake of her breath. He opened his eyes and caught the fleeting look of surprise cross her face. Had she felt his reaction?

She pulled her hand away and rubbed the spot he'd kissed. "Until tomorrow."

Wytt leaned down and kissed her on the cheek. He exhaled, letting his warm breath brush the pleasure node beneath her left ear.

She gasped, her soft intake of breath bordering on a sigh.

Wytt looked into her amazing eyes. "Until tomorrow."

The sway of her hips held Wytt spellbound as she returned to Rangar's side. The pirate snaked an arm around Ceyla's waist and locked gazes with Wytt. The challenge in Rangar's eyes made Wytt all the more determined to win the competition. Saving Ceyla had become more than his duty. The moment Wytt's lips had touched her skin his mission had become very, very personal.

* * * * *

Long after the reception and well into the night, Ceyla had pondered the meeting with Kirxx. Her skin had tingled at the touch of his hand and the press of his lips had sent a spiral of heat whipping through her. Whenever he was near, her heart pounded.

Even now, hours later, her heart raced as Kirxx walked onto the field. Ceyla figured the heightened sensitivity brought on by her annual cycle had made the contact more than it was. His promise to take her to Glacid had added to the mix of emotions.

Learning the name of her race's homeland had given her hope. Her mind begged for details with the same intensity her body ached for Kirxx's touch. The next time she had a moment to speak with the pirate, she'd asked him about the people of Glacid.

Glacid. She'd known in her heart that she had a homeland and now it had a name.

She looked down on the field of play at the nearly naked Kirxx. She wanted to feel his lips on her flesh and his hands on her body. Her sex creamed in anticipation of having sex with the pirate.

Rangar leaned down and whispered, "Soon your restless nights will be a memory."

She looked up. Grinning, the pirate king stood and welcomed the roaring crowd. He wore a sleeveless bright blue shirt with a row of crystals down the front. He introduced the advancing players. Kirxx and the remaining contestants faced the audience, but Ceyla's gaze remained on the pirate's taut ass. If he hadn't spoken of Glacid, would she still find him so intriguing?

She would, but Ceyla also cautioned her foolish heart. Kirxx was a pirate. Listening to the gossip of women had taught her many lessons, mainly never trust a pirate. Their affections were fleeting and their appetites strong. Kirxx was more than handsome. He was a means to an end.

Rangar reached out his hand. "The prize."

Placing her hand in Rangar's, Ceyla rose. She wore a new robe studded with tiny blue crystals. The pirate king liked a show and removed her robe with fanfare. Dressed in nothing but the crystal collar and belt, Ceyla strolled around the stage displaying the scarlet tear before the leering pirates.

"Gentlemen, it's time to draw lots," Rangar said.

Ceyla accepted the silver cup from Rangar and walked along the line of contestants, pausing long enough for each to select a disc.

When Kirxx reached into the cup, his hand touched hers. The mere brush of his hand sent a shock wave of heat through her middle. After the lots were drawn, Ceyla made a final turn around the field in front of the contestants. As she passed before Kirxx, Ceyla trailed her fingertips over the bright swatch of cloth covering his privates. Several members of the audience who had caught the action called out for similar treatment, but Ceyla ignored them and returned to Rangar.

The expression on the pirate king's face told her he'd seen the tease, yet he said nothing.

During the first heat between Hatip and his opponent, her gaze drifted to Kirxx, who sat on the sidelines waiting. He turned and smiled. His burning eyes communicated his reaction to her teasing touch.

"If you continue staring at Kirxx, the audience will think you are favoring him to win."

Caught, Ceyla turned her attention to the game in progress. "I thought you wanted Kirxx to win."

"I do, but you shouldn't show favor."

Her pulse leaped when Kirxx stepped onto the field to face his next opponent, a vicious-looking pirate with black curly hair. The match was long, but Kirxx prevailed. When he glanced her way, Ceyla applauded with enthusiasm.

"What is it about Kirxx that intrigues foolish females?"

Ceyla looked up at Rangar. "His smile is generous and his words are complimentary."

"He's short and his father is a Sarkian dog."

"Nay, you are tall and intimidating."

Pleased with her compliment, Rangar ran his hand along her bare thigh. "Women require a strong hand."

"Where is Sark?"

He removed his hand. "Do not ask about things that do not concern you."

Ceyla turned her attention to the match. Kirxx faced a pirate called Norg in the final afternoon heat.

"Have you studied the manual?"

Ceyla had read the requested sections of the operating manual for Kirxx's ship and was ready in case Rangar quizzed her. "Yes."

"If you don't follow my instructions, there will be consequences." Rangar gripped her thigh. "I will find you and Kirxx. I will bring you both back to this arena. The two of you will be stripped naked and staked out on this field."

His voice was so chilling, fear snaked down Ceyla's spine. His fingers dug into her thigh. She bit her lower lip to keep from crying out.

"I will sit here and watch the whips tear the flesh from your bodies. Do you understand the consequences?"

"Yes."

He released her thigh, then patted her on the knee. "Norg is a vicious player, but Kirxx will take him."

The competition was brutal and when Kirxx won, the audience was on their feet. Ceyla stood and cheered.

Tonight at midnight, Kirxx would face Hatip in the final match. Just a few hours more and she'd leave Osesar, forever.

The noise had abated only slightly when Rangar strapped on his *falx* and strutted onto the competition field. Lights flashed in rapid, erratic patterns over the crowd and one bright light focused on the pirate king.

"For your pleasure this evening, I challenge Kirxx." Rangar drew the sword and tapped the pirate on the shoulder. "To a duel."

A low, excited murmur moved through the audience. Rangar's challenge wasn't part of the set program. All eyes were on Kirxx. Blood dripping from several laser strikes to his back and legs, Kirxx swiped the sweat beaded on his forehead with the back of his hand and stood.

"I should reserve my energy for tonight's match," Kirxx said.

"You refuse a challenge?"

"What's in it for me?"

"Kirxx, if you accept this challenge and win, Hatip must beat you by two extra points."

Hatip's fans jumped to their feet and shook their fists, yelling their protests.

"But," Rangar said, raising his voice. "If you lose, you must win by an extra point."

Confident in their host, Hatip's fans cheered and resumed their seats.

Fear shot through Ceyla. The competition had taken most of the day and at midnight Kirxx would face Hatip in the final match. Rangar's challenge put Kirxx at a definite disadvantage. If Kirxx lost the sword match, he might well lose the tournament.

Kirxx's eyes took on a fierce gleam. "I accept your challenge."

Ceyla's heart pounded, beating in rhythm with the stamping feet of Kirxx's fans.

"First blood wins." Rangar lifted his sword. "The challenge begins in one hour."

The crowd erupted in wild, raucous cheers.

Chapter Six

✖

Falx in hand, Wytt stood in the center of the field watching Rangar make a dramatic descent down the staircase. Resplendent in a shimmering white shirt, snug black pants and boots, the pirate king brandished his *falx*. The crowd cheered.

Wearing a simple white shirt and loose pants, Wytt bowed to his opponent.

Holding his sword high, Rangar swaggered onto the field.

Prince Xxan had anticipated that Rangar would challenge Kirxx to a duel and the pirate king had chosen an opportune time. Wytt had defeated every opponent he'd faced, but the cost had been brutal. He'd taken numerous laser strikes. It wouldn't take much to reopen his recently sealed wounds.

Rangar had deliberately stacked the odds against him, but Wytt had no option but to duel with Rangar. Losing Ceyla wasn't an option. How could he face Queen Tayra?

As Wytt touched his sword to Rangar's, the crowd hushed. At the first clash of blades, Wytt was grateful for the hours he'd spent sparring with the prince.

Rangar was strong, wielding the long sword powerfully, but Wytt was quicker on his feet. The noise of the crowd faded, Wytt heard only the sound of metal meeting metal. After several minutes of clashing swords, Wytt realized the pirate relied on his strength rather than skill. Rangar lacked training and technique.

The pirate swung his sword in an arc, but Wytt avoided his blade with ease. After several minutes, Wytt pretended to flag. Rangar jabbed, but Wytt parried the pirate's thrust.

Swords clashed again, crossed and Wytt's and Rangar's faces came within inches of one another. Sweat ran down the pirate's temples and his breathing was labored. Wytt saw the fatigue in Rangar's face and the fury in his eyes. The pirate understood he was about to lose a challenge before the largest audience he'd assembled on Osesar.

"Think about it, Kirxx. You'll never leave Osesar alive."

"No one follows a loser," Wytt said, pushing the pirate backward.

Rangar's eyes widened. Wytt attacked, driving Rangar back and forcing the pirate on the defensive. *Falx* extended, Wytt lunged and cut Rangar's shirtsleeve with the tip of his blade. The pirate knew Wytt's next lunge would draw blood.

"Whatever you want, I'll give it to you."

"I want the woman," Wytt said, knowing Rangar would accept so easy a solution. "Tonight, before the match."

"Done."

Rangar charged. Instead of moving out of the path of the blade, Wytt pivoted to his left, taking a long, shallow slice to his lower torso. Then he jumped back before Rangar struck again and lowered his sword in defeat. His white shirt turning bright red with blood, Wytt bowed in deference to his opponent.

He'd gotten lucky. The flesh wound bled profusely, convincing the roaring crowd that he'd been badly injured.

Rangar raised his sword in victory and the crowd went wild, especially the Jagiri who now believed that Hatip was a sure winner for the finale.

The pirate king threw his arm around Wytt's shoulder in a show of camaraderie. "After the medic has treated you, come to the Fortress. You'll be allowed one hour."

* * * * *

Startled by the distinct hiss of the outer door to her chamber opening, Ceyla closed her reader and jumped to her feet. Not expecting to be disturbed, she'd been studying the operating manual for Kirxx's ship.

"Ceyla."

Her pulse leaped as Kirxx stepped into her bedroom. He was dressed in a clean white shirt and dark pants. His long hair was loose about his shoulders.

Had he lost his mind sneaking into her room? "What are you doing here?"

"Did I disturb you?"

She set the reader aside. "I was just relaxing before the finale." She wasn't about to admit to the pirate, that she'd been memorizing the section pertaining to the operation of the life pod.

"I wanted to speak with you, alone."

Rangar's friends and acquaintances weren't known for their conversation. "No one is allowed in my room," she said. "You should leave before Rangar is alerted."

"He didn't tell you to expect me?"

Despite the rigorous day he'd spent in the arena, the pirate looked energized. "Rangar knows you're here?"

"How else would I get through his security system? The place is well fortified."

He had a point. During her first day in Rangar's home, Ceyla had noted the cameras, alarms, locked gates and doors and the numerous guards. "His benevolence comes as a surprise."

"I won an hour with you."

"Won?"

"Rangar doesn't like to lose a challenge, especially in his own arena."

"You let him win?" She recalled the blood staining his white shirt. "You let him cut you?"

"What's a little blood compared to an hour alone with you?"

"That's a high price to pay for a mere hour," she said, knowing that an hour was more than enough time for a pirate to slake his lust. The amorous couples who met in the garden below her window provided nightly proof that sex had no specific time limit.

Kirxx crossed the room, took her hand in his and kissed her palm. "I needed to speak with you, privately."

The touch of his lips sent a delicious fire racing through her middle.

He looked her in the eye. "You feel it too? This magic between us."

"Magic?"

"When I look at you, my insides tremble," he said, drawing her to the bed. Ceyla sat next to him. "When I touch you, fire burns in my veins."

Was it true? Did he feel the same fire?

"I'm going to win this tournament, and when I do, we must leave immediately. Osesar is too dangerous to stay any longer than necessary. Will you be ready to leave?"

"I'll be ready."

"Pack lightly and have your bag handy. Can you do that?"

She owned little. The beautiful gowns and the jewels, except for the crystal collar around her neck, were whisked away the moment she removed them. "I can. Where are we going?"

"Aktares. It's a long way from Osesar. I know a woman who lives there who will help us."

Ceyla wondered about this woman, doubt warring with a new emotion, jealousy. Why was she so drawn to Kirxx? Since her teens, Rangar had demanded she be kept isolated with little interaction with men. Although her experience was

172

limited, Ceyla knew Kirxx was unique, unlike the residents of Osesar. He stirred her blood when no other man or pirate had aroused her.

"Why would this woman help me?"

"She's from Glacid. She'll be able to answer all your questions about your home planet and help you locate your family."

Ceyla wanted to believe Kirxx, but pirates weren't known for selfless acts. Females were expendable on Osesar, less valuable than weapons and ships. "Why would you do this for me?"

"The Glacidians honor family. Hopefully, yours will pay handsomely for your return."

Ceyla pushed aside her disappointment. Rangar used her as a prize to carry out his plans of revenge and Kirxx planned to ransom her. What had she expected, compassion from a pirate? "I haven't any family."

"Who told you that?"

"Mada. She reared me."

"How long have you lived in Osesar?"

"For as long as I can remember."

"What of your parents?"

"I have no memory of them, of anyone except Mada. She told me I have no parents, but everyone has parents, don't they? I suppose mine are dead. Most likely they were killed by the pirates who brought me to Osesar," she said, wondering if he'd confirm her suspicions.

Ceyla doubted Mada knew her history. Surely, the talkative woman would have let something slip during the last twenty years.

He cupped her face in his hand. "Even if your parents are gone, they must have had brothers, sisters, parents, aunts, uncles or cousins. Somewhere on Glacid you have family."

"And when you find them, they'll have to pay?"

He slid the pad of his thumb along her lower lip. "Everyone wins. You get to go home and I get rich."

"Richer? If you win me, you win the scarlet tear. Rangar says it's valuable."

A smile curved his lips. "The stone should fetch a good price from the Federation."

Over the years she'd heard tales of how the pirates had outrun or evaded the Federation's forces after raids on ships, outposts and space stations. The pirates struck the unarmed and the vulnerable. "Is it true that Rangar is wanted by the Federation?"

"Yes. Even I have a price on my head. Saving you from Rangar and delivering you safe and sound to your relatives should buy me some goodwill from the Federation. If I'm lucky, I'll be able to negotiate a pardon."

Ceyla needed to know more. "Tell me about the Federation."

He slipped his hand around her neck and slid his thumb over her left earlobe. "The Federation began as an alliance to protect the Aktarian Star System from outside invasion. The ruling council is made up of representatives from the three planets of the Aktarian System."

"Glacid is one of those planets?"

"Yes. Federation ships patrol the Aktarian System."

His thumb slipped over the tiny node below her ear. The fleeting touch sent a tremor of heat through her middle. "The Federation will do business with a pirate?"

"Once the Glacidian government finds out about you and the scarlet tear, the pressure will be immense."

Again, he slid his thumb over her node, but this time a flash of heat shot through her. She suppressed a gasp. Thanks to her approaching cycle, her senses were already heightened. "How will you contact the Federation?"

Another touch, slower, more deliberate.

"My friend on Aktares has government connections."

She grasped his wrist. If Kirxx continued stroking her node, she wouldn't care about anything but quelling the raging need building inside her. "How long will it take to reach Aktares?"

"If we can outrun the pirates and slip into the Akjag wormhole that connects the Aktarian and Jagir systems, it will shorten our journey from weeks to days."

Ceyla knew Rangar would be tracking them, but she played dumb. "Why would the pirates chase us?"

"Rangar's safe passage guarantee vanishes the moment my ship leaves Osesar airspace and the prize is up for grabs. They won't expect us to make a run for Federation-patrolled territory." He leaned down and brushed his lips to hers. "I don't think I'll mind the travel time."

Although the contact was fleeting, Ceyla's heart pounded in anticipation. He kissed her again, but this time, he slid his tongue along the seam of her lips.

Rangar's kiss hadn't tempted her, but the warmth of Kirxx's lips enticed her. His masculine scent surrounded her, drawing her to him. The pirate was like a hot fire on a freezing night. She wanted the heat, welcomed the burning in her blood. He placed his hand at her waist and the warmth of his skin penetrated the thin material of her dress. He deepened the kiss, slipping his tongue between her lips and moved his hand to cup her breast.

Her heart leaped as he caressed her. The sensations wrought by his kiss and his touch overwhelmed her.

He pressed his chest to hers, pushing her back onto the bed. His body covered hers, his erection digging into her belly.

His hand dipped inside the low neckline of her dress, his fingertips raking over her taut nipple. Then he rolled the hard peak between his thumb and forefinger. Hot, streaming need raced to her pussy. Her insides clenched in need. She moaned, aching to surrender to his touch and indulge in the delicious pleasure. She yielded to the fire burning inside her.

She slipped her hands beneath his shirt. His skin was hot, his muscles hard. She ached to feel his bare flesh against hers. She wanted to wrap her body around his, take him inside and hold him close.

It would be so easy to lose herself in his arms, to let go, but if she did she'd become nothing more than another female in what was reported to be a long list. Kirxx's reputation as a lover was the subject of gossip and there was much speculation among Mada's friends as to the pirate's expertise and size. Succumbing to the pirate's charm would serve her purpose after they left Osesar. Too bad Ceyla would never have the opportunity to enlighten the gossiping females.

Desperate to cool her body and keep control, Ceyla turned her head slightly, breaking the kiss. Kirxx wasn't only her method of escape, but he was her chance for freedom and the scarlet tear was her financial future. If she wanted freedom, she had to think and act like a pirate; decide what you want and take it using any means at your disposal.

He kissed her cheek, moving to her neck. Then he slipped his tongue over the nodule at the base of her ear and hot fire licked her between the legs. Was his touch accidental or deliberate?

His tongue swept over the tiny node and she trembled. "Does that feel good?"

His action had been intentional. "You know?"

He lifted his head and looked at her. "About your pleasure node? All Glacidians have a pleasure node."

"All Glacidians. Male and female?"

"It's normal for a Glad." He nodded. "Sarks, Aktarians and Jagiri don't have a pleasure node. It's unique to your kind, but it's also dangerous."

"I don't understand."

"Just the right amount of pressure and you feel pleasure, right? But too much pressure applied will render you unconscious and can bring death."

She understood the pleasure part, but death?

He smiled. "I have no intention of harming you. Unlike Rangar, I've never found it necessary to force a woman's affections." His voice was rich and coaxing. "Pleasure is best when shared by both partners."

She believed him. As long as she had ransom value, he'd get her away from Osesar. Now she needed to control the situation. Ceyla reached up and placed her palm against his cheek. "Our time is short. Once we're on your ship, heading for Aktares, we'll have time to explore that pleasure."

"What amazes me is how Rangar resisted you."

Rangar had set aside his physical desires to achieve a personal goal. Despite her attraction to Kirxx, she must do the same. "Rangar has many women. This competition is important to him and I'm more valuable as a prize than a bed partner."

"Rangar is a fool."

Thankfully, Rangar wanted revenge more than he wanted her. "You should rest. Hatip is very skilled and his reputation as a champion is on the line. You must win."

"I will win."

His lips swooped down on hers, the promise of heat and passion in his kiss. Ceyla slid her arms around his neck. He yanked her into his arms, crushing her to his chest.

Her breath caught and a surge of desire flooded her middle. She kissed him back, answering with an urgency she'd never experienced before.

He tore his lips from hers. Groaning, he rolled off her and sprang to his feet, his erection tenting his pants. "I have to leave," he said between ragged breaths. "If I stay a moment longer..."

If he stayed, Ceyla would drag him back into her bed.

He crossed the room and opened the door. He turned and their gazes locked as the door slid closed.

Rangar had counted on her cycle to keep Kirxx enthralled until he tracked the pirate down, but the pirate king had miscalculated his control over her. Ceyla had no intention of letting Rangar catch them or returning to Osesar. Now that her cycle was in full swing, would she, could she resist Kirxx's charms?

Chapter Seven

ဢ

Wytt strutted into the arena to the cheers of Kirxx's fans and the jeers of Hatip's supporters. Hatip had been given the honor of entering first and stood at center field, marking Kirxx as the underdog.

The crowd settled down as Rangar escorted a naked Ceyla down the staircase. The two made a slow circle, giving the audience a long look at the scarlet tear dangling right above the crack of her fabulous ass.

As Ceyla walked past him, Wytt caught her scent. Desire shot through him. Just a few hours ago, Ceyla had lit a ravenous fire in his blood and had whipped him into a sexual frenzy that required a long cold shower to quell.

Wytt's gaze was glued to Ceyla's ass as Rangar escorted her up the staircase to the dais. Wytt's mind and body raged with lust for the Glacidian beauty. His intense reaction was puzzling, but Wytt had no time to think. Rangar ordered the contestants to take their places on the field.

Wytt fisted his hands in frustration and faced off with Hatip in the center of the field.

"Sarkian dog," Hatip said. "After I'm done with the pale woman, I'll give you a good price."

Wytt gritted his teeth. "She's my prize. After tonight, you'll be known as Hatip the loser."

Hatip spat. "I'll tear you apart and throw your carcass into the crowd."

Wytt forced a smile. He'd die before allowing another man, especially one like Hatip, to touch Ceyla. "You can try."

The starting bell rang and Wytt slammed his knee into Hatip's gut. Caught off guard, Hatip folded over and staggered back. Taking advantage of the champion's stunned reaction, Wytt sprinted to the end of the elongated diamond-shaped field. As his foot touched the plate, it lit up, registering the first point of the match.

The fans cheered as Wytt returned to the center line for the face-off. Blood ran down Hatip's arm. The Jagiri had taken a laser hit and was spitting mad. Hatip dropped his hands in anticipation of another assault. Wytt had watched Hatip's previous matches and he knew the moment the bell sounded, Hatip would lunge forward, placing his weight on his right foot.

At the bell, Wytt dodged to his right and brought his raised elbow down hard on Hatip's shoulder. He pushed past the Jagiri and raced for the score.

The plate lit up and the crowd roared in approval.

On the next face-off, Hatip slammed into Wytt and knocked him down. Wytt rolled and regained his feet, but not before taking a laser strike to the back. Hatip dove for his scoring plate. Wytt grabbed the big man's leg and was rewarded with a vicious kick.

Hatip scored and the crowd went wild.

While Hatip walked around the field, waving his arms to incite his fans to cheer louder, Wytt took several slow breaths to recover from the blow to his chest.

The match continued, each player adding points until Wytt had scored his tenth point. Because he'd lost the duel with Rangar, Wytt had to score an extra point to win. Dripping blood from multiple laser strikes and fighting fatigue, Wytt stood at the center line, facing Hatip and waiting for the bell.

If he scored one more point and avoided getting hit by the whips, he'd win. He gritted his teeth. One more point and Ceyla was his.

Hatip swayed on his feet, but his eyes were fierce. The Jagiri sucked in a labored breath and spat blood. "I'm going to make the Glacidian bitch scream so loud they'll hear her wails on Sark."

Wytt pretended he was too winded to respond. He gathered the fury pounding in his brain and focused on winning the match. He dropped his head and deliberately swayed. When the bell sounded, Wytt lunged forward and drove his head into Hatip's solar plexus. Air whooshed from Hatip's lungs as he fell backward.

Legs pumping, Wytt ran past Hatip. A hand clamped onto Wytt's left ankle. Wytt tried to kick his foot free, but failed. Hatip twisted Wytt's foot and forced him to his knees. Wytt ducked to his left as a laser whip snapped close to his right shoulder. Rolling onto his butt, Wytt raised his right leg and kicked Hatip in the head. He dodged another whip, then landed a glancing blow to Hatip's face. Blood gushed from the champion's nose.

The Jagiri grunted and dug his nails into Wytt's flesh.

Wytt had to break Hatip's grip on his ankle or drag the huge man across the field. Whips snapping over his head, Wytt mustered his strength and kicked hard, his heel connecting with Hatip's face. The Jagiri screamed and released Wytt's ankle.

Determined to score, Wytt tried to stand, but his legs wouldn't hold him. He ducked, avoiding a whip. On hands and knees, Wytt scurried toward the scoring plate. He fell forward, extended his arm and touched the plate with his fingertips, lighting it up.

He'd done it.

Too exhausted to rise, Wytt rolled onto his back and raised his arm. The crowd screamed Kirxx's name. Two competitors, pirates he'd beaten in earlier rounds, ran onto the field and helped Wytt to his feet.

Medics rushed onto the field. Eyes closed, Hatip lay on his side. Blood gushed from his nose and his jaw was oddly bent. Wytt felt no sympathy for breaking the Jagiri's jaw.

Wytt looked up. Ceyla was on her feet, smiling and clapping her hands. Wytt glanced at Rangar. Instead of being angry that his rival had won, Rangar was grinning. Something wasn't right about that smirk, but Wytt was too exhausted to fully contemplate its meaning.

A medic walked up to Wytt and ran a diagnostic wand over his body.

The middle-aged medic smiled and gave a thumbs-up. The crowd applauded. The medic was joined by two assistants who quickly bathed the blood and sweat from Wytt's body.

The medic sealed the numerous cuts inflicted by the laser whip and treated Wytt's swollen left ankle. "Hatip has quite a grip. Nothing's broken, but you have cuts and scrapes from his nails. I gave you an injection to help with the pain and to prevent infection. You should stay off that ankle."

Wytt glanced at Ceyla. "Are you ordering bed rest?"

The medic chuckled. "I'm glad you won."

"Thanks," Wytt said.

"Rangar is waiting for you on the dais. Think you can make the climb?"

Wytt's ankle hurt, but he was determined to walk up those stairs. "I can do it."

With the audience clapping and chanting Kirxx's name, Wytt walked up the stairs to join Rangar and Ceyla. A servant stood behind Rangar.

Rangar raised his hand and the audience fell silent. The servant stepped forward and presented a black cape with the championship insignia in silver and studded with Jagiri crystals. In keeping with Rangar's taste in clothes, the cape was expensive, but flashy. As the servant placed the cape over Wytt's shoulders, Rangar addressed the audience. "I present the winner and champion of the tenth annual Osesar *Zap* Tournament, Kirxx."

Wytt lifted his right arm and thundering applause filled the arena. Three hundred pirates and a few dozen celebrities chanted Kirxx's name.

When the chanting died down, Rangar instructed Ceyla to turn around. She presented her back to the crowd and Rangar removed the narrow crystal belt from around her hips. He lifted the belt, letting the audience view the red stone dangling from its length.

"Kirxx, as champion, I present to you the scarlet tear."

Rangar handed the belt to Ceyla and she looped it around Wytt's neck. Kirxx's fans began to chant his name.

Then Rangar raised his hand and the audience fell silent. Rangar took the crystal leash attached to the collar around Ceyla's neck and handed it to Wytt. "Ceyla, kneel before your master."

Ceyla bowed her head and sank to her knees before Wytt.

In keeping with his pretense of a pirate, Wytt looped the leash around his wrist. He looked Rangar in the eye. *I'll make you pay for every year you kept Ceyla in servitude. If it's the last thing I do, I'll see you in a prison on Glacid and never again will you see the sun.*

Wytt leaned down and grasped Ceyla by the upper arms and pulled her to her feet. Then he kissed her, thoroughly.

Rangar thanked the audience for attending his event and invited them to partake of Osesar's many and varied pleasures during their remaining time in the city.

As the audience filed out of the arena, Rangar said, "I'm having a buffet at my home, a late-night celebration. My guests would enjoy meeting the champion."

Wytt knew it wasn't wise to offend Rangar, but remaining in Osesar was dangerous. He slipped his arm around Ceyla's waist. "My apologies to your honored guests, but I must seek the comfort of my bed."

Rangar laughed, then he kissed Ceyla on the cheek before leaving the arena by a private door behind the dais.

Wytt waited until the door closed, then slipped the leash off his wrist and handed it to Ceyla. "Where are your belongings?"

"In the dressing room beneath the dais," Ceyla said.

Wytt followed her down a narrow staircase to a small room with several full-length mirrors. She removed a long shimmering silver-colored dress from a hangar. "Rangar's parting gift."

Wytt slid his gaze over her perfect form, drinking in her rounded breasts, pink nipples, shapely hips and long legs. He figured this was the last time he'd see Ceyla naked.

"Put it on," he said, thinking of the fans they'd encounter leaving the area. They'd expect Ceyla to be dressed in an expensive-looking gown.

Ceyla slipped on the dress, adjusting the thin straps of tiny crystals over her shoulders. The shimmering material molded to her body, accentuating the shape of her breasts and hips. Rangar had spared no expense on Ceyla's costumes.

Wytt took the leash and looped it around his wrist. He didn't like leading her around like a trophy, but the real Kirxx would think nothing of it.

Ceyla picked up a cloth bag. It appeared she'd packed light. "I'm ready."

"Let's go."

As Wytt walked out of the area, fans gathered to cheer and shake his hand. He felt a bit foolish wearing the garish cape, but getting away from Osesar was the objective. A young man, with a bag hanging from his shoulder, rushed up to Wytt and bowed. He had long black hair and resembled Rangar. "I'm Dag. My master, Rangar, has provided transportation. I've already loaded your luggage." The servant reached into his bag and removed Wytt's sandals and placed them before him.

Wytt stepped into the sandals. "Take me to my ship."

Dag bowed, then spun on his heel. Wytt didn't move. The servant stopped and turned around. "You'll carry my slave's luggage."

Dag nodded and rushed to Ceyla. He shouldered her bag and looked at Wytt for approval.

"Lead the way, Dag."

* * * * *

Kirxx didn't speak during the short ride to the sky terminal, but he touched her, gently brushing his fingertips along the inner side of her forearm and sending shivers dancing along her spine. Her body hummed and her pussy thrummed. Soon, her cycle would overwhelm her, her skin would burn and she'd shiver as if taken by a fever.

She looked at Kirxx and saw the heat in his eyes. He lifted her hand and pressed his lips to her inner wrist. Then he smiled.

A flash of heat rolled through her. She wanted Kirxx, touching her, kissing her and inside her. Just as he leaned close, the vehicle pulled through a security gate. Within a few minutes the vehicle came to a stop beside a transport rover.

Dag jumped out and opened the door on Kirxx's side of the vehicle. Kirxx slipped the leash over his wrist and climbed out, then to Ceyla's surprise he held out his hand to assist her.

Dag grabbed her cloth bag. "My master had provided his private rover to take you to the skyport."

The rover was long and sleek with a rounded nose and sweptback wings. A pretty, dark-haired woman in a blue skinsuit with the official seal of Osesar on front stood by the door. "Welcome aboard. The pilot will be taking off shortly. I am Rizza. My instructions are to make the champion comfortable."

From the smoldering look in Rizza's brown eyes, Ceyla bet the woman would do anything the champion asked of her.

Kirxx entered the rover, leading Ceyla by the leash. Two rows of plush seats ran the length of the rover. Kirxx selected side-by-side seats, letting Ceyla sit by the window. Then he removed the loop from his wrist and handed her the leash.

Rizza stowed Ceyla's cloth bag, then addressed Kirxx. "Would you like a beverage?"

"We're fine. Thank you, Rizza."

Ceyla's heart pounded. She feared Rangar would prevent their departure and she'd be forced to live out her life on Osesar. Freedom was precious and it was so close, Ceyla could taste it. But the journey to freedom was fraught with danger.

So far, Kirxx had treated her well, but that would change if he discovered her plan. And even if she succeeded, she faced an unknown future on Glacid. No matter the dangers that awaited her, this was her chance to take control of her life.

Kirxx took her hand and slowly caressed her palm with the pad of his thumb. The contact sent a shiver of desire sliding down her spine.

With each passing hour, Ceyla recognized the signs of her annual cycle. Her womb throbbed with a simmering heat. Soon she'd be writhing and fighting the demons of lust which had plagued her for years. Before, she'd been kept isolated and away from temptation. Now it sat next to her.

Rangar had planned his revenge well. He knew by the time she was on Kirxx's ship, she'd be climbing the walls and Kirxx would be the devil who would put out the fire burning in her blood.

When the rover took off, Ceyla tightened her fingers around Kirxx's hand.

He leaned close and whispered. "Are you okay?"

She looked down and gasped. The ground was dropping away. "I've never flown before."

"Ceyla, look at me."

She turned and he smiled. "Don't be frightened. You're going home and no one will ever hurt you again. You have my oath."

Ceyla felt the strength of his hand and saw the look of determination in his eyes, but trusting the word of a pirate was foolish.

Chapter Eight

ဢ

He'd won. The rush of winning the competition swirled with the knowledge that he'd accomplished his mission. The scarlet tear hung from his neck and he and Ceyla were safely aboard the *Star Runner*. Wytt dropped their luggage in the passageway and closed the main hatch. The moment the hatch sealed, he pulled Ceyla into his arms. He kissed her and hours of sexual agitation exploded in his brain and fired his senses.

Her scent filled the air and each breath took his breath. The urge to take her, here and now, against the bulkhead, burned in his blood, but years of training won out. She was his mission, not his possession.

He broke the kiss and released her. "Ready to run?"

When she nodded, Wytt removed the championship cape Rangar had placed around his shoulders and tossed it aside. "Let's do it."

His blood was running high as he settled into his pilot's seat and initiated the control hologram. The prince's engineers had installed a new operating and security system that recognized Wytt's voice and touch commands throughout the ship.

"Fire engines," he said, speaking in pirate lingo so Ceyla would understand what was happening. The computer also recognized Aktarian and Sark.

The engines hummed to life.

Wytt's fingers flew over the emblems and images on the control hologram, running the ship through a readiness check. Before he took off, Wytt had to know that Rangar hadn't sabotaged the ship.

He directed Ceyla to take the seat next to him. "Strap in. We'll be moving fast."

Wytt programmed the ship's course. He'd head for Jagir, then once the *Star Runner* was outside Osesar's extended airspace, the ship would take a radical turn toward the Akjag wormhole.

The *Star Runner's* communication system wasn't powerful enough to contact the Merck Space Station until the ship had passed through the wormhole. Since Wytt's mission was covert, he'd have to wait until the *Star Runner* exited the wormhole to send an encrypted message to Prince Xxan for safe escort through the heavily patrolled Federation airspace.

He glanced at Ceyla. Her gaze was locked on the control hologram. "Here we go."

The *Star Runner* moved slowly away from the docking station, turned, then picked up speed. "As soon as we've put some distance between us and Rangar, I will show you to your quarters."

"I'm fine. It's fascinating watching you work. It must be exciting to pilot a ship."

"It has its moments." Wytt initiated hyper-speed and the *Star Runner* shot into space. "Now that the course and speed are set, the computer takes over navigation."

He tapped his fingers on the ship security system icon. A new screen appeared.

"What are you doing now?"

"Security check. I don't trust Rangar."

Wytt was pleased the hatches hadn't been unsealed during his absence. The hull was secure and the engines and operating system hadn't been compromised.

The upgraded security system scanned for tracking devices. A few minutes later, the scan registered an alert. Wytt glanced at Ceyla. Had she brought a device aboard?

Within minutes, the system would pinpoint the location. Wytt decided to test Ceyla. He had to know how loyal she was to Rangar. "There's a tracking device aboard."

Ceyla ran her fingers over the crystal collar. "I'm wearing it."

"Rangar planted a tracker in the collar?"

"He knew the champion would keep the collar around my neck as a sign of ownership and pride and I'd wear it until I was aboard the winner's ship. Rangar wants the scarlet tear."

Wytt had suspected Rangar would track the scarlet tear and try to steal it back. "Tell me his plan."

"I was instructed to wait until you were sleeping, then I was to steal the tear and eject in a life pod. He'd follow and retrieve the pod."

"Do you want to go back?"

"Never."

"What of the woman, Mada?"

"She reared me. I believe she held some affection for me, but she is loyal to Rangar."

A blinking red emblem flashed on the screen. The security system had located a device, the signal coming from inside the cockpit.

Wytt rose. "I'll take you to your quarters and remove the collar."

The captain's quarters were directly behind the cockpit. The crew's quarters were mid-ship and the galley and cargo area was aft. As they walked through the passageway, Wytt picked up her bag and entered the first mate's quarters. The room was small with a narrow bunk, but at least Ceyla would have privacy. He dropped her bag on the bunk and faced Ceyla.

Wytt exhaled and focused on the collar around Ceyla's slender neck. "Turn around and lift your hair."

He found the intricate clasp, releasing the interlocking crystals. Ceyla let her hair fall down her back and turned to face him. He handed her the collar and leash. "Hold this and don't move."

Wytt left the room and returned to the cockpit. The security system showed the tracking device had moved to the first mate's quarters. So Rangar was following the *Star Runner* intending to steal back the stone and Ceyla. Wytt decided to let Rangar find the life pod, but the only thing he'd find inside was the crystal collar.

Wytt returned to Ceyla and took the collar.

"Please, Kirxx. I don't want to go back."

"You're not going back, ever."

"What are you going to do?"

"Beat him at his own game. But first, I'm going to take a sonic shower and put on fresh clothing." Wytt couldn't wait to get out of his blood-spattered trunks. "I have facilities in my quarters. You're free to use the crew facilities, aft, next to the galley. Have you ever used a sonic shower?"

"I understand how the hygiene unit operates. I'll be fine."

Her knowledge of contained facilities was another surprise. Water on Osesar was abundant and he hadn't seen one sonic shower during his time on Osesar, but then, his time was limited. "The galley has instant meals. Make yourself at home."

He turned to go, but Ceyla touched his bare arm, stopping him in his tracks. She stepped toward him. "I'm so glad you won the competition," she said, placing her hands on his shoulders. "I doubt Hatip would treat me so kindly."

Focusing on the mission had kept him sane, but how did he ignore the feel of her hands on his bare flesh? Then she kissed him.

Her lips were soft and lush, her mouth warm and her female scent stole his breath.

Wytt wanted to wrap his arms around her and never let her go. Instead, he clenched his fists. His sense of duty, ingrained by years of training, warred with raw desire. His blood heated, his muscles tensed and his cock jerked. The fatigue plaguing him disappeared and his body surged with newfound energy.

Ceyla curled her arms around his neck and pressed her body against his, breast to chest and belly to groin. Sanity fled, leaving behind a hunger that coiled his insides, heated his blood and tightened his balls.

He unclenched his hands and clamped them on her rounded ass. In a heartbeat, he was erect and overwhelmed with need so fierce, he ached.

She moaned and rubbed her mons against his straining cock. Desire surged, raw and wild. Wytt pulled at the fabric of her gown and tugged on the thin straps as he backed her toward the narrow bunk.

Her passionate cry mingled with the tearing of fabric and plinking of dozens of tiny crystals hitting the metal floor. Those sounds penetrated his brain and burst through his manic desire, reaching the disciplined officer.

Ceyla was trembling in his arms, her beautiful gown torn. What was he doing?

His heart thundering in his chest, Wytt tore his lips from Ceyla's. Prince Xxan had entrusted him with a duty and expected him to execute it with honor. If he took Ceyla's virginity, how would he face Queen Tayra? He couldn't. He'd disgrace his family's name.

Drawing every ounce of strength and honor within him, Wytt released Ceyla and pushed her away.

Ceyla's eyes flew open, a look of disbelief on her face.

Gritting his teeth and balling his hands into fists, Wytt stepped back. He was an officer of the Elite, assigned to a royal prince, not a lust-driven pirate.

Ceyla clutched the tattered dress to her chest, but her breasts were exposed.

Wytt stared at her breasts. Her pink nipples were a deep rose. His mouth watered, the urge to suckle them threatening to push him to the edge of insanity again.

"Have I displeased you?"

Wytt shook his head and forced his gaze to meet hers. Her fear that she had offended him made Wytt feel like a brute. He wanted to tell her his true identity, but he doubted she'd believe he was working undercover for a royal prince.

He wanted to let her know she wasn't a pirate's prize, but until they were out of enemy territory and she was safe on the Merck Space Station in Prince Xxan's care, he dare not. He needed her support and to retain what modicum of trust he'd earned. An audience of three hundred pirates knew he had the scarlet tear and would go to great lengths to chase him down and steal it. The only way to ensure her safe delivery to Merck Space Station was reaching Federation airspace.

Ceyla saw Kirxx as her new master and expected him to act like a pirate. "You're a tempting female," he said, his flippant words denying the truth in his heart. "But you're worth more as you are."

She raised her chin. "More ransom?"

Wytt wished Ceyla could be his woman. He'd honor her with his name and give her his loyalty for life. That revelation settled easily on his shoulders. For the first time in his life, he wanted something other than the thrill of the mission. He wanted hearth and home and love.

But Wytt knew he wasn't Ceyla's destiny. So much had been taken from her already and she deserved to make her own future. She needed to take her rightful place on Glacid, among her kind.

Wytt lifted the stone he wore around his neck and kissed it. "You and this stone are worth a royal ransom, and I intend to make the Federation pay."

Her eyes flashed in either hurt or anger. Wytt's heart twisted. The last thing he'd wanted to do was cause her pain, but he didn't trust himself to comfort Ceyla. He had to get away from her before he lost control. He ached to carry her to his fur-strewn bed and make love to her. Instead, he rushed out of her room and closed the door.

In the passageway, he leaned against the wall and took several deep breaths. He returned to his quarters, stripped off his trunks and removed the bands securing his hair. He shook his head, letting his hair fall free about his shoulders, and stepped into the sonic shower.

Right now, he needed a long, cold-water shower, but that was impossible given the limited water supply on board.

Wytt groaned. The image of Ceyla's rosy nipples was seared in his brain. How was he to survive days alone with her locked inside a cylinder hurtling through space and not touch her?

She touched him on every level of emotion, from his basic sexual needs to the reverence he'd bestow upon a loved one. She was all those things, but as off-limits as if she were royalty or married.

He prayed once he delivered her into the prince's care, the need for her would subside. It had to. No man should spend his life pining for a woman he could not have.

The sooner they reached Merck, the quicker his agony would end.

* * * * *

Ceyla shivered on the narrow bunk and rubbed her thighs together. Kissing Kirxx had stimulated her needs to the point that her symptoms were heightened and urgent.

Her nipples were elongated and had changed from pink to deep rose. Her breasts were swollen and achy. Ceyla grasped her breasts and plucked at her nipples to ease her suffering. She manipulated the node beneath her left ear until she climaxed.

But even that relief was short lived. Primal urges thrummed in her womb, urges that refused to be quelled.

She needed to end this torment. She needed Kirxx.

Driven by the insistent urges, Ceyla rose from her bed and sought out the pirate. The door to his room was open. She entered his quarters. The light on the sonic shower indicated it was occupied.

Ceyla snatched up the collar he'd left on the bed. Recalling the ship's layout, Ceyla found the room housing the life pods. The *Star Runner* had two pods.

She unsealed the hatch and climbed inside the pod.

"Where are you going?"

Ceyla gasped and turned. Kirxx stood at the door of the life pod, naked with his hair loose about his shoulders. He placed his hand on the door.

Her heart hammered with fear. If he closed the door and ejected the pod, she'd face a horrible death in Rangar's arena.

"He's expecting the ejection of the pod," she said. "He'll follow the collar."

"Where's the stone?"

"In your quarters."

"Get out. Leave the collar inside."

Relieved, she climbed out of the pod.

He closed the hatch and sealed the pod. "If you want to set a false trail, now isn't the time. We're still in Osesar airspace."

She watched as he programmed the pod for ejection.

"The pod will automatically eject when we are far away from Osesar."

Taking her arm, he led her back to his quarters. The scarlet tear lay on the bed. He picked it up.

"I had no intention of stealing the stone."

"You're going to have to trust me, Ceyla. I understand why you don't," he said, tossing the stone onto the furs. "If you want to see Glacid, we'll have to work together. Then we'll both get what we want."

Her gaze flicked over him. What she wanted was him.

She'd seen him covered in blood and sweat and even now his chest, arms and legs were crisscrossed in angry thin lines from the laser strikes. The first moment Ceyla had laid eyes on Kirxx, she'd been attracted to the handsome pirate. As the tournament had progressed, her attraction had turned into admiration. He was a mad warrior on the field, but his touch was gentle and, unlike the other competitors, his words and actions were respectful.

Now, she felt unbridled lust, and something else. Something she refused to acknowledge. She pushed the confusing emotion aside and focused on his handsome face and his muscular body.

She walked up to him and touched the long line running horizontally on his side where Rangar's sword had cut him. Just thinking he'd deliberately allowed Rangar to win the duel twisted her heart. "Does it hurt?"

He shook his head.

She inhaled his clean male scent and desire whipped through her. She licked her lips and he uttered a soft groan. She ran her fingertips over the wounds on his upper chest, then traced the lines with her tongue.

He gasped.

Just touching Kirxx aroused her, but instead of agitating her, the flash of heat he wrought was strangely comforting. Perhaps her kind weren't meant to be alone and isolated during their annual cycle.

She rubbed her face against his chest. Although she'd never touched anyone, especially a male, so intimately, her sudden craving felt right and natural.

He muttered something in a guttural language, but he didn't touch her.

She kissed each of his flat nipples, then repeatedly rubbed her face against his skin, working her way down his torso, the action instinctive and appropriate.

He shuddered, the tremble was slight, but Ceyla felt it.

As she sank to her knees, he grabbed her shoulders. "Great Gods. Do you have any idea what you do to me?"

"I know. You do it to me."

His eyes widened as she grasp his cock by the root.

She kissed the tip of his cock, testing and tasting. The drumming of her heart intensified, her blood burned and the urges thrumming in her pussy were delicious instead of agonizing.

When she swirled her tongue around the broad head, he groaned.

Then she sucked him into her mouth. She took him deep, running her tongue and lips over his rigid flesh. He was hard as stone, but his skin was hot and pliant.

He fisted her hair and the action encouraged Ceyla.

The taste, the feel of him sent flames of fire racing through her veins. She suckled, hollowing her cheeks as she tugged on his length.

He cried out in a guttural language, his voice rough and his words clipped. Ceyla had no idea what he said. The more she licked him like a sweet treat, the more exaggerated his cries.

She pulled back until her lips encircled the broad head of his cock, then took him deep.

He tugged on her hair. "Fuck me. That feels good."

She pulled and tugged on his flesh and her pussy quivered on the edge of ecstasy. This was what she needed, what she'd been aching for.

"Ceyla, if you don't stop, I'll—"

She ignored his protests and sucked harder, deeper.

He groaned and a salty fluid filled her mouth. A climax ripped through her, the first she'd experienced through a method other than self-manipulation. The sumptuous release brought satisfaction and euphoria, yet left her eager for more.

The pirate was a drug, a satisfying remedy for what had plagued her for years.

She released him and swallowed the salty fluid.

He let go of her hair and fell back against the wall. His eyes were closed and his breathing was harsh and rapid.

Ceyla rose to her feet, grabbed him by the hair and kissed him. The mix of saliva and semen fueled a new fire. She'd tasted him. Now she wanted reciprocation.

She broke the kiss. "Your turn."

He shook his head.

For years she'd needed a solution to end the agony of her cycle. Only Kirxx could satisfy her raging needs and cool her blood. Yet he denied her what any hot-blooded pirate would take.

"Did I please you?"

Fire burned in his eyes. "I could die of the pleasure."

"Then kill me."

His eyes widened. "You don't know what you ask of me."

He had no idea of her suffering. She wouldn't go through it again, not when the solution was before her, long and hard and ready despite his protests.

"I don't ask. I demand. All my life, others have told me what to do, what to think, ignoring my wants and needs. You are what I need."

His eyes flashed with heat.

Ceyla's heart pounded as she waited for him to decide whether he wanted her more than the ransom.

He cupped her face. "What better way to lay down my sword."

Then he kissed her and his strange declaration was forgotten in the heat of contact.

His lips covered hers, insistent and ravenous. His arms wrapped around her, holding her tight.

Her heart pounded and her blood heated, pooling thick and heavy between her legs. His tongue slid between her lips, deepening the kiss.

She clutched at his shoulders and rubbed her breasts against his chest and her belly against the hard ridge of his erection. She wanted him inside her.

He kissed a hot path down her neck to her breast and latched on to her nipple, suckling strong and deep.

Heat coiled deep in her middle, tightening with each lush draw.

Kirxx slid to his knees, cupped her buttocks and pulled her toward him. The tip of his tongue slipped between her lips, licking her clit before thrusting inside her pussy.

Ceyla arched her back, pushing her pussy into his face. Instinctively, Ceyla understood he was the answer to her torment, only he would satisfy the needs raging inside her. This was what she needed, what she'd been missing.

Hot and moist, his mouth moved over her and inside her. Then he fastened his lips on her clit. A flush of searing heat flowed from her womb, bringing her to the precipice of climax.

"Great Gods!" she cried, using the pirate's words that had no meaning to her, but aptly expressed exactly the sensations she was experiencing.

Grinding her pussy against Kirxx's mouth, Ceyla came in a rush so intense, her knees buckled.

He caught her in his arms and carried her to his bed. Together, they fell upon the soft furs.

He climbed between her thighs and Ceyla's breath caught.

His eyes burned with purpose as he moved his hips. When he bumped against her virginal shield, he started to withdraw.

Ceyla grabbed his ass, dug her fingers into his muscled cheeks and pulled him toward her. He thrust, breaking through her shield.

Her womb contracted around him, the feeling of having him deep inside her so pleasurable she shivered.

He moved faster, thrusting faster and deeper. She clenched, squeezing his cock. He drove into her, relentless, harder, deeper, faster, giving her what her body craved. Each deep thrust made her wetter, hotter, until she cried tears of joy. The pressure built, swelling in her womb. Perspiration beaded her belly and the valley between her breasts.

His body jerked and his arms trembled. Heavy, throbbing pulses coursed his length.

She clenched, grasping at the bliss hovering just beyond a place she'd never been, never imagined, never experienced. She cried out and dug her nails into his buttocks as the sensation of heat and utter physical gratification slammed into her, then spread like hot syrup.

Reality returned, bringing her back to awareness of the soft furs beneath her and the hard-muscled body of the man lying atop her. The hair framing his face was damp and his legs were slick with sweat. He leaned down and kissed her, a languorous kiss that made her feel like tiny wings were beating in her chest.

He lifted his head and looked her in the eye. "That was worth dying for."

"I'm so glad we're still alive," she said.

He rolled to one side and drew her into his arms.

Her body hummed with joy. She loved the warmth and feel of his male body. She felt safe and secure in his arms and happy, an emotion she hadn't anticipated when Rangar placed the crystal collar around her neck just a few days ago.

Now she wanted to spend hours touching him, kissing him, making love with him. She reached down and her fingers brushed his erection. "I want to do it again."

He grinned. "My climax was so intense. I can't believe I'm still hard."

"Intense is good, right?"

"Right." Kirxx kissed the tip of her nose. "We're just getting started."

Chapter Nine

ဆာ

He rose and kneeled in the center of the bed, resting his butt on his heels. He crooked a finger at her. "Face me."

Ceyla kneeled before him.

He pushed her hair back, exposing her pleasure node. He licked her node.

Delicious heat shot through her.

He looked her in the eyes. "I'm going to suckle your node. You're in control. If you need me to stop, tell me."

"Why would I want you to stop?"

"Glads are trained how to safely manipulate the node. I understand the experience during sex is amazing."

"You've done this before?"

"I've had no formal training, but you must trust me."

Ceyla shivered in anticipation. "I do."

He kissed her on the lips, then flicked her node with the tip of his tongue. "Ready."

She climbed onto his lap.

He grasped her hips. "Slow and easy."

She sank down on his length, moaning as she rocked her hips.

He shuddered and palmed her ass. "You're in control."

Kirxx's words were as enticing as the thick cock filling her pussy. She lifted her butt, then sank down on his length.

He slid his hand up her back and cupped her head, holding her firmly. Then he placed his lips over her node and suckled.

Fire raced through her veins. Blood pooled between her legs. She squeezed down on his cock and clutched his shoulders.

Although he trembled, Wytt remained still. Ceyla understood he was exercising caution and letting her direct the pace.

She raised her hips, pummeling her pussy on his hard length.

He fastened his lips on her node, suckling deeply. His arms shook and his skin slicked with perspiration, but he remained amazingly still.

Heart pounding and wild with need, she rode him, racing toward ecstasy. Her pussy throbbed and clenched. Heat swamping her, Ceyla came. Crying out, she dug her fingers into Kirxx's shoulders.

He released her node and Ceyla collapsed against his chest.

"Are you okay?" Ceyla grinned. She'd touched the sun.

Wytt threaded his fingers through Ceyla's long hair, then trailed his fingertips along the curve of her back to cup her ass.

Her eyes fluttered open.

"I thought you had passed out. You worried me."

"I'm fine," Ceyla said. "I just needed to rest."

"Go back to sleep."

"I've had enough sleep." She slipped her thigh over his and ran her toes up and down the back of his calf. "I want you to do it again."

He understood her eagerness to experience the ultimate orgasm, but unlike his prior Glad partners, Ceyla was a neophyte. And it was damn hard for him to remain still while she fucked him like a wild woman. "We'd better stick to Sark-style sex. Glad sex can kill you."

She laughed and rubbed her breasts against his chest. "Let's do it Sark style."

Her skin was warm and soft, her body supple and inviting. He squeezed her butt cheek.

"You have a magnificent ass. During the competition, I loved watching you walk up that long staircase to the dais. I imagined taking you from behind in the traditional Sarkian fashion."

"That tradition exists on Osesar. I saw Rangar's guests and his slaves in the garden below my bedroom window."

He kissed her on the forehead. "On Sark, the ancient position had significance."

Wytt rolled Ceyla onto her belly. She drew her knees beneath her and positioned herself to receive him. Wytt kneeled behind her. "If a Sark takes a woman in this position, he honors an old tradition."

When he kissed her back, Ceyla wiggled her ass. "Show me how a Sark takes his woman."

He caressed her thighs, sliding his palm down to her knees and back again. He touched his lips to the small of her back, then slid the tip of his tongue between her butt cheeks.

"Centuries ago marriages were arranged," he said. "Sometimes the bride and groom had never met before the ceremony."

He moved his hands to her hips. "A couple wasn't bonded until the groom took his bride's virginity in the traditional position before the tribal elders."

Ceyla glanced back at him. "The elders watched?"

"They witnessed the bonding." He slid his hands over her perfect ass. "But the bride wore a hooded cape to hide her face and preserve her modesty. She was escorted to the furs by her parents. She kneeled, then lowered her head."

Ceyla bent forward, touching her forehead to the furs and presenting her perfect ass. "Like this?"

"Yes. Once the bride was in the consummation position, the elders escorted the groom into the room. The head elder would remove the groom's robe. Naked, he'd kneel behind his bride and lift the cape carefully, mindful of exposing his bride's body."

Wytt slid his hand between her legs, caressing her pussy with his fingers. "A kind groom prepared his bride for entry."

Ceyla's pussy creamed, slicking Wytt's fingers.

He removed his fingers and sucked off her silky essence. His cock strained, throbbing for the relief her wet walls promised.

"Some grooms used their fingers," he said, grasping her calves and pushing her legs apart. "Others used their tongues."

He licked her slit and shuddered as her nectar drenched his tongue. He licked his lips, loving the taste of her.

"Then the groom bonded with his bride." Wytt fisted his cock, guiding it between her thighs. He shuddered as the sensitive head of his cock made contact with her silky flesh. Gripping her by the hips, he thrust.

Ceyla moaned as she accepted his length.

Embedded deep inside Ceyla's lush pussy, Wytt remained still, resisting the natural urge to move his hips. "Then the groom addressed the elders, taking the bonding vow."

Ceyla's vaginal muscles tightened around him, clenching and grabbing his cock as he silently spoke the bonding vow. *I, Wytt Sann, take Ceyla as my lifemate.*

Perspiration beaded his forehead and the urge to climax challenged his control. "Then the elders left the room and the couple concluded the bonding ritual."

Wytt thrust, fucking her, loving her, taking her in the Sark ritual of pleasure and bonding. Immersed in her heat, he drove into her again and again. Matching him stroke for stroke, Ceyla drew him closer to ecstasy.

Pussy quivering, she clenched down on him.

His grip on her hips tightened, his fingers digging into her soft skin, but Wytt couldn't hold back. Every cell exploded, ripping semen from his balls and hurling it along the length of his cock.

Ceyla's cries of pleasure joined his groans of ecstasy.

Together, they collapsed onto the furs, unable to speak, barely able to breathe.

Although he hadn't taken her virginity in the ancient position, Wytt honored Ceyla by making love to her in the tradition fashion. His pledge of love was as sincere as if he were a groom claiming his bride.

Ceyla rubbed her face against Kirxx's damp chest. She had no idea why the action felt so good, so right, but the impulse was deep seated. She'd never felt so alive, so in touch with her body.

The connection to Kirxx was baffling. Why was she so drawn to this pirate who wanted to ransom her when all she wanted was to remain in the warmth and comfort of his arms?

Ceyla sighed. She had no explanation for the bond she felt for Kirxx, but her desire and need of him grew with each kiss, each caress and each time she took him inside her body.

"Was that a sigh of contentment?" he asked.

"Hmmm."

He rolled onto his side, then lowered his head and licked her nipple. "I'm still hard. I've experienced the most amazing orgasms, but all I can think of is being inside you."

"Shall we try again and see if we can resolve the problem?"

"This problem, I never want to solve."

Then an alarm sounded. The ship's klaxon sent a shot of adrenaline straight to Wytt's heart. He jerked out of Ceyla's warm arms and was on his feet in seconds.

Ceyla sat up. "What's happening?"

"We've got company," he said, grabbing a pair of pants out of a cupboard.

Ceyla's eyes widened. "Rangar?"

He stuffed his legs in the pants and pulled them over his hips. "Maybe. I ordered the computer to warn me if any ships were detected."

Wytt's training said run to the cockpit and assess the threat, but his heart told him to reassure Ceyla. He leaned down and gave her a quick kiss. "Everything will be fine. Get dressed and join me in the cockpit."

As he rushed to the cockpit, Wytt wondered if Rangar had managed to track them despite the ejection of the emergency life pod. The pirate's personal transport was larger with better range and speed and was well armed, but Rangar wouldn't destroy the *Star Runner*. He'd try to disable it and retrieve the scarlet tear. And Ceyla.

Wytt prayed the advanced shields installed by Prince's Xxan's engineers would hold off an attack.

He slid into the pilot's seat and fixed his gaze on the holographic star map. A red blip indicated that a ship was approaching from the Jagir quadrant. He read the streaming data. The tension in Wytt's shoulders eased a bit as the ship was identified as a Jagir patrol cruiser. If both ships remained at present course and speed, they'd intercept before the *Star Runner* entered the Akjag wormhole.

Ceyla entered the cockpit and took the copilot's seat. "Is it Rangar?"

Wytt shook his head. "A Jagir cruiser."

"Is that good or bad?"

"Depends. By now they've identified the *Star Runner*. I'm not wanted in Jagir, but right now I'm not exactly popular. If we're lucky, the captain isn't a *zap* fan and they'll ignore us."

"And if they don't."

207

"We make a run for it."

Wytt had one shot at outrunning the cruiser, but he had to wait until he was closer to the wormhole.

"How long before they intercept us?"

"It's moving fast. We've thirty minutes."

Ceyla rose. "I'm going to the galley. I think we need nourishment."

Wytt smiled as she left the cockpit. They'd spent several vigorous hours in the furs and he was running on pure adrenaline, but he felt great, better than he'd ever felt in his life.

Ceyla returned with two prepared meals. She handed a container to Wytt. "I can't read the label."

"It's written in Aktarian. You chose meat and vegetable stew."

"What kind of meat?"

"I have no idea, but it's nutritious and it tastes good."

He broke the seal and within seconds the stew was hot. Ceyla did the same. While they consumed the stew, Wytt watched the cruiser's progress.

Wytt collected the empty containers and rose. He pointed to a number on the star map. "If those numbers change, call out. I need to know if the cruiser changes speed or course."

He walked back to the galley and tossed the containers into the trash chute. On his way back to the cockpit, he entered his quarters and searched the furs for the scarlet tear.

Upon returning to the cockpit, he sealed the hatch. If they came under fire, the cockpit was reinforced and its air supply protected. If the hull was breached in another section of the ship, the cockpit was the safest part of the ship.

He placed the stone around Ceyla's neck. "Just in case this goes wrong and we're captured. Demand to speak with a Glacidian official."

"All the stone will buy me is a trip back to Osesar."

"Bluff. Rangar isn't in charge of the Jagir military and I doubt they are eager for a confrontation with the Federation."

"What will happen to you?"

If the captain was a *zap* fan, Wytt didn't want to think about the possibilities. Jagir soldiers weren't known for kind treatment of prisoners. "I'm a pirate. I'm no threat, just a nuisance."

She glanced at the map, then took his hand and gave it a firm squeeze.

Data flashed on the control hologram warning that the cruiser's shields were up. Logically, the cruiser would attack the second they were within range.

Neither of them spoke as the *Star Runner* approached the wormhole and the cruiser closed in on them. His heart pounding, Wytt waited for the right moment. His decision to act before the Jagiri attacked was a calculated risk. Aiming for the wormhole, he initiated stellar-drive, pushing the *Star Runner* to maximum speed.

His heart thundered as the cruiser released a volley of pulse torpedoes. The *Star Runner* took a hit on the starboard. The control screen flashed with alarms. The shields held, but a direct hit would destroy the *Star Runner*. The ship would disintegrate, leaving nothing but a million scattered pieces.

Then the *Star Runner* plunged into the wormhole, escaping the cruiser's next assault. Caught in the vortex, the *Star Runner* went into a spin. His fingers flying over the controls, Wytt worked to right the ship and slow its speed.

He managed to level the ship, but instead of slowing the *Star Runner*'s speed increased. The hull shuddered. The air pressure inside the ship changed so rapidly, Wytt was slammed back into his seat. He tried to move, but was held fast. Several alarms flashed on the holographic controls. The extreme speed was burning out the shields. Another series of blips and flashing lights told Wytt the computer had reacted to the emergency and had taken control of the *Star Runner*. Wytt gritted his teeth. He had no choice but to ride it out and pray they'd survive.

Did Ceyla realize the danger they faced? If the ship held together inside the wormhole, it would be shot out of the exit at such a high speed and so out of control he had no idea where they'd end up. At least they'd be in Federation airspace.

The pressure inside the cabin dropped. Wytt sucked in a shallow breath. He turned his head and looked at Ceyla. He reached out and her hand grabbed his, holding on tight.

He looked back at the controls. They were nearing the exit.

Ceyla's nails dug into his hand. No matter the outcome, they were in this together.

Then the hologram dropped. The lights began to flicker, then went out. The ship began to tumble, faster and faster. Wytt tried to speak, but just breathing was a struggle.

He gasped for air, felt himself passing out. *We're in trouble.*

Chapter Ten

ॐ

Wytt awoke to total darkness and bitter cold.

The familiar contour and armrests told Wytt he was still in the pilot's chair. He listened for the comforting hum of the engines, but the ship was eerily silent. Even the emergency lights hadn't come on, which told him that the *Star Runner* was a dead ship floating somewhere in space and their lives depended on a limited air supply. They were lucky to be alive.

If he'd been wearing his wrist unit, the illuminated face would provide light and he'd know how long he'd been unconscious. But he'd left the multi-purpose unit in his luggage.

"Ceyla."

He reached out and touched Ceyla's arm. She didn't respond. Fear raced along his nerves. He shook her.

She moaned and her hand touched his.

"Ceyla."

"Kirxx." She gasped "Why is it so dark?"

Wytt worried that the air supply was dangerously low. He'd felt like this before on a high-altitude rescue mission on Aktares. He wanted to search for an emergency light, but if he moved around, he'd use up more precious oxygen. "The ship's engines are gone and the lights are out. Are you hurt, injured?"

"Just tired and cold," Ceyla said. "Why is it so hard to breathe? What happened?"

He took a slow breath. "The high speed likely burned out the engines." He didn't want to admit he had no idea how badly the ship was damaged or how long their oxygen supply would last. "The cockpit is secure, but the air supply is low."

Her hand tightened on his. "Where are we?"

"In Federation airspace." Wytt was confident they'd exited the wormhole, but he had no idea where they'd ended up. He took a slow breath. "A ship will receive our emergency beacon. If we don't talk and remain calm, we can preserve our air supply until help arrives."

She unclipped her restraints. Then her hand touched his arm and she climbed onto his lap. "I'm cold."

He removed his restraints and drew her into his arms. He held her close, needing her heat as much as he needed to hold her close. The temperature of the cockpit had dropped. If the air didn't run out first, they'd freeze to death.

"What if there's no one out there?"

"Someone will find us."

"Don't let go."

Wytt kissed her hair. "I'll never let go."

* * * * *

The ship lurched and Ceyla's eyes flew open. The blackness of the cockpit enveloped her, but Kirxx still held her.

Another lurch threw Ceyla forward, but Kirxx tightened his hold.

She shivered. The air was cold and thin. It hurt to breathe. "What's happening?"

"I think a tractor beam has locked on to us," Kirxx said. "If we're lucky, a Federation ship is pulling us into their bay."

All her life the Federation had been the bad guys. Kirxx had admitted he had a price on his head. "What will they do to us?"

"Show them the stone and demand to be taken to Merck Space Station to see Prince Xxan," he said, speaking slowly, his breathing labored.

"You must say you have sensitive information about Rangar and Osesar that you can share only with the prince." He took another labored breath and squeezed her hand. "Say nothing more and you'll be safe."

The ship shuddered and metal ground against metal, then the floor seemed to drop out beneath them. The hatch opened with a hiss and air rushed into the cockpit. Ceyla took a deep breath, pulling the fresh air deep into her lungs.

"Remember," Kirxx whispered. "Demand to speak to Prince Xxan. Trust me."

Beams of light bounced around the cockpit, illuminating Kirxx. A blinding light hit Ceyla in the face. She lifted her hand to shade her eyes.

She saw two figures. Their faces were obscured in the darkness, but they held weapons. One spoke in an unfamiliar language and his tone was unfriendly. Kirxx responded in the same language, then raised his hands in surrender.

"Ceyla, don't ask questions. Just follow my instructions," Kirxx said, addressing her in pirate lingo. "Security Officer Uggar of Federation battleship *Guardian* wants you to slowly raise your hands and stand up. He and his officers are armed. Cooperate and they will not harm you."

Ceyla did as Kirxx asked. Her hands raised, she stood. The officer addressed Kirxx.

"Officer Uggar and his officers will escort us to his superiors on the *Guardian*. Follow me. Move slowly. Do not speak."

Hands raised, Kirxx stood and followed the officer out of the cockpit. Ceyla stepped in behind Kirxx and the second officer fell in line behind her.

They exited the *Star Runner* and stepped into a large bay that held several sleek ships. Soldiers in gray form-fitted uniforms stopped their various tasks and watched as they were marched toward a hatch.

Officer Uggar opened the doorway and stepped through. Then he led them down a long narrow passageway. He stopped, opened a door and spoke to Kirxx.

"Step inside the room, Ceyla."

"What are they going to do to us?"

"Just remember what I told you and you'll be fine."

Ceyla stepped into the room and the door shut behind her. She turned and called out to Kirxx. Then she pounded on the door.

Getting no response, she turned and looked around the room. Except for two chairs and a table, the small room was empty. The ceiling and walls were white and without windows. The floor was gray and warm to her bare feet.

After pacing for several minutes, Ceyla sat down. Locked in the white, silent room, Ceyla had no idea how long she'd waited before the door opened.

A man wearing a dark blue uniform stepped into the room. His hair was white, his skin was paler than hers and his eyes were a light green. Her heart pounded. Surely, he was from Glacid, the planet Kirxx had told her about.

He spotted the stone hanging around her neck and gasped.

Then he bowed and spoke to her in what she assumed was the native tongue of Glacid.

"I do not speak your language," she said in pirate lingo. Then she repeated the sentence in Jagiri.

Although the common tongue on Osesar was the pirate lingo, a product of the many languages spoken by the pirates who'd settled on the small planet, Mada had taught Ceyla Jagiri.

"I am Executive Officer Lydar, of Federation battleship *Guardian*," he said in Jagiri.

"I am Ceyla. I must speak with Prince Xxan at the Merck Space Station." Ceyla noticed his gaze often slid to the stone hanging around her neck. "I must deliver the scarlet tear to the prince."

"The scarlet tear belongs to the people of Glacid, not to the royal family."

She recalled Kirxx's stunning declaration about a woman ruling Glacid. "Isn't Queen Tayra part of the royal family?"

"Of course. But the Chamber of Lords rule Glacid."

The officer reached out for the stone, but Ceyla grabbed it, holding it firmly in her palm. Kirxx had told her to bluff and demand.

"I demand to be taken to Merck Space Station," she said, lifting her chin. "I have critical information to convey to His Highness, Prince Xxan."

"I am the highest-ranking Glacidian officer on this ship. You may view me as a representative of *our* government."

Years of being the outcast had taught Ceyla the art of using manners and a pleasant voice to avoid confrontation.

"I must respectfully decline your generous offer," she said. "My information must be delivered to the prince in person."

Lydar stared at her, his pale green eyes hard as glass. "You are a Glacidian, but you do not speak our native tongue."

Ceyla understood his curiosity and suspicion. She wanted to ask him about Glacid. She had so many questions, but should she trust him? If he got his hands on the stone, she doubted she'd ever see it again. "A result of unfortunate circumstances outside of my control. I must speak with Prince Xxan."

Lydar bowed, then turned on his heel and marched out of the room. The door closed behind him.

Ceyla released her grip on the scarlet tear. She'd won the first round.

Wondering how Kirxx was faring, she paced the room.

* * * * *

His wrists and ankles cuffed, Wytt looked up as an officer entered the room. The insignia on his collar designated him as the battleship's executive officer and his physical appearance was unquestionably Glacidian. He introduced himself as Lydar and his expression told Wytt the Glad had no affection for pirates or Sarks.

"You are under arrest for crimes of piracy," Lydar said. "Since you have already been convicted in absentia, you will be taken by transport to Tartic."

Wytt shrugged his shoulders.

The *Guardian* was part of the First Defense Battalion, patrolling Federation airspace. If Wytt told Lydar his true identity, he wouldn't believe him. Thanks to Rangar's *zap* tournament, the face of the notorious Kirxx had been flashed all over the intergalactic news by now. If Lydar even bothered to check out Captain Wytt Sann, he'd run into the cover arranged by Prince Xxan. Wytt's family and friends believed he was conducting a training exercise on Sark and would be out of communication for two months.

Wytt had to trust Ceyla to do her part. Once Prince Xxan realized she was aboard the *Guardian*, he'd demand that Ceyla and Kirxx be delivered to his headquarters on Merck.

Now Wytt had to find a way to stall his transfer to Tartic and his best option was to remain silent and reluctantly cooperative. Lydar had to be curious about Ceyla and the scarlet tear.

"Have you served time in Tartic?"

Wytt shook his head.

"It's in the polar region of Aktares. Prisoners must work to earn their meals. Privileges are few."

Wytt sighed as if bored. "Your point?"

"I can delay the transport."

Although decades had passed since Sark and Glacid were officially at war, the relationship between the two governments was strained. The majority of the general population of both planets remained distrustful of one another. "Why would a Glad help a Sark?"

"My concern is for the young woman we found on your ship."

"Found in my arms," Wytt corrected, remaining in character. "Glad women are amazing in the furs."

Lydar lunged at Wytt, knocking him out of the chair. His boot rested on Wytt's throat. It went against Wytt's instincts not to fight back, but if he attacked a Federation officer, he'd be on his way to Tartic at light speed. He had to force Lydar to negotiate.

"She was the prize in the *zap* tournament. Her name is Ceyla."

"What's her full name?"

"I don't know. Rangar didn't say. I didn't ask."

Lydar lifted his foot. "You don't know how Rangar got his hands on her?"

Wytt sucked in a breath and rubbed his throat. When he spoke to the prince, Wytt was going to make sure word got to Queen Tayra about Lydar. His loyalty to his people was commendable.

"No." Wytt cleared his throat.

"Would you prefer I order a mind probe?"

Lydar's eyes were bright, telling Wytt he'd give the order in a heartbeat. It was time to cooperate.

"Rangar's virgin prizes are usually Jagiri or Fants, maybe a bit of Sark blood mixed in for good measure. I was invited to participate. If you'd like to watch it, the holographic invitation is still on my ship. You can see for yourself. Offering a Glad for the prize is like poking your enemy with a sharp stick. All through the competition, I expected the Federation to invade."

"Get up."

Wytt got to his feet, righted his chair and sat down.

Lydar sat down and drummed his fingers on the table. He looked at Wytt. "What were you doing in Federation airspace?"

"Outrunning a Jagir cruiser. Right now I'm not real popular with Hatip's fans."

"You're not real popular with the Federation either."

Wytt grinned at Lydar. "You Federation guys aren't as trigger happy as the Jagiri."

Lydar's lips curved, but he didn't smile. "What were your plans for Ceyla?"

"Plans? I hadn't made any. I took my prizes and made a run for it."

Lydar's eyes widened. "Rangar offered the woman and the red stone as prizes?"

"Rangar called it a scarlet tear."

Wytt could almost see the wheels turning in Lydar's brain, asking the same question he'd pondered a few weeks ago, how did a Gladcidian beauty and a scarlet tear end up as a pirate's prize? The stones were rare and it was likely Lydar had never seen a scarlet tear.

"What were your plans for the stone?"

Wytt yawned. "Sell it. I have no use for a bauble."

Lydar visibly stiffened and for several seconds he stared at Wytt.

"Any chance I can get something to eat? Perhaps a glass of *kvass*?"

Lydar rose and walked out of the room.

Several minutes later, two security guards entered. Several sealed packets were placed on the table along with a cylinder of water. Then the guards left.

Wytt picked up one of the packets. They'd given him nutrition squares, the basic sustenance issued to soldiers. Small and lightweight, the squares maintained a moving army. Wytt smiled and broke the seal. He'd lost count of how many squares he'd eaten during his years in the military.

The square heated and swelled. Not knowing when he'd have his next meal, Wytt consumed the cake-like square in four bites. Then he reached for another.

* * * * *

Ceyla smiled at Lydar and picked up her wineglass. "The fish was delicious. Thank you."

"I'm surprised you've never eaten lake cod. It's very popular in the western provinces of Glacid."

Ceyla understood Lydar's attempts to engage her in conversation were a subtle form of interrogation. She decided to counter with a direct question. "Have you made contact with Prince Xxan?"

Lydar tossed his napkin on his empty plate, telling Ceyla her refusal to respond was frustrating him. "Your well-being is for Glacid to decide. The pirate will be taken to Aktares."

Glacid. The land of her people. Wasn't that what she'd always wanted? Freedom was sitting right in front of her. All she had to do was reach out to Lydar. Why should she care about the fate of a pirate?

Kirxx's handsome face came to mind. He'd gotten her away from Osesar and he'd treated her well. Just thinking about those hours in his arms made her tingle all over. And as Rangar had promised, Kirxx had ended the torment of her annual cycle.

Perhaps she was foolish to throw her lot in with the pirate, but her gut told her Lydar wanted the stone and she was of little concern.

"Thank you again for dinner and your kindness. I must insist on being transported to the Merck Space Station."

Lydar's mouth thinned. He stood. "I'll escort you to your quarters."

Ceyla followed Lydar along a passageway to a doorway. He opened the door and stepped back. "I hope you will find the room comfortable."

Ceyla stepped inside the small windowless room. The walls were white and unadorned except for a three-dimensional image of a frozen lake with a backdrop of ice-covered mountains. Ceyla wondered if the lake was on Glacid, but resisted the urge to engage Lydar in conversation. Beneath the picture was a bunk, her cloth bag resting on one end. A desk and chair were to her right. A door was to her left.

Lydar pointed to the door. "Cleansing facilities. Perhaps you'd like to wash the stink of pirate off your skin."

Before Ceyla could respond to the insult, Lydar spun on his heel and left the room.

* * * * *

Still in handcuffs and bracketed by security officers, Wytt was marched through a maze of corridors and into a large docking bay. When he saw the long-range transport, Wytt was sure he was headed for Tartic prison.

Wytt walked up the rear boarding ramp usually reserved for cargo. Inside the ship's cargo bay, Wytt was ordered to step into a small compartment outfitted with four seats, a cell designed for the express purpose of transporting prisoners.

Either Ceyla had failed to convince Lydar to contact Prince Xxan or she'd turned against him. Had those hours they'd spent in his furs meant nothing? Or had she seen a chance for freedom and taken it?

Wytt wouldn't blame her if she did. All he had to do was survive Tartic until the prince saved his ass.

"Take a seat, pirate."

Wytt dropped into a seat. His ankles were cuffed, then he was secured with locking restraints.

The officer left and a woman wearing a uniform with medical insignias on her collar and sleeves entered the transport cell. She was tall with light brown hair and she held an injection pistol in her left hand.

She sat down next to him and lifted his hair away from his neck.

"Is this necessary?"

She gripped his chin. "Hold still," she said, placing the nozzle against Wytt's neck.

Two hot points pierced Wytt's skin. Then he blacked out.

Chapter Eleven

ဆ

Ceyla yawned, opened her eyes and looked around the empty, windowless passenger cabin of the vessel transporting her from the *Guardian* to Merck Space Station. She had no idea whether she'd slept for minutes or for hours. She touched her chest and felt the hard lump of the scarlet tear. Releasing her safety restraints, Ceyla climbed out of her seat and stretched. She plucked her bag out of the overhead compartment and visited the comfort facilities.

She dug a packet of mouth cleansers out of the bag and popped one in her mouth. After the tablet stopped fizzing, Ceyla spit out the foam and rinsed her mouth. Then she washed her face and dug her hair brush out of her bag.

Her hair brushed and held back with a clasp, Ceyla exited the facilities and returned to her seat. She pulled out the scarlet tear and stared at the blood-red stone, wondering if she'd be granted an audience with Prince Xxan. She outwitted a pirate king, but could she bargain with a royal prince?

A young man with short dark hair and wearing a tan tunic and dark pants entered the cabin. Ceyla tucked away the stone.

The man walked down the center aisle toward her. "We're approaching Merck Space Station," he said, addressing her in pirate lingo. "Secure your safety straps."

"You speak my language."

"Knowledge of several languages is required to serve in the First Defense Battalion," he said, reminding Ceyla she was riding in a military transport and the young man was a soldier.

He watched as she fastened her restraints. "Would you like a hot beverage?"

"Tea would be nice," Ceyla said.

The young man ran his fingertips over a row of buttons on the back of the seat before her, selecting one. A compartment slid open and a tray was lowered.

The soldier walked to the forward section of the cabin, then returned carrying two slender cylinders and two square packets. He placed a cylinder and a packet on her tray. "Tea and a nutrition square. I'm sorry, but it's all we have aboard."

"Thank you. I'm Ceyla."

"I'm Daast."

Daast took the seat across the aisle and lowered his tray. Then he withdrew a small device out of his pocket and pushed a button. A screen slid from the ceiling. Ceyla gasped as an image of a silvery, multi-level object appeared.

"Merck Space Station," Daast said.

Blazing with lights, the space station looked like something had swooped down and snatched a huge, haphazardly built structure and stuck it in the night sky.

"I've never seen anything like it," Ceyla said, admiring the brightly lit station floating in the starry void. When she was aboard the *Guardian*, Ceyla had no sense of its size but she knew it was far larger than Kirxx's ship. She couldn't recall seeing a building as large as the station on Osesar. "Is it as big as it looks?"

"Merck is a military base, housing a thousand personnel. It has twenty levels and can dock more than a hundred ships. The long arm sticking out on the right is one of the docking stations," Daast said. "That's where the transport will dock. Then a chute will attach to the port hatch. You'll enter the station through the chute."

"It's quite impressive."

"It is, but this is my favorite view," Daast said as the image changed from the space station to a ringed planet. "Aktares is my home."

"It looks so close."

"Aktares is the closest planet to Merck. Glacid is that bright steady light in the upper right-hand corner."

Ceyla located Glacid on the screen. "Where is Sark?"

"It's hidden by the station." Daast ripped his packet open. "Eat. We'll be docking soon."

By the time Ceyla had finished her tea, the transport was approaching the assigned docking bay.

Daast gathered the empty cylinders and discarded packets. "As soon as we're fully docked, I'll escort you to the airlock."

Several minutes after the ship had docked, Ceyla followed Daast to the port hatch. A long cylindrical tube connected the ship to the station. Carrying her cloth bag, Ceyla stepped into the chute.

"This is where I leave you," Daast said. "Walk toward the station hatch. As soon as I close this hatch, the pressure will equalize. When the opposite hatch opens you can step into the station. Goodbye, Ceyla."

She gave Daast a final wave and walked toward the station hatch.

Ceyla wondered about Kirxx. She'd hadn't seen him or spoken to him since their rescue. As she reached the station hatch, Ceyla wondered if she'd chosen the right path. Was she a fool to put her faith in a pirate or should she have depended on the mercy of Executive Officer Lydar?

The hatch opened and as Ceyla stepped through, a strong hand grasped hers. The man was tall and his hair was brown, long and sun-streaked. His tawny eyes reminded her of the long-toothed cats that lived in the arid region of Osesar. The handsome golden-skinned man reminded her of Kirxx.

"Welcome to Merck. I'm Prince Xxan and I understand you wish to speak with me."

Stunned that he greeted her in pirate lingo, Ceyla stared at him. Surely a prince would be dressed in fine clothes. In his simple white shirt, tan pants and sandals, this prince reminded her of Kirxx. The prince wore no jewels, only a ring on his finger.

Was he a real prince? Had she made the right decision?

Ceyla glanced around. Two armed soldiers bracketed the airlock. Two more stood behind the prince. The soldiers wore black shirts, bloused black pants and black boots. They were far more intimidating than the crew of the *Guardian*.

She managed to find her voice. "I'm Ceyla."

"Welcome to Merck. If you're tired, we can speak tomorrow." The prince lifted his hand and a soldier stepped forward and took her bag.

After Lydar's reaction to the stone, Ceyla had tucked the scarlet tear beneath her long-sleeved tunic. She'd taken few things from Osesar and her clothing choices were limited. At least her green tunic and pants were clean. She considered delaying her conversation with the prince and getting comfortable in this new environment, but the tear was like a heavy weight around her neck. Now that she was with the prince she felt an urgency to bargain for Kirxx's life.

"Thank you for meeting me, Prince Xxan. I would prefer to speak with you now, privately."

The prince spoke to the soldiers and then offered his arm. "Forgive my speaking in Aktarian. My assistant, Tarren, will carry your luggage."

Tarren picked up her bag and fell in step behind them as the prince guided her along a corridor to an elevator. Uniformed soldiers, men and women, passed them in the corridor and acknowledged the prince by fisting their right hand and placing it against their chest just above the heart.

Tarren accompanied them on the elevator.

Ceyla's stomach dropped as the elevator rapidly ascended. The doors opened and they stepped into a carpeted foyer with three doors.

Tarren fisted his hand, then turned sharply on his heel and moved toward a door to his left. The prince guided her through the door directly opposite the elevator.

They entered a well-lit room with pale gray walls, twin white sofas and dark gray chairs. Through an archway Ceyla saw a table with six chairs. As she moved into the room, she noticed the photos on the walls. Her breath caught at the scenes of blue lakes and towering ice mountains.

"Glacid is called the ice planet," the prince said.

Taking her arm, he walked her around the room, telling her the name of the lake. "This is Lake Riasta. As a boy, I spent many hours fishing with my family. My baby sister always caught the biggest fish."

The expression on his face told of wonderful memories. Ceyla could only wonder what it must be like to have parents and a sister, people who loved you.

The prince touched the lower right-hand corner of the frame and the photo changed to a glistening city of ice and lights. "This is Cryss, the capital city of Glacid."

Ceyla's heart pounded. A whole new world had opened up, exciting and scary. One day she vowed to visit Cryss. "It's beautiful."

"Feel free to view the images at your leisure." The prince took her arm and they moved to the white sofas.

Tarren entered the room, carrying a tray.

The prince smiled at Ceyla. "I ordered tea."

After the tea was poured, Tarren left the room.

The prince sipped the tea, then set down his cup. "You may speak freely."

Ceyla gripped her cup. "I have something I think belongs to the Glacidian people. It's very valuable, but I'd like something in exchange."

"What is this valuable item?"

Ceyla opened the high collar of her tunic and pulled out the stone hanging around her neck.

Unlike Lydar, who had stared at the scarlet tear, the prince's gaze flicked over the stone. Then he looked her in the eye. "What do you want in exchange?"

Ceyla wondered if Kirxx and Rangar had been mistaken about the stone's value, but she'd come this far. "A pardon for the pirate, Kirxx."

The prince's eyes widened. "I'm aware of Rangar's tournament. Few in your situation would plead mercy for a pirate."

"Kirxx won me, but it was Rangar that offered me for a prize. Kirxx promised to take me away from Osesar. Rangar's plan was to track Kirxx and, with my assistance, steal the stone. Kirxx kept his promise and I am free of Rangar."

"You bargain with something you do not own," the prince said, his voice soft and unthreatening. "You must realize that I can take the stone by force and give you nothing."

"The scarlet tear is stolen goods, but Kirxx and I didn't try to sell it in Jagir, we brought it to you. To take it by force is an act that I'd expect from one such as Rangar, not from a royal prince of the Aktarian Federation."

The prince's lips curved as if he might smile. Then he asked, "You want nothing for yourself?"

"As long as I can remember, I have lived on Osesar in housing provided by Rangar. I am willing to share any and all information I know about the pirate. If that information proves valuable, I'd like to meet with a member of the Glacidian government. I do not know how I came to live on Osesar. I do not know who my parents were. I don't know my last name, but I'd like to know who I am."

"Your last request is granted. A representative of Glacid is ein route to Merck as we speak. As for your first request, I will consider it. Tomorrow, I'd like an expert to examine the stone."

"Thank you, Prince Xxan. It was Kirxx who instructed me to demand to see you and speak only with you. Please consider that when you judge him."

The prince stood. Tarren entered the room and handed Ceyla a tablet that looked like a larger version of her reader.

"I thought you might be curious about Glacid and its sister planets. I also included maps and images."

Ceyla couldn't wait to look at the information the prince had provided. "Thank you."

The prince bowed. "It was my pleasure. Tarren will show you to your quarters."

* * * * *

Wytt blinked several times, letting his eyes adjust to the light. He raised his head and looked around. He was lying on an examination table in a room of white walls and medical devices. Biofeedback bands were on his upper arm, chest and thigh. A restraint crisscrossed his body.

Was he in Tartic prison?

He released the restraint and sat up. He wasn't cuffed and sharp instruments were within his reach. This wasn't a prison infirmary. If he wasn't on Tartic, where was he?

The door opened and Prince Xxan walked in followed by a dark-haired woman dressed in white. Wytt jumped off the examination table and fisted his right hand over his heart. Lightheaded, he swayed and managed to right himself. He was stark naked.

The prince laughed. "At ease. Back on the table before you fall down."

Legs shaky, Wytt climbed back on the table.

"I was hoping to be here when you woke up. Dr. Reenn needs to examine you. I'll be in the hall."

"Ceyla?"

"She arrived on the same transport vessel, except she was in the passenger cabin."

"I thought I was going to Tartic Prison. They didn't tell me Ceyla was being sent to Merck."

"She's safe and in good health. I'll answer all your questions after the doctor has completed her examination."

Knowing Ceyla was safe, Wytt cooperated with the doctor who poked and prodded him from head to toe.

"I'm moving you into the station hospital for observation and bed rest."

"I'm fine."

"You'll be fine in twenty-four hours," Dr Reenn said. "You were given a powerful sedative on the *Guardian*. That's why you're still dizzy."

"I'd like to speak with Prince Xxan."

The doctor walked to the door.

The prince stepped inside. "How is he?"

"I'd like him to remain in the hospital for observation. After that, I recommend thirty days leave and taking a break from playing *zap*," Dr. Reenn said. "I've never seen cuts like these or so many of them. I don't know where you were competing, but the whips weren't properly calibrated. Those cuts are deep and long. Whoever sealed them did a good job, but you need to give them time to heal."

Rangar had wanted his competitors to bleed. "I can give up *zap* for a month," Wytt said. "But I'd like to go to my quarters. I can rest there."

"The captain also has a wound that wasn't the result of a laser whip." The doctor ran a gloved hand along the sealed cut on Wytt's torso. "The cut was inflicted by a blade."

"Twelve hours in hospital," Prince Xxan said. "That's an order. Dr. Reenn, can you give us a few minutes?"

The doctor stepped out of the room.

"I'm proud of you, Wytt. Job well done. But as of now you're officially on medical leave. You'll be debriefed tomorrow."

"I want to go back. If I challenge Rangar to a duel, he'll let me land on Osesar."

"Thirty days, Wytt."

"A few days and I'll be fine."

"You're on leave, Wytt."

Wytt had no choice but to accept the prince's direct order. "Yes, Your Highness."

"I'm glad you made it back alive. I understand the *Star Runner* was in dire straits when you were found."

"We were running out of air and the temperature had dropped dangerously low," Wytt said. "We're lucky the *Guardian* found us alive."

"You fulfilled your mission admirably. I'm fully aware of the danger you faced and I've already signed the paperwork for your advancement to the rank of commander. This mission was important to my mother and very personal. Thank you, Commander Sann."

Commander. For years, Wytt had worked to earn the rank. Although he completed his mission, he failed miserably in one aspect. "My mission was to bring Ceyla and the stone to Merck."

"And you succeeded."

Wytt clenched his fists. Admitting his failure wasn't easy, but he'd never regret loving Ceyla. He'd broken the oath he'd taken when he joined the Elite. "I overstepped my authority. I let my personal needs interfere with my duty."

"You and Ceyla became involved?"

Wytt wondered if Ceyla had told the prince. "If you ask for my resignation, I'm ready to relinquish my sword. But before I leave Merck, I'd like to speak with her."

"You forced Ceyla into your bed?"

"No! Never, but I deceived her."

"She believed you were a pirate, a man who had won her as a prize?"

"Yes."

"She willingly, and without coercion from you, engaged in sexual intercourse with you?"

"Yes, but she wasn't an experienced woman. I'm not a pirate, I'm an Elite. I live by our code of honor. Her honor belongs to the man she will take as her lifemate. She deserves to live out her life on Glacid with a husband who will give her the life that Rangar tried to steal from her."

The prince shook his head. "You've done nothing to dishonor the Elite. Nor do I think Ceyla feels dishonored. You coached her well. She refused to speak with anyone but me and she refused to hand over the scarlet tear to the officer aboard the *Guardian*. I expected her to give it to me, but she held on to it."

Wytt rubbed his temples. "She refused to give it to a royal prince?"

"She's using it to bargain for a pardon."

"A pardon? Was she arrested and charged by Lydar? Didn't he understand she was Rangar's victim, not his cohort?"

The prince smiled. "Lydar didn't arrest her. In exchange for the scarlet tear, Ceyla wants a pardon for Kirxx."

Wytt was stunned. Ceyla owed him nothing. All she had to do was ask for help and Prince Xxan and his mother would help her make a new life on Glacid. Instead, she'd bargained for his freedom.

"It's not uncommon for people to bond in life-threatening situations, but Ceyla asked nothing for herself. Her concern was for you. As Kirxx, you've made quite an impression on Ceyla. I wonder what she's going to think about Commander Wytt Sann."

Chapter Twelve

ॐ

Summoned by the prince, Ceyla followed his assistant, Tarren, into the living area adjacent to her sleeping quarters. The prince and a woman with short, pale hair were sitting on the sofa, speaking softly.

The prince rose to greet Ceyla. He was dressed in a black uniform with four star-shaped crystals on his collar. "Tarren has fitted you with a translator?"

Ceyla pulled back her hair to reveal the small device in her ear. Tarren had explained the device would translate her words and the speaker's words. Tarren had tested the device by speaking Aktarian. She heard Tarren's words in one ear and the translation in the other.

"I'll be speaking Glacidian," the prince said. "Let me know if you are unable to understand."

The prince introduced her to the older woman.

"Ceyla, I'm honored to introduce my mother, Queen Tayra of Glacid."

Queen Tayra? The queen's hair was as pale as Ceyla's and cut in a short, spiky style. Her features were delicate and her eyes were shimmering silver, like sun striking ice. She wore a white tunic adorned with crystals as stunning as her eyes, white pants and boots.

After meeting Lydar and Queen Tayra, Ceyla knew she'd found her people.

The queen embraced her. "Welcome home, Ceyla."

Ceyla had read the protocol of meeting royalty. When the queen released her, Ceyla dipped one knee and bowed her head. "Thank you, Your Highness."

"Xxan, I'd like a private audience with Ceyla."

Prince Xxan smiled. "I'll leave you two ladies together."

The prince left the room. The queen took Ceyla's hand and drew her to the sofa. "Please join me for tea."

Ceyla sat down and accepted a cup.

"I have spoken to my son. He told me you do not know the identity of your parents or how you came to be on Osesar."

"I have no idea who I am. For as long as I can remember I have lived on Osesar. No one looked like me."

The queen reached out and touched her hand. "Like us."

The queen's words were like a balm, healing the wounds of the outsider. "I knew Osesar wasn't my homeland."

"I will trace your family. You will know your name and your lineage. I promise."

Tears welled in Ceyla's eyes. She brushed them away with the back of her hand and silently thanked the pirate who had brought her to freedom.

"Thank you, Your Highness."

"Tracing your family will require samples of your DNA. I would like you to have a physical exam by a Glacidian physician. We are unique in many wonderful ways. If you are willing, I'd like the exam to take place after we finish our tea."

"Thank you, Your Highness. All my life I've wanted to know who I am."

The queen sipped her tea. "I have one more request, Ceyla. I would like to examine the scarlet tear."

Ceyla set down her cup. She took off the stone and handed it Queen Tayra. The queen removed a loupe out of the pocket of her tunic. She examined the stone with the illuminated monocular lens.

"Is it real?"

The queen removed the eye loupe. "Yes," she said, tucking the lens in her pocket. "It's real and it may be the key to your identity."

Ceyla couldn't imagine what the stone had to do with her. "I never saw the stone before Rangar brought me to Osesar City for the *zap* tournament."

"Do you know the history of the scarlet tear?"

Ceyla shook her head. "Rangar told me it was valuable, but nothing about it."

"Centuries ago, an artist fell in love with the fiancée of his client. The client was a wealthy man from a powerful family and although the woman loved the artist she couldn't dishonor her family by breaking off the engagement."

"The client was the newly appointed ambassador to Aktares and after the wedding the couple was leaving Glacid. The artist knew the love of his life was lost to him, so he mixed his blood in ice and bonded the mixture with rare crystals. He suspended the beautiful tear on a length of silver so when his love wore the stone it would lie close to her heart."

Ceyla stared at the stone. "It's made of ice and blood?"

"Glacid is a planet of ice and the conditions are harsh. Long ago our scientists discovered how to modify the molecular structure of ice, bonding it with other materials. Our cities are made of ice. Our buildings can withstand terra quakes and laser blasts."

"But how is the scarlet tear the key to my identity?"

The queen sipped her tea, then continued with her story.

"The husband discovered the scarlet tear and refused to let his wife keep the stone. Instead of destroying the exquisite stone, he presented it to the Supreme Ruler of Aktares as a gift from the Glacidian government. The Supreme Ruler was so honored by the rare gift, that the Glacidian Chamber of Lords commissioned the artist. The scarlet tear became the official gift for diplomatic missions. Centuries later, it's still a tradition."

"My father was a diplomat?"

The queen nodded. "I suspect your parents were part of a diplomatic mission. I find it far too coincidental that you and the stone ended up on a planet far away from Glacid at the same time. It's a mystery I intend to solve."

Excited and anxious, Ceyla felt like she was standing on the edge of the unknown. So much had happened in the last few days, she felt overwhelmed. She wished Kirxx were here to hold her hand. She missed his strength and longed to hear his voice.

"I have delivered the scarlet tear. Will Prince Xxan grant a pardon for Kirxx? He saved my life and without him the scarlet tear would still be in Rangar's possession."

"You care for this pirate?"

"I have lived among pirates all my life. Like the stone, I was Rangar's possession. Kirxx could have sold me in Jagir, instead he brought me to the safety of the Federation. The only way I can repay him is to beg for his freedom."

"It's natural to feel gratitude."

"During the competition, the players would whisper to me. I was a prize and they'd tell me what they were going to do to me. Their words were vulgar, their intentions cruel. Kirxx treated me with respect. He told me about Glacid. He promised to take me to Aktares and introduce me to a woman who would help me find my family. I feel more than gratitude. Kirxx is my friend. I care for him deeply."

"I will speak with my son."

"Thank you, Your Highness. I'm ready for my exam."

* * * * *

At the conclusion of the physical exam, Ceyla met with the queen. She'd hoped to hear that Kirxx had been pardoned, but the queen asked her about her last cycle.

"Your cycle started as you were leaving Osesar?"

"Yes."

The queen's brow knitted. "While you were alone with Kirxx, you were having your cycle?"

"Why are you asking the same questions as Dr. Saayr?"

The queen took her hand. "Please bear with me. My questions, although personal, are important. Did you have intercourse with Kirxx?"

"I did."

"When a Glacidian woman has intercourse during her cycle, there are consequences."

Consequences! Ceyla's heart started pounding. "I'm pregnant?"

The queen squeezed her hand. "Yes."

Ceyla closed her eyes. Rangar had timed the competition with her cycle. Preventing conception wasn't part of his plan. Was Kirxx's child part of his revenge?

Ceyla touched her stomach. She had to protect her baby. Protect Kirxx's child.

"Ceyla, are you all right?"

She looked at the queen and smiled. "I want this baby."

The queen hugged her. "I'm pleased you feel that way. Children are the blessing of the gods. Now that you know about the baby, what are your feelings for the father?"

Ceyla raised her chin. Perhaps the queen would think her a fool for loving Kirxx, but Ceyla didn't care. "I love Kirxx."

It felt good to admit her feelings, liberating.

"There are more consequences," the queen said.

Ceyla couldn't imagine anything more significant than being pregnant.

"Glacidian women are unique and it appears no one on Osesar provided you with the important information we learn as girls."

"The woman who reared me never told me I was from Glacid. I don't know if she knew what I was."

"If a Glacidian female has intercourse during her cycle, she must orgasm to conceive. If she conceives, she is physically bound to that man for life. There will be no other for her."

"You mean they are automatically married?"

"Marriage is a legal binding ceremony. Being physically bound to a man means you can only have intercourse with him."

Ceyla only wanted Kirxx, but what if he didn't want her or their child? "What of the man? Kirxx isn't Glacidian."

"Like Kirxx, my husband is half Aktarian and half Sark. He is bound to me. If the man loves you, the bonding is a powerful thing."

Joy swept through Ceyla, but would Kirxx feel the same joy at being physically bound only to her? Then it struck her, like a blinding light. The child had nothing to do with Rangar's revenge. He wanted Kirxx bound to her. That's why he wanted to bring her back to Osesar, so Kirxx would never to able to have sex again. The pirate king was diabolical, but she and Kirxx had foiled his plan.

"I must speak with Kirxx."

"I'm sure that under the circumstances that can be arranged."

Chapter Thirteen

ɛↄ

Dressed in his black Elite uniform, Wytt waited outside the door to the guest quarters. Heart hammering, he tugged at the high collar. He couldn't wait to see Ceyla, but how would she react when she saw him? Would she be relieved he wasn't a pirate? What would she do when she realized he'd deceived her?

He'd relished the competition and winning the prize. Playing the pirate had tapped into his sense of adventure. He liked the danger of the mission.

He'd enjoyed being Kirxx.

Would Ceyla like Wytt Sann as much as she liked Kirxx?

He'd rehearsed this scene in his head. He'd introduce himself and tell her about his mission. Wytt needed Ceyla to understand why he couldn't reveal his true identity. He'd tell her he'd remember the hours they'd shared aboard the *Star Runner* for the rest of his life.

The door slid open and Wytt stepped inside.

A vision in a pale blue caftan, Ceyla rose from the sofa. Her gaze met his.

He waited for her to remark on his uniform, but a cry tore from her throat as she ran into his arms. He hugged her tight, his rehearsed words lost as his lips found hers.

Her mouth was soft, her kiss eager and consuming. He never wanted to let her go.

Wytt buried his face in the crook of her neck. She felt so good, so right in his arms.

"Kirxx."

The name pierced his heart. He had to come clean and end the deception.

"Ceyla."

He kissed her again, taking his time and making it last.

Breathless and burning with desire, Wytt held her close.

"I'm so happy to see you," she said. "I've missed you so much."

He'd missed her too. More than he ever imagined he would miss someone. He figured Queen Tayra had made arrangements to take her to Glacid. Prince Xxan had told him that his mother had taken Ceyla under her wing and the search for her family was already underway.

Wytt released her and looked into her eyes. Ceyla looked so happy.

Wytt grasp her hand and led her to the sofa. "I have something to tell you."

"The prince gave you a pardon?"

"My name isn't Kirxx. It's Wytt. Commander Wytt Sann."

"Wytt." Ceyla's eyes widened, then her gaze flicked over him. "You're wearing the same uniform as Prince Xxan."

"I wear the uniform of the Elite. We are assigned to the royal family. I serve Prince Xxan."

Her hand gripped his. "You're not a pirate?"

"I'm a soldier. The real Kirxx was captured and the invitation to compete in Rangar's tournament was on his ship. The prince sent me to Osesar. My mission was to compete as Kirxx and bring you and the scarlet tear to Merck."

Her lips curved with a hint of a smile. "You had no intention of ransoming me or the stone?"

"Never. I couldn't tell you my true identity until we were safe."

"Weren't we safe aboard the *Guardian*?"

"My mission was covert. As Kirxx, my face was all over the intergalactic news. Even if I'd told Executive Officer Lydar my real name and he'd bothered to check out my story, he would have discovered that Wytt Sann was on assignment on Sark. The prince had a cover assignment in place.

"I put my faith in you, Ceyla. If you hadn't insisted on speaking to the prince, Lydar would have sent me to prison. Eventually, Prince Xxan would have gotten me out, but I wanted to be the one to tell you my real identity."

"Wytt. I like it." Ceyla laughed and threw her arms around him, hugging him tight. "I love you, Wytt."

Her words careened through Wytt's brain. His heart raced. "Say that again."

"I love you."

He cupped her face and kissed her. He was so happy, he hurt. "I love you too."

"I started falling for you that first evening at Rangar's party when you kissed my wrist and told me you were going to win the competition. But I kept denying what was in my heart."

Tears rolled down her cheeks. "I believed you were a pirate, so I kept telling myself you were only a means to escape Rangar. You challenged Rangar and put yourself in danger for me."

Wytt planted kisses on her lips, cheeks and forehead. "When I saw Rangar's invitation, I thought you were the most beautiful woman I'd ever seen. Right then and there I knew I had to win the competition."

"I knew I loved you when you placed the scarlet tear around my neck in case we were captured. No one has ever put me first, but you did."

He lifted her hand and kissed her wrist. "You will always be first in my heart."

"We make a good team, Wytt. Together, we bested the pirate king. He didn't get the scarlet tear or his revenge on Kirxx. His scheme failed."

"What scheme?"

Ceyla smiled and her eyes lit up. "I have something to tell you."

Ceyla revealed Rangar's plan, explaining that she'd been ordered to seduce Kirxx, how she'd been threatened and admitting her intention to escape once they'd left Osesar. After Wytt had told her his true identity and bared his soul, telling him the truth was cathartic.

"Rangar understood the consequences, but he needed my complicity. I'm loath to think how he would have treated Kirxx's child and the last thing he wanted was for my maternal instincts to ruin his scheme. Rangar had it all figured out, except you weren't the real Kirxx. He never expected us to fall in love."

Wytt hadn't said a word. Ceyla looked into Wytt's eyes, waiting for his reaction and hoping he'd share her happiness.

"I'm going to be a father." He stared at her as if in shock. "A father. You're having a baby? My baby?"

Ceyla bit her bottom lip. Perhaps she should have waited to tell him, but she was so excited she could barely contain her joy. If they loved one another, wasn't it a good thing?

"You're happy about the baby?"

"I am," Wytt said. "Are you?"

Ceyla nodded.

Wytt grasped her hands and slid to his knees. "Marry me, Ceyla. Take me as your lifemate."

"Lifemate? That means forever."

"Forever. For the rest of my life."

"There's something else I need to tell you." She related what Queen Tayra had told her. "Rangar wanted to make

Kirxx pay for seducing his favorite mistress. He didn't care about her, but he couldn't accept the affront to his manhood. He ordered me to steal back the scarlet tear and escape in the life pod. He wanted the stone and he wanted Kirxx to suffer. If I was on Osesar, Kirxx would be bound to a woman he couldn't have and he'd be denied the pleasure of another woman for the rest of his life."

Wytt kissed her inner wrist. "I've been a soldier all my life. I spent years moving from base to base, planet to space station to alien moons with no home but an assigned bunk. I want to spend my life with you. I want to share a home with you and raise a family. I want no other but you."

"Make love to me, Wytt."

Wytt jumped to his feet. "Which sleeping chamber is yours?"

Ceyla pointed to a door on her right. Wytt scooped her up and carried her into the chamber and set her on her feet. He pressed the privacy lock.

Ceyla started to remove the caftan.

Wytt stilled her hands. "I want to undress you."

He pulled her into his arms and kissed her thoroughly. Fire licked her blood and deep in her pussy, she pulsed.

Wanting him naked and inside her, Ceyla worked the buttons of his uniform.

Wytt broke the kiss and removed her caftan. Then he stared at her, his gaze moving down to her feet and back again. The caftan fell from his fingers, pooling on the floor.

"You're so beautiful, I can barely breathe."

She grasped his lapels and pushed his jacket off his shoulders. Wytt shucked his jacket and pulled off his shirt. His boots were next. His pants and underwear landed on top of his jacket. His cock stood at attention.

He fell to his knees and kissed her belly. "The gods have blessed my life."

B.J. McCall

Ceyla fisted his hair and fell back on the bed, taking him with her. She loved the weight and strength of his body. With Wytt, she'd always feel safe. "I love you, Wytt. I want you inside me, now."

He slid between her thighs. One thrust and he was inside her.

She lifted her hips, wanting him deeper.

His arms trembled and he didn't move. "Make love to me, Wytt."

He stiffened his arms, holding his weight off her belly. Muscles tensed, he moved slowly and carefully.

"I'm not going to break."

"What about the baby?"

"The doctor said lovemaking is fine, but the wild sex will have to wait."

Wytt laughed, the tension broken.

Ceyla reached up and cupped his face. "Come here and kiss me."

He kissed her soundly and made love to her gently, until her blood pounded and she throbbed with need.

"Faster."

He shook his head and grasped her hands. His strokes were measured, long and deliberate instead of fast and wild.

With each slow glide of his length the intensity built.

Ceyla moaned. "You're driving me crazy."

"Just think what you're doing to me."

Perspiration beaded his forehead and slicked his chest.

The more he held back, the more she wanted him. She clenched, grabbing at him, demanding he fuck her.

His muscles vibrated and a shudder moved down his spine.

The tension built until Ceyla was sure she'd shatter.

"Ceyla."

She opened her eyes. Their gazes met.

"I love you."

His whispered words released a dam of emotions. Her heart swelled and her pussy convulsed around him. She gripped his hands and let the flood take her over the edge.

Wytt released her hands and rolled onto his side.

Ceyla was still catching her breath. "That was intense."

"I guess it doesn't have to be wild to be great."

"It was great."

"Did the doctor say anything about stimulating your pleasure node while you're pregnant?"

"That was the best part. Bonded lifemates have an acute sensitivity to one another. They seem to know the exact amount of pressure to use, naturally."

"Even if the lifemate isn't a Glad?"

"He said proper stimulation is healthy for me and the baby. He said we should enjoy ourselves."

Wytt sat up. "Climb onto my lap."

Ceyla settled onto his lap and flipped her long hair over her shoulder, exposing her node.

Wytt flicked it with his tongue.

A sudden, intense bolt of heat shot through her.

He reached between her legs, his forefinger settling on the tiny bud of her clit.

He licked her pleasure node and rubbed her clit.

The double shot of heat slammed together. She grabbed his shoulders in anticipation of his next move.

He released her clit and fisted his cock. The thick head probed her entrance and slid home. Then he touched her clit, rolling the bud beneath his fingertip.

Ceyla rocked her hips.

"Easy," Wytt said, cupping her ass with his free hand.

Then he fastened his lips over her pleasure node and suckled gently.

She arched her back, driving down on his cock and pushing her clit against his hand.

As she increased the tempo of her hips, Wytt drew deeply on her node.

Her heart pounded and her pussy quivered.

His lips, his hand and his cock combined in a vortex of sensation. Her climax came in a rush of heat.

His cock jerking, Wytt groaned. He released her pleasure node and eased the pressure on her clit.

Heat poured off her skin and perspiration beaded her forehead and ran between her breasts.

She slumped against him and he wrapped his arms around her and held her tight.

He kissed her hair. "I'm going to be happy for the rest of my life."

Chapter Fourteen

ॐ

Two weeks later, Wytt and Ceyla entered Prince Xxan's command center. The prince had informed them that the real Kirxx had recovered from his injuries. Wytt had asked to meet with the pirate and the prince had granted his request. Ceyla had insisted on coming along.

Wytt saluted and Ceyla bowed to the prince.

"This is an informal meeting," the prince said as he led them into his private quarters adjacent to his office.

Wytt noticed none of the prince's assistants were present, not even the trusted Tarren.

Wytt spotted a man with long brown hair across the room, standing with his back to the door. Wytt had expected to see a ruthless pirate, a manacled prisoner. Instead the pirate seemed oddly familiar.

Kirxx turned and Wytt's heart stopped for a fraction of a second.

"Hadr." He glanced at the prince, then fastened his gaze on the brother he hadn't seen in almost two years.

Hadr's face was leaner and he had a scar on his forehead, but his eyes were bright. He looked fit in his black uniform.

His brother stepped forward and opened his arms. On the verge of tears, Wytt threw his arms around Hadr and pounded him on the back.

"I thought you were dead."

"I came close."

Wytt's heart was racing. Hadr was alive. "You gave me a shock. Mama must be thanking the gods."

"I haven't spoken to her. I was hoping you and your bride would go with me to Aktares. Congratulations, brother."

"Ceyla, forgive me." Wytt drew Ceyla close. Wytt was still reeling from learning he was to be a father and officially bonding with Ceyla as lifemates. Now Hadr had come back from the dead. "Ceyla, this is my brother, Hadr. Until a minute ago, I'd thought he was dead."

Hadr hugged Ceyla. "I'm glad you're safe. Seems my little brother completed my mission and won the prize."

Wytt was stunned. "Your mission?"

"I am Kirxx. I invented him."

Wytt was speechless.

"You're Kirxx? The pirate, Kirxx?" Ceyla asked.

"Two years ago I went undercover. The only way I saw to destroy Rangar's hold on Osesar was to become a pirate and challenge his authority. I learned everything I could about him and Osesar."

"So you were the man who seduced Rangar's mistress?" Ceyla asked.

"I'd been poaching his territory, pirating ships right under the nose of his crews. But I needed to get to Rangar on a personal level, so I targeted his mistress. When Rangar sold her, I had an associate purchase her. She lives on Jagir under an assumed name."

"Rangar never forgot the insult," Ceyla said.

"The invitation to the *zap* tournament was my entrance to Osesar. But when I saw Ceyla and the scarlet tear was the prize, I knew the mission had to change. I contacted the prince, but I was attacked by a Federation ship on my way to Merck."

The prince looked at Wytt. "Hadr was injured. That's why I asked you to take his place."

"Your Highness, why didn't you tell me that Hadr was alive?"

"He was barely alive," the prince said. "The doctors weren't sure he would live. I needed your focus on the mission. I'm sorry, Wytt, but Hadr had given up two years of his life. And we had to get Ceyla off Osesar."

"I wanted to visit Osesar and check out Rangar's operation. I needed him to invite me to play in the tournament, so I boasted that I was an excellent *zap* player. When I saw the tournament invitation, I was shocked to learn that Rangar had a Glacidian woman. I knew he had the scarlet tear, but I was surprised he was offering it as a prize."

"How did you hear about the scarlet tear?" Wytt asked.

"Rangar had shown his mistress the stone," Hadr said. "He'd boasted about the ship he'd attacked as a young man, a Glacidian transport. Everyone on the ship was killed, but a life pod was ejected during the battle. Rangar tracked down the pod and found the scarlet tear inside."

The prince looked at Ceyla. "There was a child aboard the transport."

Anticipating the worst, Wytt took Ceyla's hand.

"The ambassador's infant daughter was aboard, but the child was presumed dead. A diplomatic mission of twenty was on that transport. Sections of the *Tranquility* were destroyed and some of the bodies were never found. The infant's name was Ceyla."

Ceyla gripped Wytt's hand, her nails digging into his skin. "That's my real name?"

"It's logical to assume that you and the scarlet tear were put in that life pod together. Some form of identification must have been placed in that pod. A parent would sacrifice themselves for their child and they'd want whoever recovered the pod to know your name. Unfortunately, Rangar recovered it and took you back to Osesar."

Wytt saw the tears forming in Ceyla's eyes. He wrapped his arm around her shoulder, felt her trembling. She'd never met her parents, but he knew her heart was hurting.

"What were their names?" she asked.

"Arlas and Tiana Praess. There were other relatives of yours aboard, Tiana's parents. I'm sorry, Ceyla."

A soft sob tore from her throat. "At least I know their names and that they loved me."

The prince handed a package to Wytt. "I've collected everything we could find about the diplomatic mission and your family. There are personal and official records and photos. The *Tranquility* was en route to Sark on a peace mission. It was attacked in Federation territory, but the alliance between our planets was new and not well organized. Pirates took advantage of our fledging Federation."

"I'm going to take Ceyla back to our quarters."

Wytt rose and looked at his brother. "If you're going after Rangar, I want to be part of the mission."

"A Federation trade delegation is on Jagir," the prince said. "Trade with the Federation is far more profitable than tribute paid by a pirate. The Jagir Conclave wishes to be seen as a legitimate government and they want to change the perception of Jagir as a lawless territory. If the Conclave wants a trade agreement they'll have to authorize a raid led by the Federation on Osesar. Rangar's days of being protected by the Conclave are numbered."

"Take care of your bride," Hadr said. "By the time your child is born, Rangar will be on ice."

Wytt nodded. The prince and Hadr would make sure Rangar spent his last days in a prison on Glacid.

Epilogue

ﬆ

The baby kicked. Ceyla grabbed Wytt's hand and placed his palm against her belly. The baby kicked again. "Did you feel it?"

Wytt leaned down and kissed her belly. "Our daughter is healthy."

"I'd like to name her Scarlett."

Her husband lifted his head. "I thought you had decided on Tiana?"

"The scarlet tear played such an important role in my life and it brought us together."

"Scarlett Sann." Wytt kissed Ceyla on the lips. "I like it."

"You don't mind staying in Cryss until Scarlett is born?"

He looked around. "I'm getting used to the ice."

One had to adapt to live on the ice planet. The walls of their apartment were made of a blend of ice and *plastine*. Cryss was a city made of ice. The climate on Glacid was harsh and cold. Ice storms were common, but the planet had it own beauty and at night Cryss was a magical city, glistening with lights.

"As long as we're together," Wytt said. "That's all that really matters."

"After Scarlett is born, I think we should move to Aktares."

"You want to leave Cryss?"

"I have enjoyed living here, learning the language and meeting the people. The prince was gracious to give you a special leave from your duties, but you don't belong here."

"I belong wherever you are."

She cupped his face. "You're treated like an outsider and I know how that feels. My family is gone, but your mother and brother have welcomed us into their hearts. Scarlett should grow up knowing her grandmother and her Uncle Hadr."

Wytt's face lit up. "I love you, Ceyla."

She ran her fingertip over his lower lip. "Shall we go for a walk or spend the day in the furs?"

He pulled her into his arms. "You're an insatiable temptress."

About the Author

🔊

Paige Tyler is a full-time, multi-published, award-winning writer of erotic romance. She and her research assistant (otherwise known as her husband!) live on the beautiful Florida coast with their easygoing dog and their lazy, I-refuse-to-get-off-the-couch-for-anything-but-food cat.

When not working on her latest book, Paige enjoys reading, jogging, doing Pilates, going to the beach, watching Pro football and vacationing with her husband at Disney. She loves writing about strong, sexy alpha males and the feisty, independent women who fall for them. From verbal foreplay to sexual heat, her wickedly hot stories of romance, adventure, passion and true love will bring a blush to your cheeks and leave you breathlessly panting for more!

Also by B.J. McCall

ℬ

eBooks:

Deep Heat

Ellora's Cavemen: Dreams of the Oasis II *(anthology)*

Ellora's Cavemen: Flavors of Ecstasy II *(anthology)*

Ellora's Cavemen: Jewels of the Nile I *(anthology)*

Ellora's Cavemen: Legendary Tails I *(anthology)*

Ellora's Cavemen: Seasons of Seduction IV *(anthology)*

Embrace Forever

Holiday Rush

Icy Hot

Knight's Emerald

Scarlet Tear

Short, Tight & Sexy

Slumber Party, Inc.

Warrior of the Light

Print Books:

Ellora's Cavemen: Dreams of the Oasis II *(anthology)*

Ellora's Cavemen: Flavors of Ecstasy II *(anthology)*

Ellora's Cavemen: Jewels of the Nile I *(anthology)*

Ellora's Cavemen: Legendary Tails I *(anthology)*

Ellora's Cavemen: Seasons of Seduction IV *(anthology)*

Erotic Emerald *(anthology)*

The Aktarian Chronicles *(anthology)*

Things that Go Bump in the Night V *(anthology)*

About the Author

ଛ

Born a coal miner's daughter, B. J. McCall lives on the beautiful California coast. A perfect day includes writing the final chapter of a book and spotting dolphins or whales playing offshore.

Multi-published in E-book and print, B.J. writes sensual romance in contemporary, futuristic, paranormal and fantasy genres. The phrase "do what you love" applies to B.J. She loves to write and each story is special. She hopes her readers will enjoy each and every one of them.

ଛ

The authors welcome comments from readers. You can find their websites and email addresses on their author bio pages at www.ellorascave.com.

Tell Us What You Think

We appreciate hearing reader opinions about our books. You can email us at Comments@EllorasCave.com.

Why an electronic book?

We live in the Information Age—an exciting time in the history of human civilization, in which technology rules supreme and continues to progress in leaps and bounds every minute of every day. For a multitude of reasons, more and more avid literary fans are opting to purchase e-books instead of paper books. The question from those not yet initiated into the world of electronic reading is simply: *Why?*

1. ***Price.*** An electronic title at Ellora's Cave Publishing runs anywhere from 40% to 75% less than the cover price of the exact same title in paperback format. Why? Basic mathematics and cost. It is less expensive to publish an e-book (no paper and printing, no warehousing and shipping) than it is to publish a paperback, so the savings are passed along to the consumer.

2. ***Space.*** Running out of room in your house for your books? That is one worry you will never have with electronic books. For a low one-time cost, you can purchase a handheld device specifically designed for e-reading. Many e-readers have large, convenient screens for viewing. Better yet, hundreds of titles can be stored within your new library—on a single microchip. There are a variety of e-readers from different manufacturers. You can also read e-books on your PC or laptop computer. (Please note that Ellora's Cave does not endorse any specific brands.

You can check our website at www.ellorascave.com for information we make available to new consumers.)

3. *Mobility.* Because your new e-library consists of only a microchip within a small, easily transportable e-reader, your entire cache of books can be taken with you wherever you go.

4. *Personal Viewing Preferences.* Are the words you are currently reading too small? Too large? Too... ANNOYING? Paperback books cannot be modified according to personal preferences, but e-books can.

5. *Instant Gratification.* Is it the middle of the night and all the bookstores near you are closed? Are you tired of waiting days, sometimes weeks, for bookstores to ship the novels you bought? Ellora's Cave Publishing sells instantaneous downloads twenty-four hours a day, seven days a week, every day of the year. Our webstore is never closed. Our e-book delivery system is 100% automated, meaning your order is filled as soon as you pay for it.

Those are a few of the top reasons why electronic books are replacing paperbacks for many avid readers.

As always, Ellora's Cave welcomes your questions and comments. We invite you to email us at Comments@ellorascave.com or write to us directly at Ellora's Cave Publishing Inc., 1056 Home Avenue, Akron, OH 44310-3502.

Make each day more *EXCITING* With our

Ellora's Cavemen
Calendar

www.EllorasCave.com

ELLORA'S CAVE
Romanticon

Annual convention
for women who
refuse to behave

Discover for yourself why readers can't get enough
of the multiple award-winning publisher

Ellora's Cave.

Whether you prefer e-books or paperbacks,

be sure to visit EC on the web at
www.ellorascave.com

for an erotic reading experience that will leave you
breathless.

CPSIA information can be obtained at www.ICGtesting.com
Printed in the USA
243031LV00001B/41/P